Nothing to Fear but Ferrets

Linda O. Johnston

BERKLEY PRIME CRIME, NEW YORK

THE BERKLEY PUBLISHING GROUP
Published by the Penguin Group
Penguin Group (USA) Inc.
375 Hudson Street, New York, New York 10014, USA
Penguin Group (Canada), 10 Alcorn Avenue, Toronto, Ontario M4V 3B2, Canada
(a division of Pearson Penguin Canada Inc.)
Penguin Books Ltd., 80 Strand, London WC2R 0RL, England
Penguin Group Ireland, 25 St. Stephen's Green, Dublin 2, Ireland (a division of Penguin Books Ltd.)
Penguin Group (Australia), 250 Camberwell Road, Camberwell, Victoria 3124, Australia
(a division of Pearson Australia Group Pty. Ltd.)
Penguin Books India Pvt. Ltd., 11 Community Centre, Panchsheel Park, New Delhi—110 017, India
Penguin Group (NZ), Cnr. Airborne and Rosedale Roads, Albany, Auckland 1310, New Zealand
(a division of Pearson New Zealand Ltd.)
Penguin Books (South Africa) (Pty.) Ltd., 24 Sturdee Avenue, Rosebank, Johannesburg 2196,
South Africa

Penguin Books Ltd., Registered Offices: 80 Strand, London WC2R 0RL, England

NOTIIING TO FEAR BUT FERRETS

A Berkley Prime Crime Book / published by arrangement with the author

PRINTING HISTORY
Berkley Prime Crime mass-market edition / August 2005

Copyright © 2005 by Linda O. Johnston.
Cover design by Rita Frangie.
Cover art by Monika Roe.
Interior text design by Stacy Irwin.

ISBN: 0-425-20373-5

Berkley Prime Crime Books are published by The Berkley Publishing Group,
a division of Penguin Group (USA) Inc.,
375 Hudson Street, New York, New York 10014.
The name BERKLEY PRIME CRIME and the BERKLEY PRIME CRIME design
are trademarks belonging to Penguin Group (USA) Inc.

PRINTED IN THE UNITED STATES OF AMERICA

10 9 8 7 6 5 4 3 2

To pet-sitters and pet lawyers and lawyers who love pets.

To ferrets, whether maligned or justly illicit in California.

To Cavaliers and Cavalier lovers, most especially Joan and Harold Letterly, who were Lexie's first humans.

And to Fred, who learned a lot of years ago that, to love Linda, he had to learn to live with, and love, her many Cavaliers.

—Kendra Ballantyne/Linda O. Johnston

Chapter One

LIFTING HER FUZZY face, Lexie gave a ferocious growl.

Ferocious, at least, for a Cavalier King Charles spaniel who'd wakened from a sound sleep while curled into a compact ball on my shorts-clad lap.

"What, girl?" I murmured, paying a lot more attention to the study guide before me on the tiny kitchen table than the complaining canine now standing on my bent legs.

After all, the Multistate Professional Responsibility Exam, which I'd take in about a week, was all that stood between me and my ability to resume practicing law.

Not that I should have had to take the ethics exam. My law license had been suspended owing to accusations of unprofessional conduct, but I'd recently been able to prove, beyond a hell of a lot more than mere reasonable doubt, that I'd been framed for that and more, including murder.

Maybe you heard of my triumph. I'm Kendra Ballantyne, attorney at law, and the blasted media trumpeted the story of how I'd discovered who'd set me up almost as loudly as they'd blared my fall from glory in the first place. But that hadn't boosted me beyond the hurdle of the Multistate.

I blinked as Lexie leapt from my lap, faced my apartment door, and growled again—hackles on her furry black-and-white back raised ominously.

This time, I paid attention.

I closed the outline and stood barefoot on the tile floor, my own hackles playing hopscotch along my spine.

Still, I heard nothing. At least nothing out of the ordinary: the refrigerator motor, traffic in the distance, a few cawing crows outside. It was one of those regretfully rare evenings when my renter, Charlotte LaVerne, and her boy-toy Yul, who occupy the main house on my property, weren't throwing a party. Both were showbiz wannabes, and Charlotte was actually a persona of sorts, an alumna of one of those absurdly popular reality television shows. My tenants' ingenuity at creating excuses for celebrations far exceeded all talents that I'd discerned in other areas. When they were home, noise was the norm around here, though seven P.M. wasn't exactly their prime time for partying.

Even so, I continued to listen . . . nothing.

I knelt to stroke the soft back of my pointing pup, who put down her lifted paw and looked up at me like I was nuts not to be as nervous as she was. Her red brows curved in consternation I still couldn't decipher. She was a tricolor Cavalier—mostly black and white but trimmed in chestnut here and there, like those persuasively puzzled brows.

"What is it, Lexie?" I asked softly.

She ran toward the door. I stood and followed, by habit grabbing her leash from its hook on the side of the nearest cabinet. I bent to snap it on her, fast. If there was trouble outside, I didn't want her bounding down the steps head-long into it. In fact, in anticipation, I scooped Lexie into my arms.

I stood for a moment on the platform at the top of the stairs outside my apartment, surveying the situation. I didn't see diddly out of place. My beloved BMW sat in its parking place beside the garage below. Then there was my sprawling château beyond my blue, inviting swimming pool in which I was no longer invited to swim. Its availability was attached to my home, which I'd leased out to stave off having to sell it during my prior misfortunes.

Inside the tall wrought-iron fence was lush landscaping: a gloriously green lawn, some eucalyptus, a lemon tree, and—

Crash!

Lexie, in my arms, struggled so hard I nearly dropped her at the noise and my own panic. What the heck was that? It sounded as if someone had set off something a lot more frightening than a firecracker, really close by.

Like at the other side of my adored house.

The air still reverberated with the noise.

Still holding the squirming Lexie, I sped down the steps, along the driveway to its end, and stopped.

There it was, the source of the noise. It was a lot worse than misfired fireworks.

A big vehicle had plowed right through my wrought-iron fence and into the side wall of my house, about where the living room was. Or maybe the den. Or right between.

"Oh, no!" I cried aloud, hurrying forward. Was anyone hurt?

But when I peered inside the huge intruder—a Hummer— I saw it was empty. That was the good thing. Sort of.

Had it been occupied, perhaps this accident wouldn't have occurred.

Lexie must have recognized the sound of the unbraked vehicle hurtling downhill as something bad. She'd tried to warn me. If she'd spoken English, she would have. But try as I might, I was a failure at understanding barklish.

One day, I meant to try one of those gadgets from Japan that was intended to translate a dog's every comment. It would even help with my interim profession, and possibly permanent sideline, pet-sitting.

But for now, I had a Hummer in my house to contend with.

It wasn't the first time someone's brakes had failed on my two-lane, twisting street. But it was the first time my house had fallen victim. There was no indication the vehicle had been stolen and smashed like my own car was a few months ago. And now that I knew I hadn't a corpse to contend with—I'd seen too many lately—nor even an injured body to hustle to the nearest hospital, I let myself get mad.

"Damn it!" I exclaimed, still hugging the wiggly Lexie. I'd no idea whose Hummer this happened to be. Well, the cops could figure it out, and this was definitely a reportable incident. And I'd need a copy of the cops' report to hand to my insurance company when I made a claim.

Was I insured for runaway Hummers battering my fence and my house? More important, was the outsized auto insured? I certainly hoped so.

But I'd dealt with insurance companies in my capacity as litigator. All too often, clients' claims were stymied by small print in policies provided to them at hefty prices. Too many insurers were pleased to take people's money, but choked on the concept of making good on policies' promises. Most likely, I'd be in for a fight against one company or another.

"Kendra? Are you okay?" a female voice shouted from some distance.

I turned to see my next-door neighbor Tilla Thomason hurrying toward me—as much as hefty Tilla could hurry up the winding street from her home down the hill from mine. I gauged her to be about fifty, and she'd apparently added an extra pound for every year of her life.

"I'm fine," I yelled back. "Can't say the same for my house, though." I hadn't grabbed my cell phone, so I needed to go inside to call the cops. An extra five minutes wouldn't matter much, though. I waited, still squeezing Lexie, till Tilla reached us.

By the time she did, a few other neighbors were gathering, shaking their heads and offering unhelpful advice.

Lyle Urquard, our local mountain biker, braked beside me, skidded to a stop—and fell, bike and all, onto his side. He wore a helmet, which would have helped had he landed on his head. However, his legs were bare between bright green spandex shorts and the tops of socks extending up wide ankles from blue and white athletic shoes.

Lyle biked at least twice daily. I'd seen him fall before. Scraped, bleeding legs were as much an adornment as his bulging belly beneath his snug shorts. How he didn't manage to ride off his extra pounds remained a mystery to me, especially considering the admirable effort he made to pedal up our steep slope—on the San Fernando Valley side of the Santa Monica Mountains, a few blocks from Mulholland Drive. I didn't know what he did during non–biking hours, but I'd heard he was in construction.

"Are you all right, Kendra?" was the first thing he said after several of us, including Tilla, helped untangle him from his bike and set it and him upright. Sweaty hair peeked from beneath his helmet, and he flexed hands clad in gloves that covered his palms but left his fingers free.

"Better than you," I observed.

His wide grin, lower jaw obscuring upper lip, looked sheepish as he thanked those who'd dived to his assistance. "I'm fine. Really." He glanced around. "How about your tenants? Are they okay?"

"I don't think they're home," I answered.

"Oh. Well, where's Ike?"

"Ike who?" I asked, wincing as the words came out like a weak sneeze.

"Ike Janus." He looked at me as if I should know the name.

I didn't.

"Isn't he the guy who moved into the Blaskeys' old house a few months ago?" Tilla asked. She still panted from her climb, and her plump face shone with perspiration.

"That's right," Lyle said. "This is his car." He pointed

short, blunt fingers, extending from his gloves, toward the Hummer that had hit my house.

A FEW MINUTES later, the cops were on their way. Phil Ashler, my retired across-the-street neighbor, had his cell phone with him and had called 911. Was this incident worthy of an emergency call? Too late to worry about it now.

I'd seen as much damage as I could from outside looking in, but I itched to go inside my dream home to see what nightmare the Hummer had created there.

Hey, it was my house. This was an emergency—by police definition or not. I owned the place—my impatient bank and I. These days I didn't live there, and as the mere landlady, I had no right to roam inside at random. Still, my lease with Charlotte and Yul permitted me entrance without notice in an emergency, and they clearly weren't here, and—

Okay. I'd talked myself into it.

I asked the crowd of neighbors to watch for the cops.

"Are you going to check out the damage inside?" Tilla asked.

"Yes," I admitted.

"Need any help?" Lyle asked. "I mean, can you get in okay? You'll need to watch out, in case the structure's damaged, or there's something else dangerous that you can't see."

"I'll be careful," I said.

"I'd be glad to go with you," Tilla said. Obviously my nosy neighbor couldn't wait to check out the chaos and report back.

"Thanks anyway." I led Lexie to our apartment over the garage. I grabbed my extra keys from a kitchen drawer, and we slipped down the steps and around the house to the back door.

It had been weeks since I'd been in my house. The last time, I'd merely stood in the magnificent main entry and nosed around nostalgically. I'd let Yul in after he'd forgotten his keys and needed to hunt for Charlotte's passport for an impending trip. It had taken him all of two minutes to find it and flee.

I'd been invited to some of their parties but had always found excuses not to attend. It was just too torturous to enter my home now that I didn't live there.

Entering through the back door, I stood in the kitchen. Lexie barked impatiently and tugged on her leash, as if she'd scented something enticing. "Hold on," I told her.

One thing I could say about my tenants: They were good housekeepers. The kitchen was as clean as a restaurant rated "A" by the health department. My beige tile counters trimmed in Mexican designs of blue, red, and yellow looked immaculate. So did their matching counterparts on the floor. The textured beige refrigerator door sparkled, as did the stainless sink and faucet.

I had not held a lot of parties myself in the couple of years I'd lived here before—life as a litigator didn't allow time for much recreational socializing—but my kitchen had always been a gathering place for my occasional guests. I didn't have time, though, to stand here and nostalgically study my once—and hopefully, someday, future—domain. I had to find what damage the wayward vehicle had wrought on the rest of my house.

From outside, I'd gathered that the Hummer had hit the living room at the far side of the house from where we stood. Or maybe it was the den next to it that I'd used as an office, though I didn't know what use my tenants made of it.

Lexie continued pulling, and I tugged on her leash, trying to get her to do a facsimile of a heel, which she was not inclined to obey. We headed toward the far side of the kitchen.

And stopped. Rather, I stopped, slamming down my left foot audibly as a signal to my tugging pup to follow my lead, but she didn't heed. In fact, she acted as if she'd never had any training, the way she strained at her leash to be let loose. Her nails clicked on the kitchen tile as she futilely tried to pull me faster and wound up spinning her paws like tires on rain-slicked cement.

I hadn't thought anyone home. Now, though, after I opened the door from the kitchen to the rest of the house, my ears were bombarded by a shrill sound, as if a child was crying somewhere.

But Charlotte and Yul didn't have kids. No one else was authorized to stay here, and even if they'd violated the lease, they wouldn't leave an infant here alone.

It could be Yul, though. He had a voice I'd term baritone, but the last time I'd come into the house, with him, I'd called out a question and hadn't been able to make out his shrill reply.

Was he here and hurt?

All the more reason not to let Lexie explore on her own. Hanging on with difficulty, I let her lead me to the source of the sound.

Unsurprisingly, it was from the room whose outer wall had been stoved in by the Hummer—the den.

My roomy, efficient, sorely missed home office.

As I said, I'd no idea what Charlotte and Yul used it for now. If I'd known, I'd have given them written notice to cut it out—a California statutory notice to cure a lease default or quit the premises.

For they were definitely in default under the lease, namely the no-pets-without-permission-and-a-stiff-security-deposit clause.

Plus, I'd believed that showbiz brassy Charlotte—who hugged every person she met as if embracing the entire human race—hated pets. She'd unabashedly avoided my adorable Lexie. And there had to be something really wrong with someone who refused to cuddle Cavaliers.

But Charlotte obviously didn't have a phobia against all pets. The waist-high luxury wire and carved wood cage that occupied the room wasn't just for show.

I bent and lifted my Cavalier into my arms as Lexie lunged toward the cage. Fortunately, it was along the inside wall—opposite the heaps of drywall that now littered the floor beneath the wreck of the wall where the Hummer had hit.

The shrill, scared sounds emanated from the enclosure. I couldn't tell from where I stood what kind of animal made them. Still holding Lexie, I drew closer, bent down, and looked.

The cage's occupants were long, furry, and masked, and had pointed snouts. Kind of cute. But . . .

Weasels? Did anyone keep weasels as pets?

I didn't know, but I was aware that some people made pets of a similar-looking little beast. Though not in California. At least not legally.

"You're ferrets!" I exclaimed to the five chattering, nervous little mammals that scurried around the crate in a parody of a person's perturbed pacing.

None denied it.

Though I'd never had a pet-sitting client that kept ferrets, I'd heard of people who did. I'd also heard of a movement to legalize the little critters in California. One particularly avid ferret fan had even run for governor on a "free the ferrets" ticket. But then, in California everyone runs for governor, and sometimes the most celebrated wins. And if I recalled the brouhaha correctly, the ferret fanciers, some months back, had succeeded in convincing both houses of the state legislature to agree on an amnesty bill, but our celebrated governator had vetoed it, invoking the need for further environmental evaluation.

So owning ferrets remained a felony. Or at least a misdemeanor—I'd never checked. I might have to now, though, when I gave written notice to my tenants to chuck the ferrets or cancel the lease. I hoped it wouldn't be the latter, since they paid me a healthy rent—enough that I had a little to spare beyond my mortgage payments.

Sure, I'd be entitled to compensation for their default, but I preferred to continue receiving rent . . . without the illegal aliens now occupying a valued corner of my home.

I stood there attempting to control Lexie, who wanted in the worst way to make the little beasties' acquaintance up close and personal. I pondered what to do with my battered den wall. I deliberated what this particular lawyer should do with such a gross violation of lease and law right in her own home.

And then a call reverberated through the entire downstairs of the house. "Is anyone in there? This is the police!"

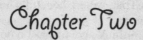

Chapter Two

DAMN! THEY'D WANT to see the damage. What should I do? Expose my tenants' possession of illicit pets?

They deserved it.

I put Lexie down, leaving the loop of her leash over my arm. As she stood on hind legs and sniffed, I lifted the large but fortunately portable cage from the floor, scaring the four long and furry ferrets all the more. As they skittered futilely to maintain their balance, I hurried them from the room.

The den abutted a hall that also led to the rear of the house and the laundry room. I aimed my awkward and unhappy baggage there, hoping the cops wouldn't barge in without invitation.

Was there any way to hush a bunch of small, squealing creatures? If so, I didn't know it. "Just a minute," I called in a feigned falsetto over the din. "Be right with you."

I reached the laundry room and deposited the cage on top of the adjacent washer and dryer. I then lifted Lexie, who was fascinated by the ferrets, back into my arms. She squirmed, obviously eager to further her acquaintance with them. Holding her as tightly as I could manage a protesting pup, I fled the utility room, closing the door behind us.

A short while after I'd moved into my beloved home, I'd been so irritated by the gurgles, groans, and belches of my electrical servants that I'd insisted on adding insulation to this utility room to keep the offensive noises inside. Thank heavens. That would hopefully muffle the ferret sounds, too.

Only then did I think about what I'd done and begin to cringe. I'd made myself an abettor, an accessory to breaking whatever law forbade harboring ferrets in California.

Oh, lord. Before, when accused of a laundry list of nasties, I'd been innocent of them all. This time, I was actually committing a crime. Would I ever again see my license to practice law? Not at this rate.

Not if I was caught.

"Hi, police," I cried out. "I'm coming."

As I'd figured, they were at the front door, two patrol guys in uniform. I was relieved not to see my suit-sporting nemesis on the L.A.P.D., Detective Ned Noralles, especially since Noralles was a homicide detective. For once, the police were around for something other than my discovery of a body whose untimely demise might be blamed on me.

"Sorry for the delay," I said. "This whole mess got my stomach churning and—well, no need to be graphic about it, though I wouldn't be surprised if you heard . . . Never mind." I daintily lifted a hand to my mouth, no easy trick while still grappling with Lexie. "Would you like to see what that darned Hummer did to my house?"

"Okay," said the younger of the two cops. His badge identified him as Officer Sallaman. His partner, Officer Elina, looked weathered, jaded, and bored, as if I couldn't show him anything here that he hadn't seen a hundred times before.

Both examined the mess that was the residue of my den wall, including rubbled piles of plaster, window glass, and broken sticks and fabric that were once Charlotte and Yul's furniture. A hint of Hummer fender showed through the hole.

Officer Sallaman made notes, while Officer Elina asked a few perfunctory questions: Who owned the house? Who lived here? Had anyone been home? Was anyone hurt?

I soon accompanied them back outside, Lexie leashed and trotting beside me. A greater crowd had gathered. Most, still, were neighbors.

A couple were reporters.

Damn.

I despised reprehensible reporters. Despite my later redemption, they'd first turned my life into a public free-for-all months ago in the guise of getting a juicy story about a lawyer who'd thrown her own case by handing a strategy memo to the opposing party. And why had she done such a dastardly deed? Because she was peeved at her client or because the opposing party had bribed her, or both.

Or so had gone all the false accusations against me.

But that's another tale. One I've tried my damnedest to put behind me, despite all the gory details I won't go into now.

That was the main reason, though, that when microphones were thrust before my mouth, I forbore from chewing on them, simply smiling secretively and saying, "No comment."

No better way to irritate irascible reporters.

Instead, I went over to where a group of neighbors had gathered—Tilla Thomason and her husband, Hal, who obviously enjoyed eating as much as his happily stout spouse; Lyle Urquard, the mad bicyclist; Phil Ashler, the sweet old guy from across the street; and a few I didn't recognize.

As we stood there, the others commiserating with my mess and clearly grateful it wasn't theirs, a jogger bolted down my street. Only he wasn't in sweats or any other exercise outfit I'd ever seen. In a suit and tie and polished shoes, he slid on the sidewalk and braked himself to a halt in the midst of my local pity party.

And stared at the Hummer and my house.

He cried out, "Oh, no."

Lyle stepped toward him, motioning Lexie and me to follow. "Er . . . Ike, have you met Kendra Ballantyne? This is her house. Kendra, this is Ike Janus." He pointed a long, scraped finger toward the nearby disaster area. "And that," he said, "is Ike's Hummer."

IN MY LIFE as a litigator, I'd come across all kinds of clients and opponents. Cynically, I'd concluded that most people should have been born with more than two index fingers, to give them more digits to point accusingly at others. I mean, I wouldn't have been shocked if Hummer Ike had dredged up a defensive argument that somehow I was at fault for putting my house in the path of his runaway car.

To my delighted surprise, though, Ike turned out to be an okay guy. Sheepishly, he answered my questions about how the Hummer had flown, with a tale of a forgotten cell phone, a missed message demanding immediate response, and a car idling in neutral on a hill, its parking brake unset.

Ike still hung around my house a couple of hours after its Hummer encounter, directing construction types he'd called in to do a temporary fix to my outer walls—mostly a frame of nailed boards to which heavy plastic had been stapled. Plus, the wrought-iron fence had been propped up. It was all a jerry-rigged fix, but would do for now to keep out early-season rain or opportunistic looters.

Not a designer's dream, though. My sprawling stone-façade château looked like a guy who'd treated a gash in his arm by hiding it beneath a big ugly bandanna instead of seeking stitches and cosmetic surgery.

"My insurance adjuster will be here tomorrow," Ike told

me as his workmen made motions as if done for the day. "I spoke to a manager, and got his promise."

Ike Janus didn't look like the kind of man to choose a Hummer. I'd always figured that people who picked huge, hulking, military-type vehicles were huge, hulking military types. On the other hand, a Hummer might be just the thing for short, bespectacled, suited sorts like Ike to manifest their masculinity. Or maybe Ike was the corporate CEO that his air of authority seemed to suggest. He certainly got things done. Fast.

"Thanks," I told him, barely noticing my own less-than-authoritative garb of faded green USC T-shirt over ragged denim shorts, floppy thong sandals held tight to my feet by my curled toes. At five-five, I was only a couple of inches shorter than Ike. Dashing from my apartment at the sound of the crash, I hadn't taken time to tame the frizzies in my hair, which had resumed its natural dark brown shade. I'd halted highlighting it during my prior troubles, which had left me, for a while, without a means of making a living. "What's the name of your insurance company?"

I got the particulars, including his personal list of phone numbers—home, office, cell, secretary—and promised to call if I hadn't heard anything from the adjuster by this time tomorrow. Hell, yes, I'd let him know. In my experience, it'd take more than a call from an insured to get the wheels grinding at an insurance company faced with the likelihood of coughing up cash to settle a claim.

On the other hand . . . "In case they ask, where is it that you work?" I was only taking a stab at being subtle in my inquiry.

Ike named a local baking company. Not just a little neighborhood store, but a major firm that distributed brand-name bread and pastries to all the supermarket chains.

"I don't just work there," he said. "I own it." He smiled. So did I. He *was* the CEO I'd taken him for. And between him and his insurance company, he was bound to have the bread to cover my loss.

And another good thing about Ike: He liked dogs. At least he liked Lexie, who behaved admirably as she sat at my side on her leash. While Ike watched the men at work, he'd bent over often to stroke behind her long black ears. That never failed to set her furry black-and-white tail happily wagging.

A neighbor to esteem, even if he didn't set his brakes as often as he should.

"Do you have any pets?" I blurted.

"A couple," he said. "Dogs. Mutts, actually, a lot bigger than Lexie, part sheepdog and part whatever."

"They sound cute." I reached into my pocket and . . . Yes, I hadn't left home without one. My card. The handy little business card I'd devised for my pet-sitting business. I handed him one. "In case you ever need someone to walk them, or to watch them while you're out of town."

He tilted his head to stare down the bottom of his bifocals to read the card, then grinned. "You're a professional pet-sitter?"

"Among other things." I wasn't about to tell him my whole life history, even if he wanted to hear about a temporarily defrocked attorney who'd taken up something fun to earn her living while waiting to figure out what was next.

"That's great. I'll definitely be in touch. And, Kendra, I really am sorry."

"Apology accepted. Again."

We exchanged smiles, and he turned to trudge back up the hill.

A tow truck from the Auto Club had already taken his Hummer. With nothing sensational remaining around here, the battery of barracudas—er, the group of reporters—had disappeared long ago. Most neighbors, too, although Phil Ashler from across the street had returned now and then to check on the patching's progress.

At that moment, Lexie and I stood there alone.

But not for long. A big black Escalade pulled up to the curb and parked. Lexie leapt to her feet and yapped in pleasure. That SUV was familiar to her. It contained her best friend, an Akita named Odin.

It also contained a friend of mine. A client.

A lover, at least when it suited us both.

I'd called Jeff Hubbard soon after the Hummer hit my house, mostly to talk about the unpleasant occurrence, but also to let him know I'd be late for the dinner we'd planned on grabbing together that evening.

A private investigator and security consultant by profession and a man who thrived on taking charge, Jeff had insisted on dropping over to make sure I was okay, though he couldn't get here right away.

I didn't need him here professionally, but I hadn't dissuaded him from coming.

And now, as he leashed Odin and they exited his SUV, I welcomed the six-foot-tall hunk to my hammered house, which I let him examine before I led dogs and him upstairs to my humble apartment abode.

Jeff liked to help solve problems. Which was fortunate, for I had a substantial one to fling at him.

What the heck was I going to do about those ferrets?

Chapter Three

THAT NIGHT, JEFF and I dined on deep-dish pizza with the works on top. The dogs devoured doggy food spiced with just a soupçon of pizza scraps. I admit it. I'm a soft touch for big, begging doggy eyes.

Over dinner around my cramped round table, we—the humans, not the canines—nibbled for a while on the progress of Jeff's current P.I. cases, then gnawed on my Multistate studies and pet-care tribulations. We tried to sink our teeth into my distasteful ferret dilemma, though no savory solution came to either of us.

"Kick 'em out," he said, taking a swig of Sam Adams from one of my heftiest beer steins. "All of them—tenants and animals."

"You're kidding." I scowled at the now-familiar face full of masculine angles that had character and class—and, when added to the hint of irrepressible golden beard beneath, was the most magnetic male visage I'd ever viewed.

His twinkling blue eyes acknowledged he was teasing. "Yes, but you'd better handle your dilemma sooner rather than later. You could always whisk the ferrets away and say they got stolen in the confusion."

"No, I won't lie about it. If I whisk them, I'll have to tell Charlotte and Yul where they've been swept. And I've no idea what to do with the illegal little buggers without getting myself in deeper."

"Send them to ferret heaven?" Jeff suggested.

"Bite your tongue." I stuck mine out at him, hoping it wasn't coated in unappetizing pizza glop. "You're talking to a professional pet-sitter. I'd never do anything so nasty to someone's beloved babies."

Taking advantage of my mugging, Jeff leaned forward and tickled my tongue with his. He tasted as spicy as pepperoni, as intoxicating as prime ale . . .

Okay, dinner was over. Time for Jeff and me to adjourn to my compact bedroom with its big-enough bed so we could feast on each other that night. Multiple courses. Delicious leftovers for breakfast, too.

Gourmet's delight.

EARLY THE NEXT morning, after extracting my commitment to care for Odin when he traveled the next week, Jeff left for work. Me, too.

Leaving Lexie at home, I spent the A.M. walking dogs, feeding cats, and visiting one of my favorite charges to make sure his defrosted mouse of the week suited him: Pythagoras, the ball python. Py had recently done a good deed for me, so I had a soft spot in my heart for the young blue-and-magenta reptile. He seemed well, and his mouse had apparently been devoured. "See ya, Py," I told his lethargic coiled carcass and headed for the next home.

My first break came at noon, and I headed to Doggy Indulgence Day Resort on Ventura Boulevard in Studio City.

My best friend in the world, Darryl Nestler, owns Doggy Indulgence. He greeted me at the door, hanging on like the expert he was to the squirmy Pekingese in his arms. "Hi, Kendra. You really are okay?"

"Sure."

He nevertheless eyed me up and down behind his wire-rims. I'd called this morning to assure him I was fine. The Hummer hitting my house had been eclipsed in the early news by some local political lunacy, which suited me fine. Still, I figured someone would hear about it and tell Darryl, so I preempted his concern by phoning him first.

Apparently satisfied that any injuries I'd suffered were internal, invisible, and inconsequential, he said, "Hold on a sec," which he was having a hard time doing with the increasingly wriggly Peke. He turned and let the furry red ball down on the linoleum floor. "There you go, Bruiser." He watched for a second as the miniature sumo wrestler bounded toward one of the spa's special areas for pampered pets, the one filled with human furniture. Bruiser leapt onto a sofa and settled down.

"No Lexie today?" Darryl asked as he turned back toward me.

Darryl's lean and lanky, and not a lot taller than I am. As usual, he wore one of his dark green Henley-style shirts, with the Doggy Indulgence logo on the pocket. It had strands of red Bruiser hair on it, which I began to pick off.

"I left her home today. Don't tell her I was here, next time you see her. She'll be crushed I didn't bring her."

Before, when I was a preeminent litigator, I'd left Lexie here a lot on weekdays so she'd never suffer from lack of attention. When my law license was suspended, I could no longer afford Darryl's lavish rates. He'd offered to let Lexie hang out here anyway, but I'd kept it to a minimum. I hadn't wanted charity, even from a chum as dear as Darryl.

Now, with Darryl's help, my pet-sitting gig flourished, and though I wasn't getting rich, I could afford Doggy Indulgence again. But my schedule often allowed me to take Lexie to jobs, so she didn't need day care as much. I nevertheless left her here a few times a week, just for the fun of it.

"So bring her next time," Darryl said. "How's the studying coming?

"Fine. Have a minute?"

"For you, I have . . ." He looked at the big black watch on his skinny wrist. "Five. Come into my office."

As usual, I ignored the too-sweet scent of pet odors sublimated by pine cleanser and followed him.

Darryl's small office had a major picture window that let him keep an eye on his four-footed charges while they were pampered by his pet-specialist employees. He motioned me to the comfortable chair that faced his cluttered desk. I slung the strap of my habitually huge purse over its back.

"What's up?" He knew me well enough to recognize when I was requesting a simple social visit and when I needed a pal's candid opinion.

"Ferrets," I replied, without pussy- or ferret-footing around. "What do you know about them?"

"Cute little critters. Has someone asked you to ferret-sit? You know they're illegal to keep as pets in California, don't you?"

"Sure, if you like creatures resembling elongated rodents, no, and yes," I rushed out in response to all his queries.

"Rodents? That's an insult to ferret lovers everywhere." He leaned back on his desk chair and crossed his hands beneath his head, obviously not a member of the offended fan club.

"I didn't say they *were* rodents, only that they resemble them."

"Not to me. Think weasel family. Or badgers. Or skunks."

"It's their owners whose actions stink," I retorted. "Or who're the weasels, sneaking them in like that."

"Like what? Which weasels are we talking about?"

"The tenant kind."

Darryl sat up straight, brown eyes wide behind his spectacles. "As in reality show Charlotte and her not-to-be-believed boyfriend?"

"You got it. So what do you know about the law against ferrets?"

"That's your job," he reminded me.

"True. And I'll do research when I have the chance, including how stringently the statutes are enforced. But what I need from you is advice. I mean, I have a clause in my lease with Charlotte that she's not to keep pets without my written permission, and to get it she's got to pay me a substantial deposit. She's violated it."

"So give her notice and kick her out."

I scowled at him. "Easy for you to say. But she's paying premium rent. What if I can't find another renter as generous?"

"Then let her stay but get more money from her."

"But what if someone learns there are ferrets in my house and I'm abetting a lawbreaker? Here I am, trying to get my law license restored, and you're suggesting that I allow someone to break the law on my own property?"

His sparse eyebrows slanted, Darryl stood and scooted his skinny jeans-clad butt onto his desk next to where I sat, deftly avoiding the mounds of paperwork. "Kendra, my friend, you don't want my advice. You just want me to listen while you figure it out for yourself."

"Who says?" I grumbled, not meeting his eyes. He *was* right, of course. I'd come here not to listen, but to talk. I'd wanted a sounding board who echoed back my ideas without an opposing opinion of his own.

Which was unusual, when it came to Darryl. Most often, when he spoke, I listened. The guy had more common sense than ninety-nine one-hundredths of the obfuscating attorneys I knew.

"Your old buddy Darryl says. And I think you already know what to do, don't you?"

"I guess."

"And *I'll* guess what it is. You have to go talk to Charlotte and tell her to chuck the ferrets."

I sighed.

"Hey, you're the silver-tongued lawyer who's nearly never lost a case in court. You'll figure out a way to tell Charlotte to lose her illegal little housemates without offending her. Piece of cake."

"Right." I stood and smiled in unqualified appreciation.

Yet why did I have such a sour taste in my mouth when I considered the coming confrontation?

Chapter Four

FRAN KORWALD CAME through the door as I was heading out. Her pug Piglet, on a leash, trotted amiably at her side.

"Hi, Kendra," Fran said with a huge smile. Though at least in her late forties, Fran dressed in snug, short, and suggestive clothes like a fashionable twenty-year-old, and looked adorable in them. Even the curls in her cropped dark hair added to her incredible illusion of youth. Today she wore an off-the-shoulder green T-shirt over short short-shorts.

She was a massage therapist and I'd made great use of her services. At a reduced rate.

But she was the one who was grateful. To me. Though I wasn't able to practice law, that didn't mean my scheming litigator's logic took a hiatus, too. A few months ago, I'd helped Fran resolve a custody matter with her ex-husband. Not over kids, but Piglet.

"How are you, Fran?" Still inside the door, now closed, I stooped to pat Piglet, who wriggled happily beneath my hand.

"Never better, but I have a friend who's going to call you. Marie Seidforth. She's not doing well at all."

"What's wrong?"

A couple of Darryl's charges from the doggy play area across the room bounded up to assert their alpha-ness to Piglet, the newcomer. Piglet scooted closer to Fran, who picked him up, and the interlopers were soon swept away by one of the alert attendants. As I watched them head back to the fenced area full of dog toys, I noticed that Darryl was now behind his big reception desk on the phone. He waved goodbye, but I didn't go.

Fran kept talking. "My friend has a house in a development in Santa Clarita. You know, the kind where you pay dues to an association, and they're supposed to keep the development nice for all the neighbors?"

I nodded my understanding.

She shook her head in perturbation till her curls bobbed. "Poor thing has been breeding boxers for years. No one minded, because she takes good care of them and keeps her yard clean, nothing for anyone to complain about."

"But someone's complaining," I surmised.

"Right. A new next-door neighbor who's made it clear she wants to run for president of the association next year. She's made my poor friend and her dogs a campaign issue, since the association's rules say only two dogs per house."

"And your friend has how many?"

Fran shrugged a slender shoulder, lifting her snug T-shirt slightly. "Depends on when. She had a new litter of puppies a few weeks ago. Rather, her prizewinning mama boxer Vennie did. I told her what a miracle you'd worked to let me keep Piglet, so she wants to talk to you."

"I still don't have my law license back," I cautioned. "What you're describing could be a legal matter, and I can't offer that kind of advice."

"A custody battle's a legal matter, too, and you helped

me by common sense, not a lawsuit. I'm sure she'll be in touch."

"Oh, Kendra, you're right on time," gushed my tenant after I'd gotten home. A pretty lady, Charlotte LaVerne was a would-be starlet who'd gotten her start in one of those reality TV shows that took the country by storm. I'd never figured out whether she'd survived or selected a mate or eaten silkworms, but apparently she'd been successful at it—for she could afford my top-dollar rent.

It was early evening, and I stood outside the carved oak front door of my big, beautiful rented-out house. While scooting from one pet I tended to the next that day, I'd taken the long way around often, to pass by here and see if my tenant had returned. Only when I'd headed home for the night did I find cars back in the driveway, lights on, my main house reoccupied.

Facing me from inside the door, Charlotte was clad in a silky blue tunic over matching harem pants, all beneath a big, frilly white apron. Though her look suggested food, her smell was her usual costly signature scent. I had to look up, from my five-five, to meet her sparkling blue eyes.

"On time for what?" I responded cautiously to her comment.

"For our party. We're celebrating that Yul and I are home from our trip to Palm Springs, and that the damage to the house wasn't worse. I'm so glad you'll be able to join us."

"But—" I found myself addressing her back, where her long black braid swung smoothly in the opposite direction of her swaying hips.

I knew that Charlotte and Yul took every opportunity to toss bashes, celebrating everything from moving in to six weeks after the summer solstice. Return from a vacation? Sure. But exultation over the injury to my beloved home?

Well, she had said they were rejoicing it wasn't worse.

And she was obviously too busy to focus on ferrets . . .

Ferrets. Where were they now? What would she do with them while her home was filled with nosy neighbors and flighty friends?

Would the cops come to celebrate—and to cart me off to jail for abetting a law-breaking tenant?

Oh, wouldn't my nemesis, Detective Ned Noralles, love that?

Fueled by my ferret dilemma, I followed her inside. My kitchen wasn't as spotless as when I'd passed through yesterday. Trays of food and bottles of wine were strewn on every surface. Charlotte, now by the big, useful island in the middle, wasn't the only one wearing an apron. A few unfamiliar women wore identical black dresses, and they wore aprons with a catering company's logo. The women picked up armloads of dressy tableware and waltzed from the kitchen.

Yul remained, though. Charlotte's golden-haired prize hunk didn't wear anything to shield his black silk shirt, but he studiously sliced salad ingredients and stuck them into a big metal bowl. "Hi," he mumbled as I walked by. The guy never talked much. I'd learned to take what mutter I could get.

"Charlotte, I need to talk to you. Yul, too."

"Great," she enthused. "We'll talk and cook at the same time."

Damned if she didn't put me to work stuffing mushrooms.

A few minutes later, my fingers full of gooey cheese cactused with sticky herbs, I considered how to approach the subject. The hell with it. I flew right in. "When I came in here yesterday—an emergency, because of the accident—"

"The Hummer," Yul interjected.

"Right," I agreed. "Anyway, I happened to—"

"Oh, *you're* the one who moved our little friends. Thank you so much, Kendra." Charlotte closed the few feet between us and gave me a big, gushy hug, as my too-friendly tenant was wont to do. I tried not to get any cheese on her. "They're still traumatized over the accident, but at least they're in a different room, though the laundry isn't the best environment for them. I keep them mostly confined when we're out or entertaining, though they love to wander."

As soon as I could, I stepped back. It would be hard to threaten a tenant while being embraced enthusiastically by her. "Charlotte, your lease says no pets without my permission."

She gave me a huge, toothy smile. "May I have your permission, Ms. Landlady?"

She apparently hadn't a clue. Or didn't want me to know how many clues she did have. "No, I'm sorry, you can't. Keeping ferrets as pets is illegal in California."

She frowned. "Well, sure, but everyone has them."

"Not everyone," I contradicted, then rephrased in case she hadn't understood. "It's against the law to keep them."

"But all the pet stores sell ferret food. No one pays attention to that silly old law."

"They're mine," said a deeper voice over my shoulder before I could protest again.

I turned to face Yul and had to look up to find that gorgeous, if vacant, face. "Then you're the one who'll have to get rid of them," I said.

"Oh, Kendra," Charlotte protested, taking her place at Yul's side and holding his hand. They made a gorgeous couple. And this particular gorgeous couple was ganging up on me. "No one will ever know."

I sighed. "*I* know. And I'm a lawyer."

"Not now," Yul said, drawing his big, bold brows together into a scowl.

"Yes, now," I contradicted, struggling not to shout at him. "I'm working hard to get my license unsuspended. And that's all the more reason I can't allow something illegal in my house."

"Our house," Yul protested. "We rent it."

I swallowed my sigh. I wasn't about to get into a lecture on real property law with this good-looking nitwit.

Or was he? Something deep in his brooding dark eyes suggested a twinkle. Was he toying with me?

The doorbell rang.

"The rest of the guests are coming," Charlotte said. "We'll talk more later, Kendra, I promise. And if we have to give up our little friends, we will. As soon as we find them good homes. Now, come help me answer the door. Wait till you see who I've invited."

I DIDN'T WAIT, but I did decide, just this once, to partake of Charlotte's hospitality. Why? Who knew? I slid out the door as some strangers came in, went up to my apartment, and changed from pet-sitting grunge to party casual.

After soothing Lexie's hurt feelings, I headed back down toward the house.

A guy in a navy sport coat came up the walk at the same time I did. "Hi," he said, holding out a hand. "I'm Chad."

He was tall and broad-shouldered and had a chiseled, Roman-nosed face that could have held its own in a handsome contest against any of Hollywood's latest male celebrities and won, hands-down and thumbs up.

I gladly shook his hand—and of course his grip was firm and sexy—and accompanied him to the front door, which stood wide open. He stood back to let me enter first. Very gallant.

"Are you from around here?" he asked. All that, and friendly, too.

"Yes," I said, but chose not to exert any explanations of my landlady status. "And you?"

"Kind of," he said. "Now at least."

He halted for a second inside the door, then threw his shoulders back. I had the impression he was bracing himself

for something. Was the guy a closet wallflower who pan-
icked at parties? What a shame that would be, but . . .

"Have a good time," he said, then hurried down the hall
with a purposeful stride.

"You, too," I called. I watched his hunky body disappear around a corner and sighed, as if suddenly deprived of
a treat I'd promised myself.

I shrugged away Jeff Hubbard's sudden glare in my
imagination. *As if you've stopped appreciating gorgeous
women just because we're sleeping together,* my mind shot
at him, and his visage vanished.

Chad wasn't my type. Assuming I had a type.

But even so I hoped for a chance to talk to him some
more.

Chapter Five

IF I'D BEEN a reality-show junkie, I'd likely have recognized a preponderance of the other people at Charlotte's party that night. As it was, I felt glad that a few familiar neighbors were also guests. At least not everyone was a stranger. But Charlotte hadn't asked them here for my sake.

The cynical little demon on my shoulder, my personal Mr. Hyde who reached in to control my mind a lot lately, told me Charlotte was just being smart. I mean, what neighbor who was a blissful participant at the party would complain about too many cars usurping precious parking spots on the narrow street, or the ear-splitting music rending the night air?

Only, if I'd known better, I wouldn't have let myself wind up in the same room as Tilla Thomason, let alone sit beside her.

My older neighbor from down the hill wore a silky floral muumuu that did little to hide her girth, which hung over both sides of her folding wooden chair beside mine. Neither of us had gotten to the living room in time to occupy the ghastly overstuffed white-and-black sofa or matching chairs that Charlotte had stuck there in what I considered a travesty of decorating. But hey, she could turn every room in the house horrendous if she chose.

It might be tasteless, but at least it was legal.

Most of the others chattering with exuberant animation over the amplified music were beautiful people, young—or youthful by age-defying artifice. Chad would have fit well among them, but I didn't see him. All were arrayed in designer outfits—a bit much for a party celebrating a hole in the side of a house, but who was I to judge?

My den, the room harboring that hole, had been sealed off with yellow tape that resembled the kind cops used at a crime scene. I knew that from experience. But this tape instead said simply, NO ENTRY. It was the big sign on the door, though, that would keep everyone out. UGLY ACCIDENT SCENE, it proclaimed. ANYONE WHO ENTERS HERE WILL BE INSTANTLY STRUCK UGLY.

With this chic crowd, that was a definite deterrent.

Were the ferrets again in that room? If so, since Charlotte was entertaining, they were hopefully confined. But had they been struck ugly? Though I'd dickered with Darryl about them, they'd struck me as fairly cute, even if their presence was anathema in this state.

On Tilla's other side, Lyle Urquard sat speaking with someone else, his back toward us. I hardly recognized my athletic neighbor without his bicycle and helmet. Or his usual Spandex, for tonight he wore an ordinary white shirt and gray slacks that bulged in front where his belly lay beneath. His sandy brown hair didn't look the least bit sweaty, either.

Ike Janus wasn't there or I'd have told my take-charge bakery-owner neighbor that I hadn't heard from his insurance adjuster that day.

As I sipped Chablis, I held the plastic glass with my left hand. Tilla had control of my right arm, screeching softly into my ear with pleasure each time someone connected with Charlotte's show sashayed in.

"Oh, heavens, that's Philipe Pellera," Tilla shrilled as a tall, slender guy with dark hair and darker features shimmied into the room, his shiny black trousers tighter than his neon red shirt. I recognized him myself from my occasional forays into music video TV stations. His singing voice was sensational, his gyrations the stuff of sensual legends. He was the latest Latin singing sensation, and with the way he humped his hips, his music videos should have been rated NC-17. Those bumps and grinds were dangerous.

I also remembered having seen a box of client files with Pellera's name on them in Jeff Hubbard's house, at a time I felt ethically encumbered from sneaking a peek. Now, seeing that sex symbol in piquant person, my curiosity was piqued even more—why had he needed an expert P.I.'s services?

Pellera took a seat on the couch, surrounded by sycophants who made room for him.

Before I'd recovered from my vision of Latin sensuality, Tilla gushed again. "That's Sven Broman." She pointed to a tall blond Viking in a tan sportcoat. "He was the next-to-last guy, the one Charlotte dumped for Chad Chatsworth. Chad was the winner, if you could call him that, since at the end of the final show, Charlotte took the money and gave Chad the boot."

Oh, really? Was that the Chad I'd met?

Earlier, most others who lived on our street had rolled their eyes as Tilla gossiped away, except for Lyle, and even he stayed occupied elsewhere. I'd gathered from some of their comments that they'd attended previous parties of Charlotte's where Tilla had identified reality show celebrities to the oblivious and uncaring, ad nauseum. None wanted to hear it anymore, even Tilla's husband, Hal. *Especially* Tilla's husband, Hal, who stood in a corner speaking with Phil Ashler.

Having assiduously avoided Charlotte's soirees before, I was a new body for Tilla to bombard with info I found less than fascinating. I'd been considering a courteous way to slip out of her grasp. Till now. Tilla had just hit on some stuff that snagged my interest. "How much money did she get?" I asked.

"A million," she replied, eyes huge in her drink-pinkened pudgy face. "And that's not all. Part of the prize was that she'd help with the producer's next reality show. Brainstorm it, pick candidates, even get paid for it. I mean, what woman could resist that?"

"Right," I agreed. Okay, she'd succeeded in snaring my attention. For one thing, I now knew which kind of reality show Charlotte had been on.

Tilla pushed her big moist lips closer to my ear. I stiffened as she said, "That Yul is one gorgeous guy, isn't he? I mean, Charlotte didn't do bad, dumping Chad and winding up with all this and Yul, too." She gestured with her empty glass around the glitz- and glamour-filled room.

"Maybe she's also got Chad," I said.

"No way!" Tilla sounded scandalized. "To prevent someone in Charlotte's position from getting it all—the guy *and* the money—it's a condition of her keeping the prize that she never see Chad again."

"Interesting," I said. "Then why . . . ? Never mind." I stifled a yawn. Chad's visit wasn't my business, and Tilla's dose of reality programming was now enough to last me a lifetime. "You know, I'm a little tired. I think I'll head to my place."

"Well . . . Okay." Tilla stood when I did, blinking as she scanned the room for my replacement. The obvious one would be Lyle, but he was slipping out the door, followed by Hal and Phil.

I guessed where they all headed: the kitchen, which served as the makeshift bar. I joined them, hoping to find my host and hostess to make my farewells. They weren't there.

That gave me a good excuse to meander about my house, hunting for them. And if I happened to spot something not being taken care of well, well . . . I already had to put them on notice to get rid of the ferrets. Adding more to it would be no trouble.

And maybe I'd see that Chad again, too. I was curious why he was there.

I went upstairs to case the bedrooms. Everything looked fine—except that the tasteless decorating had expanded to the second floor.

I headed back downstairs and along the hall between the living room and kitchen.

As I reached the door decorated with police-type tape and dire warnings, I heard voices. Startled, I stood still. So did the few other guests who traversed the hall with me.

"Someone's getting ugly," commented a pretty starlet-sort who kept going.

"Not me," said the blond Viking whom Tilla had ID'd as the reality also-ran Sven Broman. He followed the star.

My neighbors, just returning from the kitchen, glanced toward the closed door. Before any of us said anything snappy, the door banged open. Charlotte burst through it backward, but she continued staring into the room.

"Get out, Chad," she screamed. "I don't know what you think you're doing by coming here, but I want you gone."

Uh-oh.

"Get your lapdog away from me," shouted a male voice from inside the den. Lapdog? At least he wasn't howling about ferrets.

"I'll get away when you're out of here!" I recognized that voice, too, though the bellow and the high number of words in one sentence were unusual. Yul.

The Chad I'd strode in with erupted from the room. He plowed through the interested crowd in the crowded hall—me among them—with no sign of recognition on his furious face. "This isn't over, Charlotte. Like it or not, you'll see me again." He shouldered his way into the kitchen, and I heard the outside door slam.

Charlotte's usually perky face was pasty, and her white-toothed grin was as false as her measurements probably were. "We have something else to celebrate now, everyone," she said a lot too brightly. "Chad's gone."

I didn't know until a few days later how prophetic those words would be.

I WAS EXHAUSTED that night, so sleepy that I dropped off fast despite the din still pealing from next door.

The following morning, though, I woke up early and took Lexie for her walk. Though a couple years old, she was full of puppy energy, and I figured she was primed for more attention than a few fast minutes. I took her along on my rounds. It was Saturday, after all. A lighter day than the norm, since some of my professional pet care involved dog walking on days my human clients were at work. Unfortunately, Jeff was on a stakeout for one of *his* human clients that weekend, so we weren't getting together.

Same thing on Sunday—Lexie assisting me, Jeff unavailable, me studying for the ethics exam in my spare time. I also researched ferrets on the Internet. Interesting creatures. A lot of websites suggested people adored them as pets. Their problem, though, was that if they escaped into the wild, they allegedly enjoyed endangered bird species as lunch. Hence, their illegality in California. Why not other states? Good question.

The following day was Monday. Lexie and I had had such an enjoyable weekend, I asked her after our own early walk, "Do you want to come with me again today?"

Her black-and-white long-haired tail wagged eloquently as she stood on her hind legs and leaned her furry white paws on my shins. I knew that if she could speak English, her response would be a resounding, "Yes!" So, obeying as if she were the alpha of our pack, I hustled her downstairs and into my Beamer as I prepared to head off.

My Beamer was a leftover from my days as a successful litigator. I'd treated myself to it from the bonus I'd received after winning my first case for Marden, Sergement and Yurick, the law firm where I'd worked. The case that my mentor and then-lover Bill Sergement, whom I not-so-fondly referred to as "Drill Sergeant," had all but turned his back on as a big loser. Though we hadn't been lovers for a long time before I left the firm, Bill had turned his back on *me* when I'd been accused of handing a confidential memo to the other side in a more recent important case.

As I mentioned before, my usual penchant was to choose lovers of the loser persuasion.

In any event, despite some later unanticipated repercussions, the good part of that case almost ten years ago had been my winning my first courtroom combat, followed by the acquisition of the car that had stayed by my side despite my recent bankruptcy. And after its theft and wreck a few months ago, I'd had it restored to near-perfection.

Now, Lexie and I made my pet-sitting rounds of the day. I even dropped her with Darryl when I got to his neighborhood, so she could spend a few hours fraternizing with friends of the canine kind.

And then we headed back to our own digs.

As soon as we exited the Beamer, Lexie started acting excited. Though leashed, she leapt around similarly to the way she had a couple of days ago when the Hummer had hit the house, barking and tugging and behaving in general as if something significant was on her mind.

And a Cavalier with something on her mind was a dog to be heeded.

"What is it, Lexie?" I asked, half expecting to hear another rumbling engine of a runaway vehicle on our street.

But other than distant traffic, the drone of an aircraft overhead, and a few birds, I heard nothing.

Lexie tugged me toward the back door of the big house. "Just a sec," I said. I pulled her toward the garage, and peeked in a window. Neither Charlotte's nor Yul's car was there.

I headed for the front door, Lexie leading me, and rang the bell. Waited for a while, but no one answered.

Lexie's nose, in the air, kept sniffing noisily till she stood up on hind legs and scratched at the door.

"Lexie, off!" I commanded, not wanting her little doggy nails to chink gouges into my cherished oak front door.

They didn't have time to, for that same door swung open with no one behind it. I hadn't noticed that it was ajar.

"That's weird," I told my canine, who had tautened her leash as she lunged inside.

Lexie barked, straining on her nylon leash so strongly that I decided to let her lead while I followed. She headed through the entry, past the living room, and down the hall toward the closed-off den. The KEEP OUT tape now dangled down from one side. The door was shut, and Lexie lit into this one, too, with her burrowing paws. It didn't open for her.

It did for me, once I turned the knob.

And stopped with a gasp..

The ferrets were loose from their cage, and the long little varmints scrambled to stay out of the growling Lexie's way.

The stench was sickening. And in the middle of the room, Friday night's uninvited guest, the hunky, genial, and temperamental Chad Chatsworth, lay on his stomach, head turned toward the side. His clothes were in shreds, and so was he. Blood was spattered everywhere. Was he dead?

"Chad?" I whispered, crouching on the floor to find out.

I didn't sense a shred of a pulse.

But I did see a lot of what looked like small dog food chunks scattered all over Chad and the floor—and a bunch of blood puddled around Chad's throat.

It was 911 time. Déjà vu all over again, for Chad's wasn't the first body I'd stumbled upon in the last several months. But I was certain that the culprit in those cases was incarcerated.

And it appeared, since Charlotte and Yul weren't home, that the culprits in this case might have escaped from their wire prison before committing this direst of crimes.

Had Chad been their lunch?

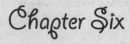

Chapter Six

I CALLED 911 and Jeff, in that order. I had a feeling I might need my own private private investigator. Unfortunately, I got Jeff's voice mail, so I left a veiled message. I didn't exactly want to blurt out over one unsecure cell phone to another that I'd just discovered a dead body—in my own house this time.

After blocking the barking Lexie in the kitchen, I tried, briefly, to coax the ferrets back into their cage—carefully keeping far from their teeth, as poor Chad apparently hadn't.

It was like trying to talk water into meandering up a mountainside. "Not bloody likely," the small, furry fellows screeched at me from beneath den furniture that was already partly mangled from the Hummer incident. Or at least I assumed that was what they were saying. It didn't help me to stay calm and convincing to see them speckled with Chad's blood.

Nor to have Chad's obviously deceased cadaver lying on the floor not far from me. And by doing anything at all about the ferrets, I was contaminating a crime scene, so I quickly decided to leave them alone.

I supposed that if I'd spoken ferret, or they understood English, I'd have explained the legal system to them. No matter how bad things looked, they were entitled to a good defense.

Weren't they?

I was reminded of a short story I'd read in my youth, "Sredni Vashtar," by Saki, the pseudonym of H. H. Munro. In it, a young boy had hated his guardian and supposedly sicced his surreptitious pet ferret on her, killing her.

I felt just terrible for Chad. No matter what the beef among Charlotte, Yul, and him, he'd seemed nice to me— not to mention alive.

I soon heard a rapping from the direction of the open front door. "Police," someone shouted. I headed that direction to greet them. It was a couple of patrol officers—a male and female this time—who'd followed the usual protocol of answering a call about a potential crime. When I showed them the body, they agreed a crime had been committed and called for backup.

Why wasn't I surprised, a while later, to see that the head of the detective detail at my front door was my old nemesis Detective Ned Noralles?

Maybe it was because he was a top-rung homicide detective, and this was definitely the kind of case that rang his chimes.

The hell of it was, despite my complete exoneration last time, Noralles didn't look surprised to see me, either. "Hello, Ms. Ballantyne. I received a call about a possible homicide here. Would you know anything about that?"

"I'd know about the homicide, Detective," I told him. "But not how the victim got that way."

"Of course," he said in a voice as smooth as his brown tweed suit. Detective Noralles was one good-looking African-American. He was also one good, determined homicide detective who clearly refused to let any case grow cold. He'd certainly kept the heat on me before, when he'd tried hard to prove I'd killed two of my favorite pet-sitting clients. He'd seemed a good sport afterward, when I'd not only proven my innocence but handed him a real, live, guilty suspect.

Maybe I would this time, too. Or rather, I'd let him go scrounge on the floor for the ferrets.

As I showed him and the two other detectives with him down the hall to the area already under scrutiny by the patrol cops, he said, "Care to tell me what you're doing in this house? Does it belong to another of your endangered pet-sitting customers?"

"No," I retorted. "It belongs to me."

That shut him up long enough for me to lead him to the discombobulated den.

"Hey, Detective," said the female cop from the patrol pair who'd first taken charge of the site. "Looks like the victim might have been chewed to death."

"Chewed? By what?"

"These little critters." Apparently the cops were cagier than I'd been, for they'd managed to round up the ferrets and deposit them back in their cage. I wasn't permitted to put a toe into the room, so I peered in from outside the door.

"What are they?" Noralles asked me.

"Ferrets," I responded with a sigh. His dark brown eyes glittered much too cheerfully, so I beat him to the punch-line. "Yes, I know they're illegal to keep as pets in California. They're not mine. They're my tenants', and I've already put them on verbal notice to get rid of them."

I'd hoped they'd have time to do it in an orderly manner, find the ferrets a good out-of-state home. I had nothing personal against ferrets, and I'd take a lot of animals over people as friends any day.

But now . . .

"You're the pet expert," Noralles said. "Care to tell me whether ferrets are outlawed because they're considered dangerous?"

"To endangered species," I said.

"Not people?"

"I don't think so." No website had suggested "Sredni Vashtar" was a true story, and I didn't mention it.

Noralles glanced back into the room, where police took photos and placed little numbers down to show the spots where they'd removed and bagged potential evidence. "Looks like *these* weasels may have been dangerous, although . . . Is the victim one of your tenants?"

"No." I decided to revert to what I'd learned as a litigator: When you answer a question, never volunteer information. It only leads to more questions.

"Do you know the victim?" His tone was a touch more severe, as if he'd figured what I was up to.

"Not really."

"Then do you know who he is?" exploded Noralles, with no attempt now to keep his cool.

"Yes."

"Ms. Ballantyne," he said through gritted teeth, "since this is your house, do you know of somewhere in it where we can go to talk? No, let me rephrase that." He obviously knew that my answer would have been a single-syllable affirmative. "Let's go somewhere where we can discuss this situation."

"All right," I agreed with resignation.

I led him into the kitchen, where Lexie greeted me with enthusiasm, though she eyed Noralles suspiciously. Did she remember him from our last ugly encounters? Who knew what went through her sharp canine mind?

I started to sit on one of Charlotte's kitchen chairs till Noralles nixed it. "This room needs to be examined for evidence," he said, "in case you killed him here."

I glared, and he had the gall to grin.

"Let's go outside," he said, all serious again.

In my backyard, enough landscaping hugged the wrought iron surrounding my estate to provide privacy.

Over the fence around the swimming pool hovered the top floor of the garage—my apartment and home. Since the Hummer had hit the house wall nearest the street, its effects weren't in evidence here.

Turning, I'd the ill fortune to find Noralles still behind me. Without asking his okay, I strolled to the fence near the pool and leaned on it.

I commanded Lexie to lie at my feet, which she did for five seconds before popping up again. I lifted her into my arms, which was good for a few moments of canine calm.

Noralles stood beside me. "Now, we can do this in a game of twenty-plus questions, or you can just tell me what you know. Which will it be?"

I preferred the former, but it would take extra time and piss him off even more. Besides, even with a suspended law license, I was an officer of the court. That meant I had to cooperate with the law, like it or not.

I therefore latched on to Noralles's latter suggestion and told him, "I believe the victim is a man named Chad Chatsworth."

"But you don't know him, even though he's now dead in your house?"

"Not really, though I met him here on Friday night." I told Noralles that I still I rented out the large house on my property owing to economic necessity. I described the Hummer accident, and how I'd found the ferrets. Then I told him about the party. "Chad and I happened to walk in at the same time. Later, one of the neighbors who watched the show my tenant Charlotte starred in said that Chad Chatsworth was the guy she dumped in favor of money and future TV projects."

"And Chatsworth was a guest at the party?"

"I think he crashed it. The neighbor also told me that one of the rules that allows Charlotte to keep her prize is that she can't have contact with her dumpee."

"You came in with him?"

"Kind of. I saw him first on the front walk. He introduced himself as Chad. No one greeted us at the door, so he just walked in. Me, too. I lost track of him and later heard Charlotte and her boyfriend, Yul, ask him to leave."

Okay, so I spoke euphemistically. But I'd been the subject of a couple of Noralles's murder investigations. I wasn't about to sic him on my tenants just because they'd had a falling-out with the victim.

Of course, that victim was found dead in the house they rented, after he'd been told never to darken its doorstep again.

But Charlotte a killer? Yul?

Ferrets?

What if Charlotte actually had been having a relationship with the guy who'd won her heart on that reality show—and tried to keep it from the world so she could keep her financial winnings, too? Did he threaten to out their relationship and jeopardize her juicy prize?

Did Yul find out about said relationship and get peeved enough to pull a Sredni Vashtar on Chad?

Or did the freed ferrets do it on their own?

If so, who'd freed them? Chad? And then he'd lain down on the floor so they could chew him to death? I didn't think so.

Could it have been an accident—Chad tripping, falling in a way that scattered both ferrets and their food while hitting his head and falling unconscious?

Then the ferrets, while scarfing up their spilled food, scarfed up some of Chad's flesh, too?

Seemed pretty far-fetched.

Before Noralles could bombard me with more questions than I'd asked myself, a woman wearing latex gloves slipped out through the kitchen door. Lexie squirmed in my arms, but I held her there. "I'd like to go over a few things with you where we found the victim, Detective. It looks as if he was attacked by those ferrets—all over, but most severely at his neck. His carotid artery was severed, and he died from loss of blood."

"Have you called L.A. Animal Services?"

"Yes, and a couple of their officers are here now."

I followed Noralles back inside the house, Lexie still wriggling under my arm. I watched as a guy and a girl in blue shirts and light pants who'd collected the ferret cage maneuvered out the den door as Noralles stood back to let them pass.

"What's going to happen to them?" I asked, holding the fascinated Lexie all the tighter.

"We'll hold them pending the outcome of the investigation into this incident," the woman said, stopping just outside the door and effectively blocking Noralles from entering the den. Though she was slighter than her male counterpart, she seemed to be having an easier time holding up her end of the cage.

"If it turns out that the ferrets were guilty only of chewing a corpse and not committing the murder, what will happen to them?"

"We'll call a ferret rescue group to come get them," the guy said, panting a little. His shirt showed a damp stain at the armpits.

I hated to ask, since I figured the answer was obvious, but said, "And what happens if the conclusion is that they killed the victim?" I didn't meet Noralles's eyes, though I knew they were watching me.

"Then they'll be humanely euthanized," the lady said, and the two continued toting the cage from the house.

Humanely euthanized. Sounded like an oxymoron to me. Ferret capital punishment.

"But why would he have let them chew his neck like that?" The words burst out before I could contain them.

"I'm wondering that, too, Ms. Ballantyne," Noralles said, entering into the conversation, then exiting as he eased past the animal control people and disappeared through the door.

I heaved a sigh as I watched out the front door while the animal control truck took off. A coroner's truck still sat behind the vacated space and in front of my wrought-iron fence.

The killings before had involved me because my pet-sitting clients had been the victims.

This killing involved me, too, since it took place on property I owned and loved. Plus, I'd met Chad . . . sort of.

My tenants might be involved, although I hated to imagine that. But one way or another, their ferrets were at best witnesses, at worst small murderers.

The investigator on the scene had implied that Chad was chewed to death. But I had too many questions just to bite into that as the answer. It sounded as if Noralles did, too.

One thing I knew for sure. After all I'd already gone through, I wasn't about to let anyone get framed for something she didn't do.

Not even those weaselly little ferrets.

Chapter Seven

IF A LITTLE thing like a Hummer hitting a house brought out the neighbors in force, imagine what an assemblage of law enforcement vehicles, including a coroner's van, did.

As Noralles finally left Lexie and me standing alone outside, the same group who'd gawked at the damage to my home descended. My pup and I headed outside the fence toward the street, to prevent them from sticking their noses closer to the crime scene.

Phil Ashler, the retired guy from across the street, appeared as if the excitement had interrupted his dinner, for he clutched half a submarine sandwich in one hand and a water bottle in the other. Thin enough to fit nearly anywhere, he insinuated himself at the forefront of the crowd. Lexie sniffed the air, obviously enthralled by the scent of his snack, but I held her tight at my side to prevent her angling for handouts.

"What happened, Kendra?" demanded Tilla Thomason, usurping my other side. I winced, recalling her gossipy tirade at Charlotte's last party. Though Tilla's face was a plump frown of concern, a potential new scandal brought a gleam to her watery brown eyes.

Not about to ignite a conflagration that would undoubtedly consume the neighborhood anyway, I simply said, "There's been an accident. Someone got hurt inside the house."

"I'll say," said Tilla's husband, Hal. Daylight revealed even more that though he was not as overweight as his wife, his girth straining his white knit shirt suggested he was a proud participant in the culinary largesse that added to her mass. Hal stared at the gurney being wheeled out of the house. On it was a closed body bag, and every eye in the area joined his in watching as it was loaded into the coroner's vehicle.

When I turned back, I saw Hal eyeing Tilla expectantly. Dutifully, she began barraging me with questions. "Accident? Are you sure? It looks as if someone died. Who was it? How did it happen?"

"Sorry," I said. "As you can see, this is a police investigation. I can't talk about it."

She screwed her features up to prepare a protest, but I was saved from it by the screech of bicycle brakes as Lyle Urquard stopped abruptly, sliding to a stop at the curb so fast that his cycle slipped. So did he. I grimaced in empathetic pain as the already bloody sides of his legs slid along the pavement. Again. This time not even his helmet had helped, for his cheeks were scraped, too.

All we needed was Ike Janus and his Hummer to make our little horde complete. Or maybe that wasn't irony oozing from my thoughts, for the guy had seemed the take-charge sort. Maybe he could have taken charge of this horrible situation, dispersed the crowd, and gotten the cops to hurry.

Sure. Like he'd gotten his incommunicado insurance adjuster to hurry. He'd sworn he was on top of it when I'd called to remind him, but still no one had contacted me.

Right then, I needed air. I needed privacy. I needed for the whole horrible situation not to have happened.

Just like Chad would have said, had he been able.

"But, Kendra," Tilla protested, "you've got to warn us. This is our neighborhood, too. If someone's been attacked by a burglar or something, we all need to know so we can stay alert."

"That's right," Phil Ashler seconded, his mouth full of sub sandwich.

I doubted they needed to fear ferrets sneaking in during the night to feast on them. But I still hesitated to cast verbal stones at the furry little creatures.

"I don't know what happened," I dissembled, though it was far from being a big, fat lie. "I'm sure the police will tell us what they can." Now *that* was a large, obese prevarication.

"We need to call a Neighborhood Watch meeting," Lyle suggested, still blotting his bleeding leg with a tissue.

"As soon as we know what to discuss," Hal Thomason agreed.

They all stared at me once more.

This time, what saved me wasn't an awkward bicyclist but an even more awkward situation, for a small sports car came up to the driveway and the gate began to slide open.

Charlotte and Yul were home.

Yul was driving, and I stood nearer the passenger side as the car started through. The window rolled down, and Charlotte shouted out, "What's going on, Kendra?"

I wasn't about to reply in front of this entire assemblage that someone she'd argued with had died in her den.

I didn't need to, for even as I inched forward after the car, the front door opened and Detective Ned Noralles leached out. Even from this far away, I could make out the crocodile-snide smile on his face.

"Oh, Charlotte," I whispered after them. "Yul, too. I don't envy you your next few minutes." Or days. Or even weeks.

Even though I'd not become best buddies with my huggy, gushy, rich reality show graduate tenant or her strong, silent, and possibly smarter-than-he-acted boy toy, my sympathy definitely swayed me, for now, into their corner.

But if it eventually turned out that either or both had actually conspired to kill someone in my beloved house, heaven help them!

NOT THAT I was surprised, but less than five minutes later the media descended. Actually, I wondered what had kept them.

The vans that appeared looked prepared to lift off and hover if their dish antennae on top started rotoring like helo blades. They jostled for the few remaining prime parking places on the constricted, twisting lane. Before they could negotiate the street or settle their pecking order, swarms of reporters leapt out and thrust microphones in front of whoever didn't thrust them back. Camera jockeys followed, gesturing cues to their on-screen personalities.

My cue to leave.

"Let's go, Lexie." I gave my trained pup a small jerk on her leash to let her know to stand and heel.

That apparently was a cue for one of the untrained reporters to swoop and shove a mike at my mouth.

"You're Kendra Ballantyne, aren't you?" The short-skirted TV newsmonger flashed me a nasty grin of the Cheshire cat variety.

"Never heard of her." I turned my back.

"What happened, Ms. Ballantyne?" came the shout from behind me. "Was someone killed in your home? Who was it?"

Too bad it wasn't one of you, I thought, immediately retracting the ungenerous thought. Dead was dead, and I'd seen enough death lately to last for several litigators' lifetimes. I didn't wish permanent termination on anyone, even my worst enemies—which included reporters.

A little well-directed damage, though, like someone else snatching up their news scoops . . . that was a taste of just deserts that I'd eat up, given the opportunity.

I hustled Lexie and me back inside through the gate, ignoring the hapless uniformed officer assigned there to hold back the hovering hordes.

"Hey," he called, hurrying after me.

"Sorry," I said to him softly. "I live right there." I gave a fast gesture with my head toward my upstairs apartment. "Feel free to check with Detective Noralles."

"I'll do that." Harried dismay turned the young man's forehead into one big frown as the reporters took his momentary distraction for invitation and started spilling through the gate.

Ignoring me, he gestured for backup and began shooing them all back again, his hand hovering over another item on his belt—his holstered weapon—that attracted everyone's attention a lot more pointedly than his radio. The group began to recede.

For that moment. But cops would be combing my property for clues for the rest of the night. And wherever law enforcement engaged in a homicide investigation, the media wasn't about to slink away.

I had a phone call to make. Only, my wall phone rang even before I'd let Lexie off her leash.

Did I dare answer? My only caller ID was on my cell phone. One of the diehard reporters could have somehow latched on to my unlisted number, and simply saying hello could lead to beating off a whole new barrage of questions.

But I was once a litigator. Would be again, soon. My mouth was my most skilled instrument, and I readied it to spew curses and threats if the caller was someone I didn't want to hear from. I snatched up the receiver and growled, "Yeah?"

"Kendra?"

My braced body nearly buckled. "Jeff, I'm so glad it's you."

"I'll bet. What's happened? The news is full of pictures of your house and speculations you're involved in another murder."

"Tell me about it. No, on second thought, don't. I'll tell *you*. At your house, in about half an hour. Do Odin and you feel like a couple of overnight guests tonight?"

I could hardly have felt more relieved when he assured me they did.

Chapter Eight

OTHER THAN WHEN Jeff had initially hired me to pet-sit for Odin—he'd been my first customer when I'd begun to wonder whether Lexie and I would wind up begging on street corners—I can't recall a time I'd been so happy to slip my Beamer into the driveway at Jeff's home.

The pseudo Mexican ranch-style house was located in the flats north of Ventura Boulevard in Sherman Oaks. It had become my home-away-from-home, even when—especially when—Jeff was out of town, since I was Odin's surrogate human and usually moved in to look after the Akita along with my Cavalier.

Of course there were many times since initiating our business relationship when I'd been more than a little happy to see Jeff himself. Even aside from the sex, he'd become pretty important to me.

And counting our definitely delightful sexual exercises, he was even *more* important to me. But who was keeping count?

Odin greeted Lexie at the door with a woof and a house-thorough romp. Jeff greeted me at the door with a glass of wine and a kiss that tossed into oblivion the day's most terrible trials and tribulations. Temporarily.

"Do you want to talk first or eat first?" he asked. The sleeves of his white shirt were rolled up unevenly, exposing unmatched lengths of hair-sprinkled arm. Sexy.

Then there were his faded jeans, snug in all the sexiest places. Okay, so it wasn't just refuge and a repast on my mind. Not after that kiss.

"Let's talk while we eat," I replied, tearing my stare from his big and beautiful bod.

For an instant, I thought of Chad and how good-looking he'd been. What a waste—even if he hadn't been the great guy my initial impression suggested.

Jeff had brought in Peruvian takeout, some *lomo saltado* sautéed beef for him, and *pescado sudado,* steamed fillet of fish, for me. Good stuff, and filling, with aromas obviously enticing to our respective imploring canines.

But unlike Lexie and Odin—whom we made settle for simple dog food despite their exceptional begging efforts—I hadn't a huge appetite as I told Jeff about Lexie's earlier excited behavior, leading to the discovery of Chad's unenviable end.

"Ferrets?" he said after swallowing a chunk of bread. "Chewed on a corpse?"

"Or converted a living person into a dead one," I replied. "Is that in their nature?"

"Doubtful, but . . . have you ever read 'Sredni Vashtar'?"

Unsurprisingly, he hadn't, so I described the century-old story that had been circulating through my synapses since I'd discovered Chad Chatsworth with the ferrets in my den.

"And the ferrets killed the kid's guardian?" Jeff said as I finished, his dusty blond brows dipped dubiously.

"That's the implication."

"We'll see."

I wondered for a minute if he intended to find a few ferrets and test their fondness for human flesh—not an easy task in a state that turned ferrets into fugitives.

Instead, he headed for the Internet, used some of the most-sought-after search engines, and spent an hour checking out ferrets on some websites I'd visited before and many I hadn't.

We learned that ferrets are in a classification of mammals known as mustelids, along with weasels, wolverines, badgers, polecats, and similar sorts.

Like their cousin skunks, they have simply awful smells unless their scent glands are removed, which is often done when they are pets.

Fortunately, the ferrets Charlotte and Yul had brought into my house had apparently been deskunked, since I hadn't smelled anything putrid the first times I'd seen them. And the last time, what I'd smelled had most likely been human corpse.

Speaking of which, we found nothing at all that suggested that ferrets are lethal to anything but small animals such as rabbits and birds, including some endangered species of the latter—which I'd already learned was what rendered ferrets unwelcome in California. But the long, furry, mostly masked-looking little buggers are definitely adorable.

And are not reputed to be homicidal.

Eventually, we got our fill of finding out about ferrets. Especially when, sitting beside him, I rested my chin on Jeff's shoulder. He turned, I turned, our lips locked and . . .

Well, you can guess what we did for the remainder of the evening.

THE NEXT DAY, Tuesday, I got up later than I should have—I was distracted from getting dressed upon awakening in Jeff's bed—and kissed him goodbye. Lexie and I practically flew out the door toward my pet-sitting rounds.

I'd be more prompt next week, I promised myself, when

I'd wake up only with Odin and Lexie around. Jeff would be gone on business.

The early routine went well, despite a couple of disgruntled housebroken hounds all but attacking to get outside to do what they'd been waiting for.

Late morning snuck up on me all too soon. I'd picked up a new client a couple of weeks before—a cute terrier mix named Widget. Widget's temperament was of the manic kind, which was why I'd been hired to step in a few afternoons a week to give him a midday walk. Better yet, a run, to burn off his excess energy. Heck, the ten-month-old pup was *all* excess energy. And unfortunately, the word *training* had eluded his owner's vocabulary, so Widget bounced all over the place even on a leash.

That meant leaving Lexie at home or dropping her at Darryl's while I dug in for a little Widget discipline. That day, she was already along for the ride. Since I didn't want to take more time fending off any dawdling reporters with manners worse than Widget's, I eschewed my apartment and left Lexie at Darryl's doggy resort. He was out when we got there, probably a good thing since I still needed to hurry.

I'd cry on his shoulder later about finding Chad Chatsworth among the unwelcome ferrets.

Widget's owner lived in a small stucco home in the northern Valley. That house, and all its identical neighbors, abutted a flat, broad boulevard with a nice-sized sidewalk. That day, I felt especially energized when the whiskered black fireball that was Widget finally sat, for the first time, on my command. Not that he stayed more than a millimoment. But Widget's temporary obedience hyped my petminder's self-confidence nonetheless.

Too bad it didn't carry over to my lack of confidence about the pending ethics exam. I'd passed it before, years ago, as part of the California Bar Exam. That was right after I'd graduated from law school and was still used to studying—and nothing in my life interfered with my immersing myself in the study guides.

Certainly nothing like a murder in my own off-limits house.

"Okay, Widget," I finally said to the terrier, who was tugging so hard on his taut nylon lead that he was choking himself on the training collar.

I scooped the wriggling thirty-pound pup into my arms. My annoyance with his wayward disregard for my training evanesced when he looked at me with his huge brown eyes and licked my chin.

"You're welcome," I said with a laugh, settling him back in the small storage room that was also his dogdom when his owner wasn't home.

Then it was time to retrieve Lexie from Darryl's.

I delayed leaving there when he pulled me into his office to ask questions about the latest newsworthy incident to impose itself into my life.

"Yes, another murder," I told him, rolling my eyes and spilling my guts once again. I explained who Chad Chatsworth was and how I'd found him.

"You're not a suspect this time, are you, Kendra?" Darryl demanded, holding the edges of his desk with bony fingers as if to brace himself.

"Only if Detective Noralles gets stumped and needs a scapegoat," I said with a sigh. "But before me, he's got some ferret suspects. And their owners, since they're the ones with easier access to the house where Chad was found, plus a grudge against him. Or at least that's what I gathered at Charlotte's party."

"So Charlotte LaVerne might have offed the guy she'd once chosen as her perfect lover? You really believe that?" Darryl's thin brows rose skeptically over his wire eyeglass frames.

"To keep a million dollars and the possibility of a lot more? I'd hate to think so," I said with a sad shake of my head, "but that's easier to believe than the ferrets decking Chad and chewing him to death on their own."

BUT A FEW hours later, back at my home, I decided that my acceptance of Charlotte as a viable suspect would be more unlikely than I'd thought.

Lexie and I had just arrived. I'd driven around slowly before pulling the Beamer into its spot, making sure no reporters still lurked to spoil our constitutional. I intended to take Lexie on a neighborhood walk of our own before settling down to study till Jeff arrived.

I'd peered into the garage window before heading upstairs to our apartment. No cars had been inside.

Had Charlotte and Yul fled?

Nope. I learned they hadn't as I heard an engine and peeked out to see Yul pull onto the property. I soon felt my floor vibrate as he drove his grumbling sports car into the garage below. He was alone. No Charlotte riding shotgun.

I waited till he was inside the house before leashing Lexie and heading downstairs. I wasn't in the mood for a single-syllable conversation about what had happened to Chad Chatsworth.

No sooner had Lexie and I gotten to the front gate than it began to open for Charlotte's brand-new brilliant red luxury sedan. As she pulled in, I waved.

She stopped. Her window rolled down.

So did her tears. I'd never seen the perky brunette with perfect makeup so upset. "Oh, Kendra," she sobbed, laying her head down on her steering wheel.

Only she hadn't parked yet, and the car crawled forward, not to the right, toward the garage, but straight toward the parking space beside it.

"Be careful, Charlotte," I called to her. I cringed as her auto approached the rear bumper of my Beamer. "Charlotte!" I shouted. "Stop your car!"

She did, maybe an inch away from stoving in my poor Beamer's butt.

Giving Lexie a little tug to tell her to follow, I hurried back up the drive toward her stopped car.

The driver's door stayed shut.

As I looked in, I beheld Charlotte, head still down, crying uncontrollably.

"Sorry, Lexie," I murmured. "Looks like our walk will have to wait until later." To Charlotte I said, "Let's get you into the house, okay? Then you can tell me all about what's wrong."

As if I couldn't guess.

Chapter Nine

TO MY SURPRISE, Charlotte invited herself upstairs. My usually high-flying tenant had never before seemed interested in visiting my modest second-story flat. All our landlord-tenant interaction had been in my much-missed mansion or on its grandly maintained grounds.

She even led the way, Lexie and I bringing up the rear as we all mounted the garage-side steps. I held back to make sure that *her* rear, sashaying from side to side as she scaled the steps, stayed far from my face. I had to catch up and squeeze around her, though, to unlock the door.

My little kitchen would have fit into one corner of my much more magnificent culinary environment in the main house, but it was still where I did most of my meager entertaining. I showed Charlotte to one of the chairs at my round table, and sighing, she sank into it, resting her small chin on trembling hands. Her perfume began to permeate my apartment, and I made a mental note to open some windows later.

"Would you like something to drink?" I asked. "I've water, apple juice, diet soft drinks, red wine—a nice Bordeaux, I believe—amber beer or—"

"Rum and cola, if you have it," she ordered. "Mostly rum."

I turned before she could see how my brows reached for my hairline. I considered joining her in something strong. I had a feeling that whatever she was about to spill to me wouldn't be easy to imbibe. I settled on a beer.

A little later, Lexie at my feet, I sat across from Charlotte at the table, watching her swig her strong rum concoction as if she were an overheated runner just handed a bottle of water. I sipped my Sam Adams from a mug to brace myself, then began, "Tell me why you're so upset, Charlotte—though of course I can guess. I'm sorry about your friend Chad. It must have been a shock to learn what happened. Especially because it was in the house where you're living." I'd developed tremendous tact as a litigator. The idea was to start the wheel turning with what I intended to learn, then let her respond with her own spin on it.

"I feel terrible that he's dead, even though he wasn't my friend anymore," she said, sounding surprisingly sad after what I'd witnessed the other night.

"Chad crashed your party," I said to Charlotte, "so I wondered how close you were. Especially since you and Yul didn't welcome him with open arms. But I heard that Chad and you were an item not long ago."

"Only in front of the cameras," she shot back, the glare from her blue eyes so pointed that I felt the stab in my cheek.

"But from what I gathered, he was the last guy standing on a show where you had to choose the supposed love of your life."

"Well, yes." She shrugged a slender shoulder beneath a snug, white shirt whose hem barely met the top of her gray sweatpants. Then she took a good stiff swig of her drink.

"Were you just acting for the camera?" I pushed.

"Not really." She sighed. "He was the best of the fifteen-man pool I started with. I knew that right off. And . . . well, by the end I actually was in love with him." Another hefty swill.

"I see," I claimed, while my mind mulled over this revelation. "Did you know you'd have to choose between him and a bunch of money when you picked Chad?"

She shook her head. "No, but there've been a lot of reality shows that have a catch. A few made the main player choose between *mucho* money and supposedly true love. Some shows were straightforward about their endings, some weren't. I figured something like that could happen in this one, too, and I was fully prepared to pick love over money."

I felt floored. That wasn't what I'd anticipated. Charlotte had Yul now and a whole lot of loot. Plus a burgeoning career in reality TV.

And she'd chewed out Chad but good at her party, without hiding it from any of her house full of guests.

"But you dumped Chad on the last day, right?" I asked.

She nodded sadly. As she spoke, her speech was slurred. "That was when I found out he was really in it for the fame and fortune. Not that *he* was offered money and a show to dump *me*, but he accidentally let slip about his girlfriend from home, how his being on the show had been her idea, and how she was still in the picture."

"That doesn't make sense."

"Sure it does, sort of. Hardly any couples in these shows actually stay together long enough to still be an item months later, let alone get married. But most major contestants became media celebrities, at least temporarily. There's lots of money in that. It's what Chad and his girlfriend apparently counted on—together. Only when I found out, I decided that if I couldn't have him, I might as well settle for fortune and fame, and a reality show of my own."

"Might as well," I agreed. My mind was definitely boggled. I'd already decided that, huggy habits or not, Charlotte was probably a mercenary queen, ready to kick a guy who was down on his knees to propose to her right in his impoverished teeth.

Instead, she'd settled for a bushel of money as second best.

"And then Chad showed up at your party. Didn't his visit threaten what you'd gotten?"

"Yes," she acknowledged. This time, she just took a sip, maybe because her drink had nearly disappeared. "I was pretty damned mad about it, especially since he and his girlfriend nearly made a fool of me. I guess I made a spectacle of myself."

"Everyone understood," I said sagely, then added, "Of course it also gave you a good motive to kill him."

"Kendra, you can't believe that!" she squealed. "I mean, that nasty detective said the ferrets had human help, but not even he has accused me of having anything to do with Chad's death." She paused, eyes rolling upward as she pondered. "Not directly, at least. He really upset me."

Hence her histrionics in the car? Maybe.

I'd found out the hard way that Noralles wasn't a nitwit. I wondered how he'd become certain the ferrets hadn't acted alone in killing Chad—the autopsy?

And whom did he suspect, if not this possible perpetrator who'd had motive, means, and opportunity? Or was he playing cagey with Charlotte, waiting for her to implicate herself?

"I suppose, by 'nasty detective,' you're referring to Detective Noralles?" I asked dryly.

"You know him?" She looked at me in confusion till her blue eyes narrowed in understanding. "He was the one who tried to pin those murders on you, wasn't he?"

"The same," I acknowledged with a smile as wry as I could grin it. "What has he asked you?"

"Mostly about ferret habits." She swung herself to her feet. She had to hang on to the table, I figured, since she'd chugged the hefty helping of rum in less than a minute. To make sure the table and Charlotte stayed erect, I held on, steadying it, feeling it tilt in my tenant's unstable grip. My beer stein was nearly drained, but I set it on the floor anyway to ensure it didn't slide off and smash. She went to the counter and refilled her glass with rum, not even a hint of cola this time.

"Like what?" I asked.

"Their favorite food, for one thing." She sat once more, swaying unsteadily in her chair and taking another swig. "But he knows that. It was all over the place. I asked *him* questions, too. Sure, the ferrets chewed on Chad, but whoever killed him dumped ferret kibble all over his body, especially around his neck. Of course the poor little creatures would chew on what they thought was just an extension of their food."

My sudden shuddering segued into a valiant attempt to deactivate my gag reflex. I croakingly continued, "Then the police believe someone killed Chad and set the ferrets up—scattering food to make them feast on him, and hoping the evidence would indicate they did it all?" As much as I hated discussing the disgusting details, that sounded feasible. More feasible than pinning the murder on the ferrets.

"Yes, poor, innocent creatures."

Well, not totally innocent. I'd seen some treacherous teeth marks. My voice shook as I said, "Did you ask if there were any marks on Chad to suggest someone killed him before he sank to the ferrets' level?"

"I kind of asked, but the detective didn't answer."

"So I don't suppose he told you who they think would do such a thing."

"Like I said, the detective didn't tell me much, but some questions he asked make me sure he thinks *I* did it. Or Yul did."

Big surprise. Only, wasn't that a little too obvious? Okay, maybe I was doing an about-face, but my suspicions were turning elsewhere, to suspects as yet unknown.

Chad had been killed in the house Charlotte and Yul rented, after a party where they'd all but punched him out. The ferrets may have been set up to take the fall. But would either Charlotte or Yul have tried to do that to such prized pets?

Probably, if it would eliminate them as suspects.

Which it apparently hadn't.

Charlotte's mind seemed to stagger along the same initial lines but stopped short of what I'd concluded. "We wouldn't do that to the ferrets. They're Yul's, but I adore them, too. And now they're in ferret prison." Her voice broke, and her eyes brimmed with tears. "I don't know whether the cops have determined yet how much the ferrets actually did contribute to Chad's death. The best scenario for them will be if they're found totally innocent. Then, they'll be shipped off to some ferret rescue place, probably in another state. The worst case . . ." Her voice trailed off as she dropped her face into her hands.

She didn't have to finish. I heard the Animal Services lady in my head: *They'll be humanely euthanized.*

Charlotte's tears became contagious, though I contained mine in moist eyes.

Shaking so hard that the table between us started to shimmy on the tile floor, Charlotte swept her hands from her head and stood again. Her reddened eyes grew grimmer. "The thing is," she said hoarsely, "that even if the ferrets are cleared, the police will still want to know who killed Chad in the first place . . . and that detective might accuse Yul. Or me. But we didn't do it."

I genuinely hoped they hadn't. Either of them. "You're sure Yul—"

"We're each other's alibis, for whatever good that'll do." Though her sigh was soggy, she took yet another swig of rum. "We'd gone to Vegas for the fun of it, but I was supposed to have a meeting on my show ideas yesterday so we didn't stay overnight but decided to come back. The thing is . . . Well, you might have noticed that Yul's a sexy-looking guy, and in this case looks aren't deceiving. We took a little detour, pulled off the road, and spent the night . . . I'm sure you get the idea, but we won't be able to prove it."

I chose not to pursue questions about where they'd been or what they'd been doing. A picture glowed graphically in my mind, though, till I switched to something else. "Did you have any idea Chad would be in the house when you were gone?"

She shook her head so vehemently that her long braid gave a whiplike lash. Her ensuing unsteady blink suggested her drinking, plus her head movement, had made her dizzy.

"And do they know how he got in?"

"The police shed . . . er, said, that some of the plastic stuck to the wall that the Hummer smashed in was loose." She slurred an occasional word despite the clarity of what she said.

When I'd arrived, the front door was ajar. How had it gotten open in the first place? Maybe the killer and Chad came in through the plastic and only the killer exited from the front . . .

"Chad had no business being there," Charlotte continued. "He knew I never wanted to see him again, and I told him that once more at the party. But he wanted to ruin everything, out of revenge. Only he was the one who hurt me, you see?" She paused till I nodded. "Never mind that he'd planned all the time to stay with his girlfriend. He was so pished . . . pissed off after I dumped him on the last show that he made it clear he'd do anything to convince the producers I was really madly in love with him and intended to see him secretly. And he knew full well that my seeing him would mean I wouldn't get to keep the money or be able to help develop new shows. Spite, that's all it was."

"And a good motive," I muttered.

She shot me a horrified, if fuzzy, stare. "You don't think I did it, do you, Kendra?"

"Of course not." I wished I was as convinced as I hoped I conveyed.

"Honest," she said, holding up some fingers unsteadily, as if she was either attempting a Girl Scout oath or was too soused to sense that the bird she flipped me wasn't flying. "I didn't know Chad was there the night he died. Neither did Yul. He must have sneaked in to try again to sabotage everything for me."

"So you killed him. Okay, okay, I'm just playing devil's advocate," I said in response to the look of horror on her face.

"You've got to believe me." Charlotte's grasp was firm, her unfocused blue eyes beseeching. "The ferrets may have been framed, but if those sweet little guys get off altogether, *we'll* be framed instead. Please help us. I'll hire you, because I know that, of all people, you'll understand. You went through the same kind of thing, didn't you?"

"Yes," I admitted reluctantly. "And I agree you need a lawyer. I can give you a referral, but you can't hire me, Charlotte. Even if I had my law license back, I'm a civil litigator, not a criminal defense attorney."

"We don't need a lawyer, at least not yet. You solved the murders in your own case. Can't we hire you to find out what really happened?"

"I'm not a private investigator, either." Although I knew a damned good one. One whom, if I asked, would help me figure out what really went on among Chad, my tenants, and their ferrets.

Hey, I was actually considering it. Did I buy her story?

My pondering must have been legible in my expression, for Charlotte cried, "You will help us. I know you will. You believe me, don't you?"

"What I believe is that I've got a lot of questions that need to be answered before—"

Before I knew what she was doing, Charlotte had sprung to her feet and drawn me into one of those hugs that had so repelled me when I'd first rented my adored house to her.

The movement must have startled Lexie awake, and she leapt up, woofed, and lapped excited circles around Charlotte and me.

My mind began to churn inside my skull. When, over the last few months, had I actually begun not to loathe my bubbly lessee? And when, over the last few minutes, had I started to sincerely entertain that she might be telling the truth?

"No guarantees, Charlotte . . ." I finally said to her slowly, my mouth muffled against the thin shirt over her bony shoulder. She was at least five inches taller than my five-five. "But I'll try to help figure out who really killed Chad."

Even as I said it, I wondered what the heck I was letting myself in for.

Chapter Ten
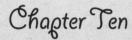

MY ANXIETY WAS as high-strung as a tennis racket by the time I reached Jeff by phone that evening. Or rather, he reached me, on my cell.

I'd planned on an intense night of study at home alone, since the ethics exam was only days away. But right now, my head was too hyper to let me focus.

"Where've you been?" I demanded without preamble when he finally responded to my multiple messages. Lexie and I were just scaling the steps again to our apartment after her latest evening constitutional. And mine. Walking was supposed to have helped me clear my chaotic mind.

Right.

"I'm delighted you've missed me." Jeff's reply was far from an answer to my inquiry.

"I need to talk to you," I said.

"Good. I need to talk to you, too. Why don't Lexie and you come over to my place and plan to spend the night?"

"Why don't Odin and you come to my place?"

"Uh-oh. A power struggle. Want to compromise and book a hotel room?"

"With the dogs?"

He laughed. "Obviously I can't win. I'll come there."

"No," I grumbled perversely, "I'll go there."

"Okay."

The fact he let my offer stand elevated my dander even higher. But I was tired of this discussion and let it drop.

Besides, I needed a change of scenery. What if I ran into Charlotte and Yul before I'd had a chance to vent about my quasicommitment to them?

"I'll bring takeout," I said. "Thai?"

"How about . . . Never mind. Throwing in another nationality for consideration will only start us off again. Thai it is."

Forty-five minutes later, Lexie and I parked my Beamer in Jeff's driveway, and I bent back in to pick up the bags of aromatic Asian dinner delights. I knew Jeff's preferences in Thai foods, as he knew mine.

Odin wagged his curled tail as Jeff let us in the door. Our host's cargo shorts did justice showing off his hairy male legs, and his snug black Malibu T-shirt made me feel glad I hadn't changed from the similar stuff I'd thrown on in anticipation of studying. Only my shirt said CABO SAN LUCAS, it was green, and the bulges it hugged on me were boobs, not biceps and pecs.

I caught Jeff's appreciative ogle as he took one of the bags from me, and I figured my bulges blossomed in all the right places.

The two pups sniffed each other, then swooshed off for a romp through the house. I knew they'd end up in the kitchen with us. The aroma of food would be too hard to resist, even if the nasty old humans refused to share.

Which we didn't. Not totally. I'd opted for our usuals of pad Thai and mee krob, but had also gotten an order of barely seasoned sticky rice thrown in. Rice is good for a sick doggy's stomach. Neither of our pets needed that kind of pampering, but I nevertheless figured I'd let them join us for more than their usual food.

Over dinner on Jeff's round kitchen table, I related my conversation with Charlotte, finishing with the pièce de résistance: my promise to help find who killed Chad and tried to frame the ferrets—and thereby, at least peripherally, Yul and her.

"Did she give any details about how the cops think Chad really died?" Jeff asked when I was finished.

"No details, I gathered. Only innuendoes."

"Okay, so some unidentified suspect did something to Chad, then let the ferrets out to hide what really happened. Why wouldn't that be Charlotte or Yul?"

"Because," I said, "Charlotte wants to hire me to figure out who it really was."

Jeff laughed. "Maybe that's because she figures you'll fail." I stood and scowled, till Jeff threw his hands up. "Okay, let's assume you're right and they're innocent. How did you plan to figure out who the real killer was?"

I sat once more, but stayed on the edge of my seat. "The way I did it before—make a list of candidates, then go corner all of them and see where it leads."

"It nearly led to your own murder the last time." It was Jeff's turn to scowl, and it had nothing to do with the fact he'd just swallowed a big bite of the sweet-and-sour noodle concoction that was mee krob.

"But I survived. Not only that, I figured out who was framing me."

"And that makes you an expert."

"No, but I have one who could advise me, if he decided not to be an insulting and conceited jerk about the whole thing."

"What if he's a concerned jerk?"

I sighed as our eyes caught. His were blue and shadowed by his straight brows, and right now they radiated the concern he'd chucked out between us. He had me there. My righteous irritation puddled into a big glob of gooey happiness. "No need to worry about me, Jeff," I said softly.

"Yeah, there is. Besides, I'm going out of town again to-morrow, unexpectedly. Can you stay here and take care of Odin?"

I nodded. "I'll get your advice by phone."

"You're not a licensed investigator, Kendra." He'd dredged up another dilemma in his attempt to dissuade me. "There's a lot of looking around that you can't do."

"A P.I.'s employees who are learning how to become the real thing don't need their licenses right away," I reminded him. "You even suggested hiring me before, when I successfully investigated my own case."

"But you said no. And now you want to be a P.I. rather than an attorney?" He shook his head in skepticism.

"No, but I can say I'm on your staff if anyone questions me." Before Jeff could craft a denial, I continued, "The thing is, if Charlotte and Yul are being framed, directly or indirectly, well . . . after what happened to me, I can iden-tify with their fear, the sense of fatalism, the whole scary scenario. I have to help them, Jeff, assuming they're inno-cent. And even if they're not, either way I'll hand over whatever evidence I find to Noralles."

"But—" Jeff bit off whatever he was about to blurt out, replacing it with a bite of rice. "Okay. Whatever I say, it won't change your mind. So all I can do is to tell you again to be careful."

"I will."

Later, we both rinsed dishes, stuck them in the dish-washer, and went outside for our final romp with the dogs for the night.

And then it was time for bed.

When I'd first started pet-sitting for Jeff, my space had been a guest bedroom he also used for storage. The boxes he kept there had stoked my curiosity. Still did, truth be told. One of them was labeled PHILIPE PELLERA, and now I'd actually met—well, seen from several feet away—the Latin singing sex symbol.

But my legal ethics, though unjustly besieged, hadn't let me look in those boxes before.

And now my spot in Jeff's home was with him, the dogs resting near each other on the floor by the bed.

We showered together, then dove headlong into bed for recreation of the most creatively sensual kind.

Later, worn out, we wound limbs around each other and waited for sleep to snatch us mentally apart, but physically, for tonight at least, we were together.

"Where are you going tomorrow?" I asked.

"Chicago," he murmured drowsily into my ear. His breath against me there made me consider waking once more, but I was too drained to tender the idea. "You'll stay here with Odin?"

"Mmm-hmm," I assured him sleepily. "Or I'll bring him home with Lexie and me."

"Why don't you just move in here?" he asked. "And not just while I'm away." He sounded a little less dream-beguiled, and I froze, priming myself for the punch line.

It didn't come.

"Did you hear me, Kendra?" he asked. "This isn't just pillow talk. I've been thinking about it. You know there's plenty of room even when I'm here, and it'll give you distance from your new sort-of investigative clients who happen to be your tenants, too." Not even a hint of haziness remained in his tone.

He was serious.

I didn't let myself move, for fear I'd roll away so far we'd never come together again. "We've only known each other a few months, Jeff," I reminded him.

At the same time, my own mind reminded me that I'd finally begun to feel that my taste in lovers had vastly improved lately.

Yeah, but was I ready to make it permanent?

Moving in didn't make a lifetime commitment, announced my bold internal devil's advocate.

But it did imply some kind of commitment, my shivering sense of self-preservation countered.

"It's been an intense few months," Jeff said, starting to nibble my neck all over again.

"That's for sure," I agreed.

"You don't need to give me an answer now," he said, still nuzzling. "Just think about it."

"Oh, I will," I said, and turned to meet his mouth with mine.

Between kisses, Jeff murmured, "I love you, Kendra." At least I thought he did. He didn't repeat it. I didn't meet it with a pronouncement of my own.

But even long after, when we'd made luscious love yet again, that soothing dream state I'd been in failed to return.

And it wasn't just whether my tenants' ferrets were being framed that frazzled my wide-awake mind.

Move in with Jeff?

Love?

Oh, Lord, this freight train was moving too fast!

WE SAID GOODBYE with another big kiss the next morning before Lexie and I headed for our day's pet-sitting assignments.

It hadn't been just pillow talk, since Jeff pressed me with a reminder after escorting us to the Beamer. "I could always move in with you," he said, "but we'd be a little cramped."

"Say hi to Chicago for me, Hubbard," I countered.

"I won't tell you again to think about it," he said. "You will."

"Yeah," I admitted, "I will." And then I backed the Beamer out.

I stopped home to change my clothes.

My home. My little apartment beside the big house that had been my home. The big house now occupied by

Charlotte and Yul, who needed my help to seek out who'd really killed Chad Chatsworth—if it wasn't them.

That's what I needed to concentrate on.

And having Charlotte come dashing out of that very house in a slinky peach silk nightgown was a good reminder. She wore matching floppy mules trimmed in feathers, too.

"Have you found anything helpful yet, Kendra?" she began breathlessly. Her hair wasn't braided at this hour, but its black length was held back from her face by—what else?—a matching peach ribbon. I had never seen her without makeup before. She was still pretty, but didn't appear as glamorous as usual.

"No," I admitted, "but I've gotten expert advice from a private investigator I'll be sort of working for while I help the ferrets and you. Right now, I want you and Yul to make lists of people who don't like you much. You don't have to focus on bitter enemies, though you can asterisk their names so I'll know."

"The bitterest was Chad himself," Charlotte said gloomily.

"Well, think about who else. Leave the list in my mailbox. I'll come back for it later, though I'm going to be spending the next few nights at a client's, watching his dog." Or a lover's, deciding whether his home would become my concurrent castle . . .

Lord, Jeff hadn't lied. His unanticipated invitation was already messing with my perturbed mind.

Chapter Eleven

As soon as I'd hurried through my early-morning routine of rounding up cats, raking out their litter boxes, and feeding them, plus walking dogs and watching them inhale morning meals, Lexie and I sped toward Darryl's doggy spa.

Lexie was full of extra exuberance since I'd mostly left her locked in the car, parked in the shade, windows carefully cracked, during my morning pet encounters. The problem was, her presence, though always a pleasure, never failed to impede my intended quick progress.

I figured she'd dash around Darryl's and work off some of the energy that caused her to bounce from one side of the Beamer to the other. More often than not, she landed smack on my lap, mostly while I attempted to navigate the most challenging of turns on San Fernando Valley streets. At least, with my current cadre of clients, I mostly steered clear of freeways.

But it wasn't only because of Lexie that I needed a Darryl fix. I craved his company. I required his counsel. I was the lawyer, but he had more common sense than a courtroom full of arguing attorneys.

It was okay for me to say that, since I was previously a

proud member of that much-maligned clan. And I intended to engage again, as soon as the ethics exam allowed.

The ethics exam. Oh, heavens, it was coming up in just days, and I was far from comfortable that I'd do well, and—

At the same moment I was angsting over that thought, I negotiated a left turn on a yellow light through a well-traveled intersection onto Ventura Boulevard, Lexie leapt on my lap, and my cell phone signaled a call coming in. My cell used to sing the "Ode to Joy," but I'd grown jaded about so much joviality. It now blared a rousing rendition of Bon Jovi's "It's My Life."

Fortunately, there was a gap in the parallel-parked cars along Ventura, and I slid the Beamer into it. Phone still shrilling, I gently shoved Lexie onto the passenger's seat and said, "Stay." Only then did I feel undistracted enough to reach for the phone. The caller ID showed a local number but I hadn't an inkling whose it was.

"Kendra Ballantyne," I answered as smartly as if I'd slid back a few months and sat in my law office accepting client calls.

"Hello, Ms. Ballantyne. My name is Jon Arlen. I'm a friend of Fran Korwald's. She referred me to you."

I remembered running into Fran at Darryl's. She'd said she was sending someone my way who needed help handling a homeowners' association complaint. But wasn't that someone a she, not a he?

"Hi, Jon. What can I do for you?"

"Well, it's kind of a difficult situation. Would it be possible for us to meet to talk about it?"

"A homeowners' association dispute?" I asked.

"No, no. That's not me." Jon Arlen's chuckle sounded like static over the cell phone. "You're thinking of a mutual friend of Fran's and mine, Marie Seidforth. Have you heard from Marie? She's afraid that getting an outsider involved will only make things worse, though Fran and I tell her they can't get much worse. Not if she wants to keep living where she is and not get rid of her house full of boxers."

"No," I said, "I haven't heard from her. And the thing is, Jon, I hope Fran told both of you that though I'm an attorney by background, I'm temporarily not practicing law."

He chuckled again. "Fran's so enthused that she's talked about little but you and your background lately. She told us you helped to psych out that psycho ex-husband of hers so she got custody of her pug. You're the famous lawyer who was in all the papers not long ago. You had your license suspended for something you didn't do, and when you set out to prove your innocence, you also solved some murders. Right?"

"Something like that."

"And your license hasn't been restored yet? That sucks."

I suddenly liked this guy a lot. "Sure docs," I said. "As long as you understand I can't give legal advice, I'll be glad to get together with you to talk over your problem."

"Tomorrow?" he asked.

"Sure." I set it up for him to meet me at Darryl's, since Fran had referred him there, too, and he was going to start leaving his dog during the day.

I slipped the cover shut on my cell phone and sat grinning, till Lexie leapt over and gave me a slobbery kiss on the cheek.

"Okay," I told her. "Next stop, Darryl's."

AFTER LETTING LEXIE off her leash so she could zoom around the playroom, I asked Darryl for an audience in his office.

"Sure, Kendra." He motioned for me to take my regular seat in the chair facing his overloaded desk. "What's up this time?"

"Are you ever going to dump your problems on me?"

"You wanted to see me to ask me to dump on you?"

I grinned. "Not hardly. I'm here to dump on you. I just

thought I'd give you the chance to get back at me first."

"Dump away." He nudged his wire-rims down his thin nose and peered at me over them.

I informed him about my call from Fran's latest referral, and asked if he knew anything about the matter Jon Arlen had in mind for my sage nonlegal counsel. He didn't, and since Fran hadn't left Piglet at the resort today, he wouldn't be able to ask.

He seemed amused that Fran kept recommending me. Not that she was the sole client he'd sent my way for services beyond pet-sitting.

Take a doggy stud fee disagreement, for example. About three months ago, soon after I'd helped Fran resolve her problem with Piglet's custody, Darryl had directed to me a different resort customer's dilemma. Cheryl Sallar's champion Bedlington terrier, Lamb Chop, had retired from the show ring in favor of showering stud service on panting female Bedlingtons . . . for a fee, or pick of the litter. In this case, it had been the latter, but the damned owner of the Bedlington dam had reneged. Even if I'd had my law license back, it didn't make economic sense for Cheryl to hire an attorney to recoup the stud fee or the prize puppy, though the principal of the dispute drove her to desperation. So of course I had to help—indirectly. I'd suggested that Cheryl sue for the disputed pick-of-the-litter's value in small claims court. And sure enough, the clash was quickly resolved once the filed action was served on the bitch's bitchy owner.

Then I told Darryl of the quasicommitment I'd made to Charlotte. "I think Jeff's decided I'm nuts. He's willing to let me play P.I.-in-training under his license—or at least he didn't order me not to—but he doesn't seem to understand how much I don't want to see someone else, even ferrets, get framed for murder."

Darryl pushed his glasses up on the bridge of his nose again and leaned his lanky body back in his chair. "Oh, I think he understands just fine. The guy's crazy about you, Kendra. He doesn't want to see you get hurt, that's all."

"That's too much," I grumbled, almost spilling my guts about Jeff's invitation to cohabit. But to my surprise, I wasn't ready to spill those particular beans yet, not even to my dear buddy Darryl. "Anyway, I'm going to do what I can to help Charlotte out."

"I thought you didn't like your ditzy tenant."

I admitted to Darryl that she'd grown on me. "The main thing, though, is that since I was there myself—"

"You hate the idea of anyone being railroaded. I get it. So how are you going to investigate, Ms. P.I.?"

"Jeff's going out of town, so though I'll get some help from him, I'm mostly on my own. Care to brainstorm?"

He did and we did, and though we didn't come up with much I hadn't mulled over myself, I appreciated the opportunity to solidify my strategy.

I took notes to rearrange later into one of my more interesting lists. As I've said, I'm a confirmed listaphile. It's how I got through my days as a litigator, and the practice assisted immeasurably in keeping a log of my pet-sitting clients.

Besides, strategically speaking, sticking all my ideas onto a list helped me keep track of them.

I gave Darryl's skinny bod a big hug when we were done. And then I looked for Lexie. She was lying in the area filled with human furnishings, finally worn out enough to sleep on the sofa.

"Do you want to leave her awhile longer?" Darryl asked.

"Thanks, but not today. I have to go give Widget his midday walk, and then Lexie and I are going to take our own stroll around the area where Chad Chatsworth lived, assuming Charlotte knows where it is."

SHE DID. WHILE I sat in the shade in the Beamer, outside Widget's home with Lexie in my lap, Charlotte also gave

me a preview over the phone of the lists of potential enemies that Yul and she had been preparing. She was under-
scoring those she particularly considered ferret foes.

In addition, she prepped me on the identities of some important people in Chad's life, or at least those he'd told her
of while off camera during the throes of their reality show.

"He has an apartment mate. They've been in the same
flat together in the Palms area—on the west side—for
about a year. His name's Dave Driscoll, and he's a techy
nerd. Not even interested in The Industry." Charlotte made
it sound as if anyone not totally immersed in the business
that was Hollywood had to have a screw or two loose. Or
maybe, since the guy was apparently a computer geek, his
silicon chips were cracked.

She gave me the address in Palms, and I planned to head
there next.

"Anyone else I should know about?" I asked.

She mumbled something I couldn't quite make out over
the phone.

"Pardon?"

"That damned ex-girlfriend of his," Charlotte grumbled
again, this time loud enough that I could hear. "Or not so
ex, as it turned out. Her name is Trudi Norman."

"And where does she live?"

"In la-la land."

"Where in L.A.?" I prompted.

"Not Los Angeles. *Her* la-la land is in her head. The
woman is just too sweet to be believed for a dirt-bag,
scheming bitch."

Charlotte had said that Chad plotted with his girlfriend
to reach the top male spot on their reality show, planning
all the time to shun what was to appear as true love for reality show fame and fortune.

Might she have had a reality of her own that caused her
to kill her fellow plotter, the handsome cad Chad?

"I need a better address," I told Charlotte. "Phone number, too, if you can get it."

"I'll try," she said with a sigh.

I gave her a bracing pep talk to buck up her obviously sagging morale, then hung up.

Commanding Lexie into her copilot's place in the Beamer, I checked my map book and proceeded south toward Palms.

Chapter Twelve

THE STREET IN Palms where Chad Chatsworth lived before becoming an alleged ferret feast was an apartment-laden urban avenue.

I squeezed the Beamer into a spot barely longer than its bumpers, snapped Lexie's leash securely to her collar, then slid out, Lexie leaping over me to be first.

I noticed right away that a couple of the scanty parking spots were occupied by police units—a marked vehicle and a crime scene van.

· I figured the police presence was related to the investigation of Chad's murder and then was convinced of it when I saw one cop head out of the building where Chad had lived and another go inside. I doubted I'd have any luck checking out his flat and neighbors sans hassle, so I decided, for now, to walk the streets to see what I could learn. That tactic had served me well before, while searching for clues in the murder investigations I'd conducted to save my own skin. Plus, I'd gained another pet-sitting client that way, as well as the idea that had helped me solve Fran Korwald's pug custody problem.

Lexie and I started strolling the sidewalk.

Greenery and flowers were scarcely to be seen, though some property managers had gamely attempted to grow gardens in the narrow setbacks between sidewalk and buildings. The five- to six-story structures were distinguished from one another mainly by the shade of beige of their stucco facades. The smell was of musty heat radiating from the irregular pavement, interspersed with diesel fumes from delivery trucks rumbling by.

Surprisingly, no gawkers blocked the area. Maybe parked crime unit cars were so common around here that a couple more failed to capture an excited crowd.

I, on the other hand, needed to get a dialogue going with someone with something helpful to say. I noticed two sweats-clad women striding determinedly toward us on the sidewalk. Their quick clip—despite the fact they each pushed baby strollers—suggesting they were out for exercise. I took a small step to plant Lexie and me in their path. Ignoring their irritated stares as they separated their strollers to swing around me, I called, "Is that where that poor Chad Chatsworth lived?"

That stopped one in her tracks—the one whose hot athletic outfit blazed magenta. She was maybe mid-thirties, with blond hair that might have looked natural if not all a single shade, and large brown eyes with laugh lines scoring her skin. Only she wasn't laughing now. The kid sitting in her stroller looked about two, and his hair was definitely dark.

"Oh, yes," the woman said. "He was quite the neighborhood celebrity. It's so hard to believe he's gone."

"Did you know him?" I maneuvered Lexie a little on her leash, then gave her the signal to sit so she wouldn't get trampled if the strollathon continued without my leave.

"Who didn't?" she asked, looking infinitely sad, as if she'd lost her best friend.

The other woman glared at her and grumped, "*You* didn't, Dee. Unless you call waving as he jogged by knowing him." She was shorter and younger-looking. Her black hair formed a wind-tossed cap, and her sweats were a nondescript gray—like her attitude. Her kid was a sleeping baby in pink.

"You could have introduced me," Dee countered. She turned back to me. "Helene lives in his building. She knew him well enough that he and his roommate invited her to a party once."

I must have reacted without realizing it, since Helene said defensively, "We're both single mothers." Only then did I dare a surreptitious glance toward her empty ring finger.

I definitely liked Dee better than her chum, for she moved past her stroller, stooped on the sidewalk, and held out a hand for Lexie to lick—giving me a glimpse of her bare finger, too. "You're so sweet. Look at the doggy, Tommy."

The kid repeated "doggy" and his mom laughed.

"So Chad had a roommate?" I asked to get back on the subject, knowing the answer. "Was his roommate in show business, too?"

"Hardly," huffed Helene. "I never did figure out why someone as good-looking and charismatic as Chad roomed with a boring computer geek like Dave Driscoll."

That conformed with what Charlotte had told me.

"Probably because the last guy standing on *Turn Up the Heat* didn't want any competition," Dee said drolly, earning her a glare from her companion.

Turn Up the Heat. So *that* was the reality show Charlotte had been on. I'd not paid much attention to it while it was airing, and had other things on my mind when I'd taken her application to lease my house. But I'd definitely heard about the show. A lot about it. Who, with any hormones, hadn't?

Helene confirmed my impression of it in her next aggravated riposte, one hand on a skinny hip. "Well, there isn't much competition for Chad Chatsworth . . . or wasn't." Her blazing gaze dimmed again to gloomy. "I mean, he was definitely the most creative of all the guys on that show as far

Nothing to Fear but Ferrets   87

as coming up with sexy and romantic dates to tempt Charlotte. *I* was certainly tempted, and I wasn't even there."

"Do you think she actually sampled all the contenders on the show?" Dee asked with interest. Her son stretched his hand out toward Lexie, who sniffed it.

"That was the whole point," Helene said scornfully. "Of course she did."

"That makes the producers of the show p-i-m-p-s, then, don't you think?" Dee said, glancing down as if assuring herself that her son hadn't comprehended.

"Of sorts," Helene agreed, with the first grin I'd seen on her otherwise dour face. It disappeared promptly.

"I'm sure the speculation didn't hurt the ratings," I chimed in, then faced Helene. "At the party you went to, was anyone from the show there?"

Before she replied, I noticed a few people exit Chad's building—in suits. Cops? Could be—the detective kind. I kept my eyes peeled for my old nemesis Detective Noralles. But this area was in a different L.A.P.D. division—West Bureau, I thought. I was unlikely to be recognized by anyone there.

"Not Charlotte, that's for sure," Helene said, answering my question. "Did you see the last week? It was really something. Talk about hot—and I don't mean sexy. Hot tempers, because of a lot of cool cash." Her baby fussed, and she bent down.

"But Chad had no hint ahead of time that being the last guy standing wasn't enough?" I persisted. I wasn't sure how well she'd known her neighbor, but she might have heard some gossip and snickers while at the party at his place.

"No." Helene stood, her baby in her arms. Cute. Even cuter, the tot wasn't crying. "The guy really seemed upset at being dumped like that, and who could blame him?"

Yeah, but was it real or just for show? Or had he been upset because it ruined his well-conceived plan—the one he'd made with his real girlfriend?

"How well did you know him?" I asked Helene. "Did he live around here long?"

A uniformed cop by the car glanced toward our neighborly conclave. I bent toward the still-occupied stroller, not eager for him to notice me, let alone describe a loitering pet-walker in his report.

"Actually, no," Dee said, kneeling at her kid's other side. "He moved here between the time the show was filmed and when it aired. At least that's what everyone here who met him said."

She looked up at Helene, who nodded haughtily, as if she felt her importance was being usurped by a blabbing interloper who'd never even met the man. Still, she stayed quiet.

"Everything was taped ahead but the end of the last show," Dee continued. She stood again, and I did, too. "Charlotte had already chosen Chad, but they weren't allowed to get together till the final episode was aired for fear they'd give the ending away. But neither knew the final twist till the live part at the end, after they showed the clip where Charlotte chose Chad. Did you see it?" She looked at me.

"Sorry, no, but I wish I had." Both women eyed me as if I'd claimed not to have showered for a week.

"Well," Dee continued, "there he was all over Charlotte, pleased as punch to see her again, vowing eternal love. And she seemed happy, too. Who wouldn't? I mean, she'd made the best choice. Chad was a total hunk, and I figured she'd had sex with him before the last episode. But then, in that last show the host came in and told her about her final choice. So what if the sex had been super? Chad became history immediately."

"How sad," I said, then turned to Helene. "Did he tell you at the party how awful it felt when he thought he'd won the woman's heart, and instead she booted him for the booty instead? Embarrassing, wasn't it? In front of the entire country—maybe the whole world."

"I didn't know him well," Helene admitted. She swayed

back and forth as her baby's little hands clenched the air. "But at that party—it was Dave Driscoll who invited some neighbors, to make sure the place was packed. He didn't want Chad to feel worse because no one wanted to come to his condolences get-together. Anyway, Chad seemed depressed. Drowned his sorrows in so many pints of Guinness that I lost count. Kept talking about how much he'd cared for the Big Bad Bitch—his words, not mine." She flushed a little and gave a guilty look toward her sweet-faced daughter. "His old girlfriend showed up to try to make him feel better, but I don't think that helped."

Aha! The co-schemer, Trudi, right on the spot.

"Since it sounds as if he was pissed at the Big Bad Bitch," I said, not reluctant to repeat her epithet and run with it, "any idea why he happened to show up in that same bitch's house?" Alive first, then dead, though I didn't say that.

"Revenge," Dee crowed. "The rules said they weren't to see each other afterward or Charlotte would forfeit everything." Nothing new in that. "He probably wanted to latch on to her like glue so she'd wind up with nothing, too. Charlotte would have been furious. No wonder she killed him."

Which was the conclusion probably the entire viewing world would draw, even with ferrets sitting there like furry scapegoats.

I turned again toward Helene, who seemed to grow noticeably cool in her warm sweats despite bouncing her increasingly fussy baby. "Did anyone mention at the party Chad's roommate threw—?"

"Are you from around here?" she suddenly demanded. "I don't remember seeing you before." She must have realized they were wasting perfectly good gossip on a total stranger.

"Actually, I live in the Valley." I waved vaguely north. No way did I intend to spill that Charlotte, her boyfriend, and the suspect ferrets were my tenants. "I'm a pet-sitter," I continued truthfully, pulling on Lexie's leash so she stood and eyed me attentively. "Do either of you have dogs you'd like walked during the day? Or pets that need care while you travel?" Were they stay-at-home single moms? *Did* they travel? For once, I hoped for a nice, nasty negatory. Not that my business cards contained an address that would arouse anyone's suspicions about my unrevealed ulterior motive, since I only had my cell phone number printed on them. Still, I'd kept my pet-sitting services confined to the Valley, for ease of jaunting between clients as fast as possible. Palms was way too many miles away to take on assignments here.

"Not me," Helene sniffed. "Allergies." She looked around her kid and down her long, mean nose at Lexie, who took a step backward before settling into a sit.

Dee let out a sorrowful sigh. "I had a cat, but she was old and I had to have her put down last year. I think Tommy was too young to understand and haven't wanted to take on that heartache again. But if I ever do, I'll be sure to think about you. Do you have a card?"

Discretion seemed a better course than truth. I patted one pocket, then the other. "Not with me, but next time I'm around I'll bring them. Hopefully we'll run into each other again."

They'd given me a lot of food for thought. Would I need a second helping from them? Brazenly, I asked for their last names and addresses.

Wisely, both demurred giving out vital statistics to this nosy nonneighbor.

Well, I'd probably gotten all I could from these particular people. They'd mostly known Chad from his fleeting stardom.

I'd need more than awed fan info to figure out his murder.

Chapter Thirteen

BACK AT THE Beamer, still sitting in the tight parking space, I let Lexie leap into the front passenger seat beside me. I turned the engine on long enough to crack open the windows to let in some air, for despite fall's having supposedly arrived weeks ago, the car's interior had morphed into a ceramics kiln while we were out canvassing the neighborhood.

I reached beneath Lexie's seat to extract notes I'd been accumulating in response to Charlotte's appeal for assistance. I added the names *Helene* and *Dee* to my growing list of players in the Chad Chatsworth ferret fiasco.

Not that they were suspects, but they were witnesses of sorts. Maybe their kids, too—but they weren't talking. Helene and Dee had added to my short supply of information that might eventually clear Charlotte and Yul and their little furry buddies.

The ferrets. I couldn't help feeling sorry for them, too. They'd gnawed Chad, sure, but they'd most likely been set up. I wanted to visit them in their ominous incarceration, ensure they were being treated humanely.

Humanely euthanized. The phrase from the animal control officer reverberated in my miserable mind. No, that had to be a last resort, only if they were found guilty in the court of animal control evidence of more than chewing the food left for them.

I was eager to rescue them, if humanly possible.

But not now. This afternoon, I had a person with a pet problem to talk to—Jon Arlen, Fran Korwald's friend.

And as I studied my schedule, I was bluntly bashed in the face with one little calendar detail that I'd unsuccessfully attempted to store deep in the recesses of my mind.

This was Wednesday. The Multistate Professional Responsibility Exam—the test that had for so long seemed much too far off for me to wait to resume my law license—was now only two days away. It was scheduled for the second Friday in November, starting early afternoon. I'd elected to attack it at the Cal State Northridge campus.

Or rather, it might assail me, with lots of questions I might not be able to answer, particularly without adequate preparation.

"Let's go, Lexie," I said with a shaky sigh. Her black-and-white tail beat a keen cadence that showed her pleasure at being addressed. I started the car like I meant it this time, and slowly eased my Beamer from its tight space.

Before I stepped harder on the gas, I glanced at the clock on the dashboard. Time for Widget's early-afternoon walk. Then, to Darryl's for my meeting with Jon Arlen. My discussion with him would be the final frolic and detour I'd undertake before immersing myself for final hours of uninterrupted ethics study. Or rather, interrupted only by scheduled pet-sitting services.

An excellent reason to ignore one big gorilla-like invitation that had been constantly crouching at the edge of my thoughts, even when I'd purposely turned my focus in faraway directions.

Should I move in with Jeff?

Bad idea. Hadn't I already convinced myself that my preferences in picking lovers were the pits?

But I'd also asserted to myself that Jeff was the exception. He was a great guy. A super lover. Someone unlike my last long-term lover, "Drill Sergeant" Bill Sergement, who'd used his influence as mentor at my former law firm to seduce new female associates, including me and many since I'd extracted myself from his attentions. He was a louse. A user.

And I was already living a lot of the time at Jeff's. Lexie and I both were, since it was the optimum place to be while watching Odin.

Was I honestly considering it?

Maybe. But not now. I had Widget the terrier to tame for a while, a meeting with someone named Jon Arlen, more pets to tend, then total immersion in studying.

That was enough to fill this fool's thoughts for the next few days.

As I LEFT Widget's later and headed for Darryl's, my cell phone sang out, "It's My Life!" I hummed along as I lifted it and said, "Hello."

"Kendra, it's Avvie. How are you?"

"Fine," I answered, surprised. I hadn't heard from my former protégée at Marden, Sergement and Yurick since I'd made it clear that, once my license was restored, I had no intention of returning as an associate to the law firm that had been less than supportive during my prior problems.

Not that they'd actually offered . . .

I'd called Avvie a couple of times after our last get-together, tried to schedule another lunch, but she'd always been too busy.

Firm loyalty, I'd figured, won out over our friendship.

"Are you still pet-sitting?" she asked.

"Sure," I said. "Unless you're calling to offer me my old job back." I knew full well that Avvie wouldn't have the authority to tender that offer, even if I was tough enough to

want it. I was just having fun at her expense. Mainly because I was irked. She'd acted so supportive before, then
had absented herself from my life for months.

Of course, that might have something to do with the fact
that, last time I'd seen her in person, I'd all but accused her
and her lover, Bill Sergement—yes, Avvie was one of his
current associate conquests—of being involved with the
murders I'd been trying to solve.

I had intended to upset them then, hoping one or both
would spill something helpful. Like a confession.

As it turned out, something Avvie said had in fact
helped me figure out who'd done it.

"Are you really interested in coming back here?" Avvie
asked. "If so, let me warn you. Things aren't great."

"No?" So much for my assumption of firm loyalty. I'd
have thought she would be singing the Marden firm's
theme song while standing on her head, if it would help her
stay on partnership track.

Or maybe while lying on her back, while Sergement
and she . . .

Bag it, Ballantyne!

"Then you hadn't heard. I told you before that old Borden Yurick had gone off the deep end. He's gone through
with his withdrawal from the partnership. And he's taken
all his clients with him. The firm tried to stop him, and it's
gotten ugly."

I didn't want to hear the awful details. Only . . . "So are
there any clients left?"

"Fewer than half," she said with a sigh. But then, resum-
ing her perkier self, she continued, "But that's not why I
called. I want to hire you, if you're still pet-sitting."

"You have a pet?" That was a surprise. She'd enthusiastically visited once while I'd stayed with a mama dog but
had acted more excited about meeting Jeff than the pups.

"Yes," she said. "Bill hasn't had as many evenings free
lately for us to stay late and work together." I was amazed

that she said the word *work* without a hint of hesitation. "I've started taking more things home to do instead of staying in the office, and to keep me from getting too lonely, he bought me the cutest potbellied pig. Pansy is her name."

"Really? That's sweet of him." I had to say something nice, after all.

"We have a trip coming up—some depositions in Las Vegas."

How convenient. I wondered if Bill's wife would come along to gamble while the two attorneys diligently deposed witnesses. At least Bill hadn't been married when he and I had been a clandestine couple.

"Would you watch Pansy for me?" Avvie ended pleadingly.

"Of course, if I can," I hedged. "When is your trip, and for how long?"

It was next week, for four days. I agreed to make myself available, promised to get the particulars from her, and gracefully gestured away her profound gratitude.

She'd be a paying customer, after all.

What did I know about caring for a pig?

As much as I'd known about caring for a python, before I'd gotten lessons on Pythagorus.

Avvie would teach me what I needed to know.

WHEN I ARRIVED at Darryl's, he was in his office convincing an indecisive canine owner that Doggy Indulgence was the Valley's prime resort for her pampered, pompadoured poodle.

I knew this because my thin, spectacled friend, appearing more frazzled than he was prone to, ducked out long enough to greet Lexie and me. He explained his situation and motioned for his most obnoxious assistant, Kiki, the bleached-blond self-styled starlet, to take Lexie to play with the pups in the penned-in sports area at one end of the resort's big room.

Darryl told me Jon Arlen was already waiting. He'd planted Fran Korwald's latest referral in the kitchen to talk to me. It was the most private area in the place, except for Darryl's office, which was occupied, and the bathrooms, which were hardly suitable for our meeting.

I headed that way. Dwarfing the table in the tiny room where the resort's staff ate lunch was a very large man with dark, curly hair. He stood as I entered, as did a sturdy russet-and-black dog at his side. The dog had a wiry coat and a squared, bearded face.

"Hmmm," I deliberated. "He's not an Airedale. And he's not a wire-haired fox terrier. Give me a clue."

"The breed used to be called black-and-tan wire-haired terriers," the man said in a rumbled rasp. "They were originally bred for hunting in the British Isles."

"Okay, I'll bite," I said. "What is he—he is a he?"

"Yes, that's Jonesy. I named him after Tom Jones, the singer, because—"

"Ah!" I interrupted. "That's the clue I needed. He's a Welsh terrier."

"You got it!" The man held out his hand. "Jon Arlen. You're Kendra?"

I acknowledged I was as we shook hands. His grip was what I'd anticipated in such a large man: firm, focused, and fast. When it was ended, I knelt to jostle Jonesy a bit, which quickly got out of hand when the dog decided I was fair game for a round of let's-wrestle-the-human. My kneel soon ended when the pup pinned my shoulders to the linoleum, licking my face proudly with a long, wet tongue.

"Jonesy, no!" Arlen commanded.

"It's okay," I assured him. "He's just being friendly." But I didn't object when Jon jerked his terrier off my face and into a sit.

"So," I said when I'd risen and planted myself on a

molded plastic chair, "Fran Korwald suggested that you talk to me?"

"Yes." Jon wore a short-sleeved shirt as wrinkled as the edges of his eyes. Its whiteness emphasized the man's tan, and if I'd had to guess, I'd deduce Jon's job kept him outdoors. He rested thick, bare arms on the small slab of wood that was the table. "It has to do with Jonesy, and something he did."

I glanced down at the culprit without yet knowing his crime. His tan tail was covered in wiry hair and stuck straight up. As I eyed him, that tail began to wag, and I had to smile. "And what was that?" I asked.

"Well, as I said, Jonesy's ancestors were bred to hunt. That included badgers, which live in underground tunnels, so—"

I guessed. "Jonesy has a digging addiction."

"That's right," Jon said.

"And he's pissed off some neighbors or your landlord by leaving holes in their property?"

Jon sighed. "If it was something as simple as that, I could handle it. I have a tree-trimming company, so I'm used to dealing with yard issues. I'd work something out."

So I'd been right about his outdoors occupation, but not about his problem.

"So what did Jonesy do?" I asked.

"He's discovered some buried treasure," Jon said, "but it wasn't buried on my property. I need to figure out how to keep it."

Chapter Fourteen

I SAT SPELLBOUND at that little table, my mind filled with visions of ancient Spanish doubloons and their valiant and determined doggy digger, Jonesy. Jon's tale wasn't complicated, though his dilemma might defy satisfactory solution.

"I live in the hills over Cahuenga Pass," he said. "My home's near Lake Hollywood reservoir. There've been rumors forever that when the Treaty of Cahuenga was signed back in 1847, ending the Mexican-American War in California, some Spanish-ancestry Californians left for Mexico in such a hurry that they couldn't take all their belongings with them. Supposedly, they buried a bunch of gold."

"And you found it? Rather, Jonesy did?"

"Some, at least. The thing is, it wasn't on our property. Jonesy was digging one day in the yard next door. Fortunately, I found him and was ready to shoo him home and replant the evidence when I happened to look in his hole. And there they were—a bunch of old coins. I dug 'em out, all I could find, took them in small loads to my place, and was just finishing when the neighbor came home. I'd already been calling her Beatrice the Bitch, at least in my mind, since she keeps a dog that howls like a coyote. And *she* complains about Jonesy's barking, and his skill at finding ways out of my yard. When she saw Jonesy's hole that I'd expanded, I thought she'd have a stroke."

"But you offered to fill in the hole with a tree," I surmised.

"Sure, or whatever landscaping she liked. At first, I thought that would satisfy her—till she spotted a coin I'd missed. She picked it up, and like a fool, when she asked if I'd found any more, I admitted I had. She held out her hands for it. Of course, even if I had been inclined to give it to her, she couldn't have held it all."

My head began to throb. That much unburied loot?

"I told her where she could put those greedy hands, and she didn't like it. She said whatever I found, it had been on her property so it was hers. But I just recited that old adage we all learn as kids."

"Which is?" I prompted.

" 'Finders, keepers, losers, weepers.' Of course that didn't satisfy her. She's promised to sue me."

I sighed. "Jon, what you've described is a legal matter. I warned you over the phone, just as I told Fran. I'm a lawyer, yes, but right now I can't practice law."

"But Fran said you told her you're taking an exam this week, and when you pass it, you'll get your license back?"

"The deity of legal ethics willing," I agreed. "But it'll take weeks before scores are released, and even then I'm no longer affiliated with a firm." Which meant no malpractice insurance, and I sure as hell wasn't going to practice law naked. "I can refer you to someone, but—"

"I want *you*," he interrupted. The way his rasp had turned into a roar, and his body half rose from his too-snug chair, reminded me that this was far from a miniature man. Still, I didn't feel threatened—too much. "Who wouldn't? Have you heard Fran Korwald sing your praises? She says you're a legal genius. And a nice person. And a pet-lover to boot. Plus you helped her put one over on her bastard of an ex-husband—and made him think it was all his idea. Genius!"

I'd liked the guy before. Now, I adored what he was doing to my ego. But that didn't reframe reality. "That was something practical that didn't involve the practice of law," I said.

"That's what I'm asking for, too. Something practical that will make Beatrice the Bitch get down on her knees and beg me to keep those old coins Jonesy found in her yard."

"But—"

"Besides, this all just happened a couple of weeks ago. I can keep Beatrice busy for now by ducking her phone calls, pretending to play along. Then when you can practice law again, you can send her one hell of a letter on my behalf telling her to butt out. Jonesy found the treasure fair and square."

I should have told Jon Arlen to go elsewhere to endeavor to keep his buried treasure. But the issue was too enticing for me just to throw away.

"Tell you what," I said. "I can't even think about this until after Friday—that's when I take the exam. Then I'll do some legal research—for myself, not you. If I think you've a legal leg to stand on, I'll hand what I find over to someone who's licensed now, and—"

"No," he growled. "If you find research stuff that'll help me keep what's mine, fair and square, then I'll wait until you can do whatever's necessary for me to keep it. Deal?"

"As long as you understand that if I don't pass the exam this time around"—*Please, no, no, no,* shrieked my stressed-out psyche—"you'll have to hire someone else, then, yes. Deal."

I DON'T WANT to discuss the rest of that Wednesday, or Thursday. I did little but study and pet-sit and nibble on snacks when my stomach grumbled. Sleep was out of the question, except for a discreet doze here and there.

And all the while I tried to keep every synapse of my beleaguered brain focused on ethics and study guides and practice exams. Yet too often, things I didn't want to think about tiptoed in and played kickball against the lining of my skull.

Buried treasure near Barham Boulevard in Cahuenga Pass. A gripping legal mind game to ensure that my potential clients, Jon Arlen and Jonesy, got to keep their ill-located treasure trove.

And each instant that I studied, despite the fact that he was out of town, Jeff Hubbard's presence loomed large over my shoulder—even between his evening phone calls to check how we were getting along. It didn't help that Lexie and I stayed at Jeff's to keep Odin company, as part of my paid pet-sitting gig.

What if we moved in permanently?

Concentrate on civil and criminal sanctions, Kendra!

And then the time came for me to leave Lexie at Jeff's with Odin and head the Beamer deep into the Valley, toward Cal State Northridge and the ethics exam.

It took two tedious hours. All multiple choice—like that TV game show where no one ever wins the million dollars—and I could only conjecture how well I did. In a room full of other aspiring attorneys sweating it out, I read each factual situation as carefully as if my career depended on it—which it did. I anguished over the described conduct, then selected which choice I thought was correct. Would the conduct toss the hypothetical legal professional deep into a boiling cauldron of ethics enigmas, or was it okay to do without worrying about appalling consequences?

Usually, two answers seemed conceivably correct. I used my best legal judgment about which eye to close while letting my finger drop onto the response to choose.

When done, I felt as drained as if I'd run a thousand-yard dash. How did I think I did? Who knew? I was a damned good litigator, could argue my way through any issue and make a credible showing for a client's most favorable position. But I couldn't talk my way out of a multiple-choice problem.

Results would be mailed in four weeks. I'd have to wait until then to find out.

GOOD THING MY Beamer was filled with gas, for it had all the energy between us late that afternoon. I still had to do normal pet-sitting rounds, and it seemed as if all my charges had saved up their extra energy until a time when I was utterly exhausted. Dogs that had hitherto heeled without balking took up barking on their walks and lunging at cawing crows, who simply took wing and soared off with taunting cackles. Litter-accustomed cats had chosen to shun habitual boxes and leave smelly urine samples all over their owners' homes.

And Jeff would be home that night.

I wasn't ready to face him, for I hadn't had sufficient time to consider his cohabitation offer. Not that I'd ignored the idea—not when it sat on my back and shrieked for attention at the most awful times. But I'd not come to a decision.

And so, when I was finally done with everything petrelated, including an enervating late-afternoon outing with Widget, I fed Odin and scrammed from Jeff's with Lexie.

We'd spend that night in our own digs. I'd have to face Jeff the next day, but surely it would be easier while wide awake.

Only, when Lexie and I reached our home in the hills, it was obvious that Charlotte and Yul had chosen to throw one of their inevitable, irritating shindigs. The front gate was open, against all lease rules. The Beamer's reserved parking spot was subject to a squatter—a Porsche Carrera that could only give my poor, ten-year-old car an inferiority complex.

I parked on the street, trying to pump up what energy

still resided in my downtrodden body, snapped Lexie onto her leash, and headed home.

I was stopped almost immediately by the across-the-street neighbor, Phil Ashler. "Hi, Kendra," the thin fellow said. He wore a starchy white shirt and beige trousers, and in one hand he carried a bottle of wine. His thin silver hair was slicked back with shiny gel. "Glad you're here. I wasn't sure which neighbors might be at this party."

"I'm not—" I began, but the words were smothered inside me by a huge, hard hug from our would-be hostess—Charlotte.

"Oh, Kendra, I'm so glad you're here." That thought was becoming a bit repetitious. "I've invited a whole bunch of suspects in Chad's murder over tonight. I figure the cops will want to arrest more than a few ferrets and will eventually go after us and anyone else who could have killed in their name. That's when they'll arrest one or all of us. Oh, Kendra." Her voice ramped up into a wail, and she hugged me again, her pale but powerful perfume wafting about us.

When Charlotte first rented my nice, large house, I used to shudder each time she graced me with an enthusiastic embrace. Hugging was a showbiz thing—and definitely uncomfortable for a cynical litigator like me.

But as I'd gotten to know Charlotte, I came to realize that gusto for everything around her was as natural as the way the long, black braid down her back swayed the opposite way from her rump when she sashayed. Her penchant for throwing parties with the most ridiculous of rationales was still tedious, especially on nights when I had no intention of joining the ruckus but ached for sleep in my upstairs apartment.

But a party for possible murder suspects? Talk about bizarre. Especially since Charlotte had chosen to wear stripes. Not the old-fashioned jailhouse kind, at least, but a slinky black-and-white creation decorated with diagonal bands.

On the other hand, I'd promised Charlotte I'd see what I could do to take the heat off all my tenants—two-legged and four—as Detective Noralles's top suspects. For me to question some of the possible perpetrators tonight seemed a good thing.

"Am I included?" Phil Ashler inquired of Charlotte, hiding his bottle behind his back.

"Sure," she said, pulling away from me. "Oh, you mean do I think you're a potential suspect? No, you're just invited because you're such a dear neighbor." Phil's turn for a big hug, which was fine with me. Him, too, I guessed, by the way his sallow complexion shifted to bright pink. I watched Phil as Charlotte led him inside, then I took Lexie up to our apartment.

Suddenly, I'd gotten my second wind. Me, a party animal? Perish the thought. But I had people to watch. I washed my frazzled face, added a smattering of makeup to mask the pastiness, then headed back toward my main house.

I realized that days had passed without my hearing squat from Ike Janus's insurance company about paying to heal my house's wounds. I'd remind him tonight if he was here. Worst case, I'd wait till my law license was restored and then suggest strongly to the insurer how much I loved to sue.

Plus, it had been exactly a week ago when I'd last attended a party at Charlotte's. That had been post–ferret finding, but pre–Chad murder.

Most of the same cast of characters was in attendance. Neighbors Tilla and Hal Tomason and Lyle Urquard had already arrived and tarried in the kitchen with tall glasses in their hands. This time, when I went into the living room, I recognized a couple of reality-show players whom Tilla had eagerly identified to me, including the south-of-the-border music phenomenon Philipe Pellera and the next-to-last-guy-standing in Charlotte's show—tall, blond Sven Broman.

"There are a couple of people I want to introduce you

to," said a soft voice in my ear. I didn't have to turn to know it was Charlotte, for I recognized her signature costly scent. "Just in case, though, can you recommend a lawyer to me? That Detective Noralles keeps smiling at me every time I see the guy, so I figure he either wants to do a reality show with me or he's waiting for me to confess and clear the sweet little ferrets altogether. Either way, I'm afraid it's about time I hired a lawyer."

"Sure," I told her. I jotted Esther Ickes' number on a cocktail napkin. Esther was an incredibly effective attorney who'd kept me from being arrested for murder when I'd skated on the thinnest of criminally laced ice. Since I still didn't seem to be a suspect this time, I figured I could share her.

Charlotte then urged me to the conversation area where Yul stood among a crowd. He was clad in a shiny black sport coat that contrasted sexily with his sleek golden hair. In this crowd, his height didn't stand out, but he still was a handsome hunk.

"Everyone, here's Kendra," gushed Charlotte. And then she introduced me to a plethora of people, most of whose names I forgot as fast as she fed them to me.

Except for two. One was Dave Driscoll, the guy I knew was Chad Chatsworth's former apartment mate. The other was Trudi Norman. She was the girl Chad had allegedly left behind to find fame and fortune on the West Coast. Instead, if Charlotte was to be believed, Trudi had plotted every instant of Chad's reality TV career. Had she plotted his murder, too?

Dave was as geeky as I'd been led to believe—not very tall, very bespectacled, and teeth as buck as a bunny rabbit's. He stuck out a hand that turned out to be clammy and shook mine with a smile. "Welcome to my roommate's unofficial wake, Kendra," he said. His voice was nasal but not unpleasant. "And also the first meeting of the Chad Chatsworth Murder Suspects Pre-Prison Fraternity."

"That's not funny, Dave," snapped Trudi. She was about my height—that is to say, five-five, considerably shorter than Charlotte. Her hair was an even mousier brown than my natural, unhighlighted shade, the way I currently wore it now that my income was no longer litigator-enhanced. Where mine was shoulder-length and somewhat sassy, hers was blunt cut and rather blah. But she had a sweet face, makeup-free except for some soft lip gloss, and a smattering of freckles across her nose. Sweet and wholesome-looking. Were her looks deceiving?

"Who's laughing," Dave countered, then bent down and gave her a fast, loud kiss on the cheek.

And then it was Trudi laughing, if a little.

No better time than the present to form an opinion about her involvement. I sidled my way beside Trudi, then said to her softly and sincerely, "I understand that Chad and you were close."

She nodded, tears in her pale brown eyes. "I even encouraged him to try to get on one of those shows, since it was his dream." Or hers? Charlotte had said his old girlfriend pushed him into it. That same old girlfriend sighed and stared down at the floor. "What a nightmare."

"I'm sorry for your loss," I said, not totally swayed by her show of sorrow. "I'm the one who found him, you know."

She glanced up immediately. "No, I didn't know. Was he—I mean, the police haven't said much, and the media always exaggerate. But I heard there were some awful little animals all over him." Her voice rose before she choked it off and took a stiff shot of whatever clear liquid was wetting the inside of her glass. By the smell of it, it wasn't water.

"I think the ferrets got a bum rap," I told her. "Have you ever seen any? They're actually kind of cute."

"If you happen to like weasels," she countered with a shudder. "Where I come from, they're sometimes shot on sight to keep them from getting in with the chickens."

"Oh, do you live on a farm?" If so, no matter what she seemed to think about the "awful little animals," if she'd been raised near livestock, she might not have been loath to loose the ferrets and scatter their food over the remains of the rascal who'd loved, and possibly left, her.

"No, though there are a lot in the area in Nebraska where I grew up. I work at my father's plant nursery. So did Chad. That's where we met."

"I see." Well, that didn't foreclose the possibility that she had the fearlessness of a farm girl.

"A toast!" came a shout from nearby, and Dave Driscoll raised his glass. Geek or not, he was the life of tonight's party, especially when he proposed his paean to his former roommate: "To Chad Chatsworth, reality show winner, loser in love, and loser in life. Chad, wherever you are, we miss you. *I* miss you, though I have to say I don't miss your puking in our powder room all night after drinking and singing ribald songs to Charlotte in the solitude of our apartment, songs she'll never hear—and a good thing, too. Anyhow, the joke's on us, roomie, since every one of us is a possible suspect in your murder. Care to say a few words, Chad, and let the rest of us off the hook?"

Dave grew silent, as did the crowd around him. In a moment, though, the silence was broken by a crack from none other than Yul Silva, who almost never said more than a word or two at a time. "You forgot some witnesses, Dave." His speech was slurred, and I realized he was breaking his own tradition thanks to courage cadged from a bottle. "Here's to my poor pals the ferrets. If we don't figure out who really killed you, Chad, you may wind up with ferret companions in hell, and though you belong there, they don't. Now, Chad, is the time to speak up."

Again, silence.

Again, no chatter from Chad's unseen shade spewed out to identify his slayer.

Fascinating evening, I thought. But I doubted I'd learn

anything more now to help me keep my promise to figure out what really happened.

But I had made some interesting acquaintances. I'd consider whom to follow up with, and how.

I hung out only a short while longer before heading to my apartment, where Lexie was waiting.

MUCH LATER, AS I lay in bed and Lexie lay on me, my phone rang. I answered.

"Kendra, it's Jeff." As if I couldn't tell. "I was hoping you'd be here waiting for me tonight."

I didn't want to explain the real reason I'd fled his domicile that evening, so I told him about Charlotte's party. "I need more information to figure out who set up the ferrets that night," I finished. "I've a few more suspects in mind now, thanks to Charlotte's ingenuity."

"And you think you'll be able to keep the ferrets from being put down and Charlotte from being arrested?"

"I'm going to try," I said. Gad, but it was good to hear his voice. I wondered if I'd made a mistake after all, still leaving miles, though fewer, between us this way.

As if reading my mind, or sharing my sentiments— maybe a bit of both—Jeff said, "I'll miss you tonight. Have you thought about what I said?"

"I sure have," I admitted. It was a good thing he didn't urge an answer right then and there, or I'd have agreed to nearly anything. And I wasn't sure I wanted that kind of commitment—was I?

"Well, we'll talk about it tomorrow night when we're together. Okay?"

"Okay."

And maybe then, when I was rested and rational and ready to think, I'd nevertheless say yes.

Chapter Fifteen

I ALMOST OVERSLEPT the next morning. That's what came of trying to get to sleep with so much on my mind—*trying* being the operative word till three A.M. or after.

With my pet-sitting charges stuck in their homes, legs crossed and tummies rumbling, I had to speed my own spaniel through her morning routine. I apologized profusely to Lexie as I plopped her bowl of premium breakfast kibble before her even as I climbed into my clothes. Good thing she already wore her fur coat without my help. Of course, I owed it a firm brushing, but that could wait till later.

Her usual moderately long walk turned into a fast near-run on the hills around our street. As we returned, I saw someone sneaking around our gate. A thief breaking in?

No, a guest from last night breaking out, or at least so it appeared. Philipe Pellera, Latino singing legend, gyration king of the cosmos, was finally leaving Charlotte's party.

An opportunity for me to ask about his knowledge of Chad Chatsworth?

Why not? I ignored the biggest reason, apologizing mutely in my mind to all the animals in my care. My errant late-night attention was focused on the suspects I'd spoken to last night, including his former roomie Dave Driscoll, and his ostensibly dumped damsel Trudi Norman. I'd not talked to Philipe about any interest he might have had in framing the ferrets while seeking Chad's demise. Till now.

"Hi." I edged up to him at the gate. He wore the same white shirt and dark trousers as last night, the oodles of wrinkles in both suggesting he'd slept in them. "Guess I left the party too early. Are Charlotte and Yul awake?"

I looked into his dark bedroom eyes and wondered if I ought to have hung around for last night's orgy. If there'd been one. But what woman could have resisted, having Pellera not only in their dreams but in the same house?

"I think so," he said in his sexy Spanish accent. "I did not want to disturb them, though, so I just snuck out." He gave me a cute conspiratorial smile that made my insides turn sloppy.

"Silly reason for a party, though, don't you think?" I managed to maneuver Lexie and her leash so we blocked Pellera's path to the street. "I mean, inviting everyone they knew who could have cheered on the ferrets."

"The ferrets did nothing wrong, Kendra, and you know it." The deep male voice that slapped at me hadn't a hint of Spanish in it. I looked beyond Philipe to see Yul stalking toward us, jeans hugging his hips beneath his tight tank top. I knew he was annoyed from the number of words he'd hurled into his sentence.

"Hey, I saw what I saw," I replied truthfully and with a wince. As much as I'd like to clear the ferrets from all accusations, they *had* gnawed on Chad. What I didn't know was whether they'd be made to pay. "Did you know anything about Chad that would cause you to kill him, Philipe?" I knew what Yul's answer would have to be. "I mean, if the ferrets were really framed."

I grinned at the obvious humor on the performer's face. "Do you think I would tell you if that was so?" He gave me a wink that made my tibia and fibula go flaccid.

"Probably not," I admitted as Charlotte and Yul formed a phalanx around their former guest. "But I promised Charlotte I'd try to help her learn what really happened."

She wore a different dressing gown from the one I'd seen her in the other day. Instead of peach with matching mules, this one was nearly diaphanous white, which again put me in mind of whether I'd missed one heck of an orgy.

And then I recalled another, larger part of what had kept me from sleeping in the first place—Jeff. Good thing I'd hung out at my own place after all. Participation in an orgy with the nearest beautiful people would only have complicated my consideration of his offer even further. And after all, I hadn't even been invited to that part of the party.

"I do not want Charlotte or Yul to take any blame," Philipe said. "Or the ferrets, for that matter." I looked at him sharply, for his words and tone suggested he wouldn't want them to take the blame for *him*. Or was that simply my interpretation of his nonnative English? He turned to look at his friends. "But that new deal Chad was working on, Charlotte, that he wished for you to join him in—it could have made you a lot more money than your staying away from him to keep your reality show winnings, right?"

"I wouldn't know," she said frostily, looking down her perfect nose at Philipe. Which was hard to do, since he had her by at least half a foot. "I didn't let him tell me about it."

"He told me," Yul said. "Too speculative." Wow, a big word for him. "Possibilities, yes. But no guarantees his deal would be better than Charlotte's for another reality show. Who knew?"

"Who indeed?" I queried. "And you described his ideas to Charlotte, I trust?"

"Of course he did," she replied.

"And they were . . . ?" I prompted, curious.

"Private," Charlotte responded.

Oh, well. "So who do you think killed Chad if it wasn't

Charlotte or Yul setting up the ferrets?" I asked, turning back to Philipe.

He put his long, elegant fingers up to ward off any insinuations on my part. "Not me, of course," he said.

"Of course. But you knew him?"

"Yes. He had approached me with his ideas, too." His dark eyebrows rose. "They had possibilities—several different ones, of course, to let the producers choose, but all, he said, would lead to a different kind of reality show. And all would star me."

"Not Chad himself?"

"I would draw a bigger audience, because I am more famous," he said with a glorious smile. "Or at least I was, until he was killed in so interesting a manner."

Surely that wasn't envy I heard. "What will happen to his ideas now?" I asked.

He shrugged sexy shoulders in an expressive gesture that would make his fans swoon. "I don't know. He fired me from his ideas before they got this far."

Ah-ha! He did have a motive for murder—maybe.

"Did he get another singer involved?"

"Sure did," Yul cut in. "The guy was a bastard."

I didn't deign to ask if he meant figuratively or literally. Philipe was working his way around Lexie and her leash, and I was fast losing my opportunity.

"Are you still having security problems?" I blurted out.

That stopped him. "What do you mean?"

"I happen to know you hired a private investigator who specializes in security matters. Is everything all right?" Of course, I was taking a stab without having all the facts—just the sight of Pellera's name on a file box at Jeff's that I hadn't dared to peek into. Could have meant anything. Still . . .

"Everything is fine," Pellera retorted in a tone that contradicted his comment. "I will see you soon, Charlotte and Yul." With that, he managed to disentangle himself and dash away—nearly into the path of bicyclist Lyle Urquard.

Of course Lyle's wheels slipped out from under him, and he slid on the street. Lexie and I dashed toward him, just in time to keep him from totally dumping off his cycle.

When he was steadied, he slid off and thanked me, then hurried to the still-open front gate. "Hi," he called to Charlotte and Yul. "Thanks again for inviting me to the party last night. I had a great time." He reached Charlotte and said with a huge, jaw-stretching smile, "When's the next one?"

"Soon," she replied, though she looked more glum than glad about it. "If we're not arrested first. Thanks for trying, Kendra, but I think Lexie and you are barking up a lot of wrong trees." She slid the corner of her mouth up as if in appreciation at her own lame jab at a joke, then said, "I'll let you know about the next party, Lyle, if there is one. Come on, Yul. I want to get dressed."

And I needed to get my pet-sitting day started. I warned Charlotte that a contractor was coming to look at the Hummer damage. Amazingly, Ike Janus's insurance company had finally returned a call and told me to expect an adjuster, since they needed an estimate.

And then, with a few amenities hurled at Lyle, I bundled Lexie into the Beamer and we were off.

FORTUNATELY, ONLY A few manageable messes awaited me despite my lateness. I left Lexie locked in the Beamer at each house, since combining her with my charges always took more time. Because it was November, with rain threatening even this early in the season, I didn't have to find shade for her. As far as I could tell, the Los Angeles basin was *all* shade, thanks to the layer of low-level clouds shrouding it. The air was comfortably cool.

As I cleaned, fed, walked, and chatted with my charges, I also kept my mind on my three most major dilemmas of the day—which I'd also stuck, in order, on one of my inevitable lists. Though I left the list in the car with Lexie, I'd updated it on my way while stopped at traffic lights, so its contents remained fresh in my memory.

Could I solve Chad Chatsworth's murder? My queries last night and this morning had seemed lame. Just because Charlotte was in an odd mood and had invited everyone she figured might be a suspect didn't mean that *all* possible killers had made her guest list. But it had included everyone I could think of, too—each inserted on my jotted agenda for investigation.

Except, of course, the ferrets. I didn't know them by name, assuming they had names. I'd have to check with Yul.

Which would also slip me an opening to talk to him further about his ferrets. I didn't know all that Noralles did about Chad's death, but how much could the little critters possibly have contributed to the act? I'd ask when I found Yul separate from Charlotte—a rare occurrence.

"Okay," I told Lexie as I slid into the Beamer and started the engine. "We're making progress. Halfway through our visits, I think. Maybe we'll have time to stop at Darryl's later." I slid us out of our parking space and onto the quiet residential street toward our next stop. My mind continued to maneuver around its issues du jour.

My Jeff situation would continue this evening, since he was in town and so was I. I could no longer use studying as an excuse to keep clear of him, even if I wanted to. Which I didn't. I had to face him and the quandary he'd stuck me in. I wouldn't necessarily need to hand him an answer yet. But I did have to hang out with him with the question dangling in my mind, to see how I reacted. How he did, too. He could have changed his mind by now. It had been days since he'd blurted out his proposition. Maybe he'd already decided it was a blunder.

As if he'd make it that easy for me.

There was nothing I could do now about my ethics exam, so it hadn't made it to the big three on my list. No, it had been jostled off by Jon Arlen and his digging dog, Jonesy.

Buried treasure. Wow, what an exciting legal issue!

Too bad I wasn't, at this moment, a practicing attorney.

On the other hand, nothing said one had to have an active law license to leap into some legal research—one of my favorite practices. I loved to perform research and craft clever arguments, argue them in court, and outclass the opposition. I only hoped my brain and tongue weren't atrophied from disuse.

Now that I wasn't with the Marden firm any longer, my subscription to online legal research services was as dead as my former livelihood. I needed access to Lexis or Westlaw to extract legal precedent about real property law and buried treasure—better access than I could get on my own at this moment.

It was Saturday. If I gained an entrée to the Marden offices, I was unlikely to meet up with anyone I wanted to avoid. "I'll call Avvie," I told Lexie as I pulled up to the next house—Py the python's place. He wouldn't mind my being another couple minutes late. He'd already ingested his mouse of the week. I was just stopping to say hi and make sure his habitat remained at comfortable temperatures for a being as cold-blooded as he.

I used my cell to call Avvie's home. I owed her a visit anyway, to meet her pig that I'd play with when she left town.

"Oh, hi, Kendra," she said.

I confirmed that she'd be in town till next Tuesday, though I suggested I stop over earlier to learn my porcine duties.

"Absolutely, but not today," she told me. "I'm buried in the case that Bill and I will be doing depos on when we're out of town. Tomorrow afternoon? I'll introduce you then."

"Fine," I said, then asked, "Are you heading for the office today?" I crossed my fingers, for that would be a fine opening for me to join her and log on to the legal websites.

"No, I'm working at home."

I decided to dump my problem on her anyway—in general, since I had no intention of even hinting about my specific treasure-bound legal issue. I explained I'd found a nonlegal way to help a friend of Darryl's out of a dilemma, and since then others had asked for my assistance. "There's a problem that contains legal issues. I won't advise the guy, of course, but I'd like to learn the law myself so I can steer him to the right attorney if he needs it. That means I have to get in some computer research time. Is there any way you can get me hooked up—preferably today?" I could pay by the search for an online legal research service, but I'd fare better financially by using a law firm's rate.

A pause as she pondered. Was she thinking of a way to let me down easily since she needed my pet-sitting services? But no, when Avvie finally spoke, she had a solution.

"I'd bring you into the office today if I could, but I can't. But I visited Borden Yurick's new place yesterday to discuss a couple of matters that he's taking over."

She didn't sound happy about it, but she'd already explained that the former Marden partner had had the temerity—obviously because his brain was mush after his mental breakdown—not only to leave his former firm but to take his clients with him.

"He's leasing a suite in Encino. You're in the Valley, aren't you? I'll give you his number. You can ask if he'll let you use his online service. In fact, maybe you can work out using one of his offices and other facilities in exchange for doing work for him when you have your license back. At least that way he'll have someone competent looking over his shoulder."

Hmmm. Avvie might have something there. The exchange, not the competency. I wasn't about to brand Borden without checking his mental state for myself. Though as to the rest . . . "Isn't he soured on everyone from the old firm?" I asked. "He might not even want to see me, since I'm not handing over files or information."

"He specifically asked about you when I was there,"

Avvie said. "It won't hurt to approach him."

Assuming he was even in on a Saturday. On the other hand, since he was just opening a new office, maybe he'd be about. I got his phone number from Avvie, thanked her, and set up a time to pop in at her place the next afternoon to meet Pansy.

And then I called Borden.

Chapter Sixteen

I WAS DELIGHTED with Borden's new digs.

Whereas the Marden offices were the stuff of stuffy big-firm lawyers, Borden's was a former single-story restaurant in a trendy area of Encino, on Ventura Boulevard. Its nearly empty parking lot was as shady as the rest of L.A. that day, plus a large picture window overlooked it from the building. It seemed safe enough to leave Lexie in the Beamer, though she obviously wasn't in love with the idea. In fact, if she'd spoken English, I suspected she'd have told me off in no uncertain terms for leaving her in the car so much that day.

As it was, she simply ignored my command to stay, and I had to scramble from the car carefully so as not to let her loose. "I'm sorry," I told her. "I'll try not to be too long." Which might be hard if Borden was kind enough to let me sponge off his online research service. There was a lot I wanted to look up.

But it all didn't need to be done today. I'd just have to gauge how amenable Borden might be to seeing more of me.

In the meantime, Lexie announced her displeasure at being left alone by barking after me as I followed the path from parking lot to entrance. I sighed, wishing I could reason with her, but I fully forgave her temper. I'd make it up to her later, with a nice long walk, just her and me.

And maybe her best friend, Odin, and my biggest conundrum, Jeff . . . ?

On the street side, no big sign designated the eatery's name, but a simple plaque near the door stated, OFFICES OF BORDEN YURICK, ATTORNEY AT LAW. Opening the portal, I popped in.

I gathered that the office's reception area was once where the restaurant's hostess had awaited patrons. It was part of a larger open room, with a door to the right that had led to the bar—the drinking kind, not a lawyers' group. From here I saw a long counter of wood but no booze behind it. No aroma of spilled liquor or cooking food, either. A hint of cologne, though, wafted from behind the reception desk, where a perky young person sat up straight and smiled at me. "Can I help you?" she sang.

"My name is Kendra—"

"Ballantyne!" she cut me off with a squeal. "Bordon said you were coming. It's so nice to meet you." She shot around her desk and stuck out a hand tipped in red nails that looked razor sharp. The auburn curls surrounding her face didn't stop bouncing until she did.

"Thanks," I said, feeling foolishly at a loss. "What's your name?"

"Mignon. As in filet." She giggled, rolling dark-lined blue eyes as if this was a joke as old as she was—which couldn't have been more than twenty-two. "It means 'dainty' in French, which is kind of silly, don't you think?"

I had to agree, for though she wasn't exactly overweight, certain parts of her were curvy enough beneath her frilly white shirt and pencil skirt to bring to mind someone not dainty but *zaftig*, a term I heard sometimes from Yiddish-speaking cronies. Meaning "built."

"Anyway, it's so great to meet you," she said again. "I

mean, I saw you in the news when you were all over it because of those murders you supposedly committed, and then you proved who really did it! And today Borden said you were coming and that you used to work with him and—"

"Down, Mignon," commanded a soft voice from somewhere behind her. I looked over her shoulder to see Borden Yurick coming toward us from what had once been the dining room. I'd been used to seeing him in suit coat or sweater, and always with a tie. Now, he was clad in one of those soft-looking Hawaiian shirts where the material is turned inside out, and beneath it he wore white pants. All he needed was a lei around his scrawny neck to complete the effect. "Kendra. Welcome."

I'd pondered how to approach an aging man who'd recently had a mental breakdown. Supposedly. I hadn't really been able to learn whether that was solely a fabrication of his former Marden partners to explain his defection. I figured I'd treat him as I always had—professionally polite.

Which was soon squeezed out of me when he threw his arms around me and constricted me in a heartier hug than anything Charlotte—or even Py the python—had ever tried on me.

"Good to see you, my dear," he said, stepping back. His smile was as sweet and lopsided as ever, and was his third most prominent feature, after old-fashioned large-framed bifocals beneath a huge shock of silvery hair. "Come into my office. Mignon, please get us some coffee, would you?"

"Right away, Borden," she chirped.

He preceded me through the former dining room, which was now refitted with an assortment of empty cubicles on the inside, with offices framed in as-yet unfinished wood toward the walls. I heard noises from inside a couple and figured they were occupied.

"I'm still remodeling," Borden remarked unnecessarily. His office was at the end, and its walls were well established, lined with oak paneling. His desk was an antique, his client chairs an eclectic assortment probably bought with the restaurant building. "Take your pick," he told me as he took his own place behind his desk. "So what have you been up to?" he asked. "Besides what I read in the papers."

"Depending on which papers you read," I told him, "you probably have a pretty good idea." He hadn't asked why when I'd asked to see him in our phone call earlier, so I decided to lead into it. "You haven't been around the Marden offices for a while, so you might not have known when I was accused of turning over a strategy memo to the other side in some litigation. That led to the suspension of my law license. I took up pet-sitting to earn some money while figuring out what to do next, and really liked it. I'm still doing it, though I just took the MPRE yesterday, the last step in getting my license reinstated."

"And you're not going to mention all those murder victims you keep stumbling over?"

"No," I said. "Sounds as if you heard about them anyhow."

He laughed. "At least my problems weren't made public," he said. "And no, before you ask, I didn't really have a mental breakdown. It was something my esteemed colleagues made up to explain why I was cruising around the South Pacific when there were so many clients clamoring for my attention at home." He held up a thin, bony hand. "Oh, I worried about them, all right, when I thought about who was going to be taking care of their legal matters in my absence. Bill Sergement." He grimaced. "Royal Marden." His grimace grew uglier as he shuddered. And then he grinned again. "I was burned out. I needed some time to get my head on straight. Isn't that the current phrase?"

"Sure," I said.

We paused in our conversation to take a couple of big, steaming mugs from Mignon. "Call if you need anything else," she sang, then left.

"So when I came back," Borden continued as I took a

sip of deep, dark, delicious coffee, "I knew exactly what I needed. That's when I withdrew from the partnership and contacted the clients I'd brought in. And do you know, nearly all of them decided to stay with me, despite the bad-mouthing I'd received while away and especially when I returned."

"So I heard," I replied.

"Of course, everything's still in transition. I've got some old—and I do mean old—law school friends coming out of retirement to join me here. We're going to have a lot of fun practicing law. That's what I want."

I laughed. "What an oxymoron!"

"Anyway, what can I do for you, Kendra? I assume you're not here to try to keep clients for the Marden firm."

"Not hardly," I huffed. "I'm through with them, too. Talk about unsupportive to a junior partner they should have backed. They're lawyers, for heaven's sake. Didn't they ever hear about being innocent till proven guilty?"

"Only when it's convenient for them."

"Anyway, I have to admit that Avvie was the one to suggest I call you. I intend to rent access to one of the online legal research services but I don't want to subscribe till I have my license back and settle somewhere to practice law again."

"You mean you're dumping pet-sitting?"

"I didn't say that. But it's led to some other stuff." I told him about how I'd helped Fran Korwald resolve her pug custody problem, which led to referrals of others whose issues were pet-related. "I've got something I might have to refer to someone with a license if things break before mine's back, but for now I'll do the legal research without providing advice."

"So you'd like to use my Lexis hookup?"

"Yes," I admitted. "I'll reimburse you for the cost."

"No need. I have a flat rate. Only one little fee to you."

"Which is?"

"Tell me the kind of issue it is."

"One that's utterly fascinating," I said, wanting to tantalize him without telling him too much. "Believe it or not, it's about buried treasure."

He laughed, then leaned toward me, pushing his large glasses back up his elongated nose. "Okay, I'll have Mignon give you office keys. Come in anytime to do research, at least till I tell you to stop. The only charge will be that you'll tell me everything that client confidentiality will allow. Deal?"

"Deal. Borden, you're a dear."

"Tell that to the Marden firm folks," he said with one of his sweet, signature grins.

I SAT IN one of the makeshift offices, choosing a parking-lot view as I used one of Borden's brand-new computers. Lexie had apparently given up trying to bark her way out of the Beamer, for I only occasionally saw her stick her nose by one of the windows I'd left cracked open.

Because it was late and I still had clients to cater to, I didn't get far into the law of treasure trove. The initial stuff, though, didn't bode well for Jon Arlen.

California Civil Code Section 829 provided that the owner of land has the right to the surface and to everything permanently situated beneath or above it. At least buried treasure was unlikely to be considered a permanent fixture by the courts.

Then there were the laws relating to trespass. Jon Arlen and his dog probably had no right to be on the property where Jonesy had dug up the long-buried goods.

But I was a lawyer, even if I wasn't a practicing one at that point. Past experience, not to mention my passion, convinced me: I'd come up with excellent arguments on behalf of my client somehow—though I wasn't sure yet what they'd be. Maybe something would come to me by the time my license was actually held once more in my eager hands. In the meantime, I'd take advantage of Borden's kind indulgence as often as I could.

While I was there, I usurped the use I'd previously made of Jeff's top computer geek, Althea, and also took advantage of the special subscription databases to do searches on people in Chad Chatsworth's sphere who might've had cause to kill him. Not that I had the hacking prowess I posited that Althea had. I printed out pages to study later, since I was running late.

I needed to go wind Widget the terrier down with his afternoon training. And then I'd get busy with the rest of my evening rounds.

But I was ever so grateful to Borden for granting me the right to return at will to do whatever research I wanted, gratis.

I WALKED—OR rather ran—Widget. My other pet-sitting clients had been tended to. I was about to call Jeff, to let him know Lexie and I were on our way.

What would I tell him? I hoped I'd know it before I said it. But before I dialed Jeff on my cell, it sang out, "It's My Life." I lifted its cover.

"Kendra?" A female voice blasted hysterically into my ear, and I had to pull the phone back to listen.

"Yes?"

"It's Charlotte."

"Oh, good. Did the insurance adjuster come today? Did you let him in?"

"Yes, of course. But that's not why I'm calling. Please come home. That awful detective is on his way here, and I think he's going to arrest me. Please help me." And then she hung up.

Chapter Seventeen

TIME TO CALL in the big guns. And that wasn't me.

First, while driving east down Ventura, ducking cars slipping in and out of parallel parking spots, I phoned Charlotte back. She was crying too hard to hear me, so I demanded that she hand her cell to Yul.

"Has she called Esther Ickes yet?" I demanded.

"Who?"

"Esther Ickes. The criminal lawyer who helped me when I was dangling by my fingernails, trying my damnedest not to get arrested for murder. Among other things."

"Ickes?"

Yul was up to his old single-syllable tricks. "Esther Ickes," I repeated. "Do you have a pen and paper?"

"Yes."

I gave him Esther's phone number. "Call her now," I commanded. "Use my name and tell her the problem. As long as she's not in court, she's the kind who'll drop everything and be there for a client, new or old. Got it?"

"Yeah."

I edged the Beamer onto the freeway on-ramp, then juggled the phone while I merged and called Jeff. I was pretty adept at patting my head and rubbing my gut at once, when I had to. Multitasking was my middle name.

"Hi, Kendra," Jeff said immediately, obviously extracting my identity from caller ID. "Coming over tonight?" His voice was sweet, deep, and seductive, and it made me remember exactly why we had to talk—and told me what my answer should be.

But not yet. "Yes," I said, "but right now I'm calling to beg a bit of your P.I. expertise."

"You're not solving everyone's problems on your own?"

"Don't get smart. But do get over to my place, right away." I filled him in on my conversation with Charlotte.

"My old buddy and yours, Detective Ned Noralles?"

"None other. No wonder the poor woman needs help."

"And you'd like nothing better than to show him up again on another murder investigation."

"Wouldn't you?" I countered.

"Come to think of it . . . See you at your place in a bit."

Lexie and I beat Jeff there. Esther, too. But not the neighbors, for with all the cop cars clustered around the place again, they'd begun to gather once more.

"What's going on, Kendra?" Tilla Thomason demanded as I wended slowly through them, car window open so I could call out to people to get out of my way. I'd have honked and scared them out of their skins, but they were, after all, my neighbors. I'd leave their skins—and nerves—intact.

"I don't know," I called to Tilla. Which was somewhat true. Charlotte could have been wrong about her impending inquisition or arrest. Though if Noralles was involved, I doubted it.

I parked the Beamer in its usual spot and left Lexie upstairs at our place. Then I headed for the main house.

I was just in time to find a way to finagle a path for Esther Ickes to join me. She'd parked her jaunty red Jaguar somewhere on the street and seemed lost in the middle of the massing crowd. I knew better, of course. Esther might look like a frail septuagenarian, but she had the street smarts of an alley cat. Better yet, she knew her way around a court better than the criminal attorneys of which legends were made.

I slunk back through the opening in my wrought-iron fence and led Esther in. As always, she was clad in a suit, this one lime green and long-skirted. Her blouse was cream crepe, which only underscored the abundance of wrinkles that added character to her aging face.

"Kendra, my dear, what a delight to see you," she said as cool as if the crowd that had grudgingly parted to let her pass weren't there at all. "This isn't about another legal problem of yours, is it?"

"Don't you think that after bankruptcy, alleged ethics violations, and murder accusations, I've had more than my share?"

"Absolutely." We reached the house's front door. "So this isn't about you? The man who called wasn't clear what he wanted, but he said it was an emergency and dropped your name."

"No, it's not me. It's my tenant, Charlotte LaVerne." I gave a one-minute overview of her reality show results, Chad Chatsworth, and his demise here in my house, complete with the presence of ferrets.

Esther nodded sagely, causing the wattle of skin beneath her chin to bob. "I wondered. I've been reading about how those nasty little animals killed someone around here, but I didn't realize it was actually at your house."

"I'm sure they were set up, and I suspect Charlotte's soon to follow, if we don't help her."

"We? Do you have your law license back now?"

I felt myself flush. "Well, no, though I'm hoping it's only a few weeks off, since I just took the MPRE. But Charlotte asked for my help, and I'm kind of acting as a quasi-P.I. In fact"—I stared over her shoulder at the big

black Escalade creeping up the street amid the crowd—
"I'm helping Jeff Hubbard. Or maybe he's helping me.
That's him now." I pointed behind her, and she turned.

We still hadn't rung the doorbell, and once again I
opened the gate to allow an invited someone inside. I
grinned at all buff six feet of Jeff as he covered me with
equally hungry eyes. "Later," I said, feeling my insides
turn mushy. "Let's see Charlotte first."

A uniformed officer who looked familiar opened the
front door after our ring. "Yes?" His name badge identified
him as Elina, and I recognized him as the older and less enthusiastic of the cops who'd come to my door when the
Hummer had bashed an entry of its own.

Esther took over, identifying herself. "Ms. LaVerne is
my client. I understand she's currently being interrogated."
A couple of leaps to conclusions, but what the heck? It got
us inside, even Jeff and me when she introduced him as an
investigator she'd hired and me as her assistant. She didn't
say assistant what. I could have been along to answer her
phone.

She asked to see Charlotte but told me to take her wherever by way of the infamous den that had been stoved in by
the Hummer, haphazardly and temporarily mended, and finally inspected by the insurance company—the same den
that had formerly been occupied by the ferrets, and the
scene of Chad Chatsworth's last stand.

Ignoring Officer Elina's protests, I pushed open the
door. We peered in one by one, then I led my entourage
down the hall toward where I heard voices. Sure enough,
the living room, in all its ugly black-and-white furnished
nonglory, was occupied by Charlotte and Detective Noralles. Yul was nowhere to be seen, which gave credence to
the assumption that Charlotte was being officially interrogated. Another potential witness wouldn't be permitted to
hear, because that might lead to meshing of their stories.

Noralles stood as we appeared in the doorway. He

didn't look happy. I wondered if he ever smiled, except snidely. Maybe a real one would make his good-looking face crack.

Charlotte, on the other hand, gave a huge grin and threw herself toward me, engulfing me immediately in one of her hugs. "Thank heaven you're here, Kendra," she shrilled.

When she stepped back, I introduced her to Esther. "And you remember my private investigator friend Jeff Hubbard, don't you?"

"I sure do." Our presence must have eased Charlotte enough that she assumed her usual enthusiastic sex-pot persona, eyeing Jeff with a feline smile. Even with her hair held back in its normal black braid, her body covered with a loose tunic and slacks, she was one sexy reality show star. But when she caught my gaze, she must have remembered herself, for she had the grace to flush and look at the floor.

"I thought you said you were her lawyer," Officer Elina said irritably to Esther.

"I am," she said amiably.

"Then how come you're just being introduced?"

"Never mind, young man," Esther said. "Now, if you two nice policemen would just give us some private attorney-client time with Ms. LaVerne . . ." She obviously remembered Detective Noralles from when she'd been around during his interrogations of me. He remembered her, too, judging from his glower.

But he had little choice. Charlotte had requested to see her lawyer, and Esther was it. Privilege could attach even with Jeff and me here, as long as we were consultants hired by an attorney on behalf of her client.

Noralles split, heading for the kitchen. That must have been where Yul was sequestered, for he shot from that end of the house as fast as if he'd been ejected from a damaged fighter plane's cockpit.

"You okay?" Yul demanded of Charlotte.

"Yes," she said, grabbing his arm. Then, "No," she said,

nearly sinking to the colorful Pakistani area rug. Yul helped her over to one of the ugly sofas and sat beside her. I let Esther sit on an overstuffed white chair near her new client, and Jeff and I grabbed others facing them.

"The detective said he received an envelope, sent anonymously," Charlotte finally continued in a subdued voice.

"We'll want to see it," Jeff said, his eyes on Esther, whose silvery hair shimmied as she nodded.

"I did see it, kind of," Charlotte said. "Its postmark was from the post office near the studios where *Turn Up the Heat* was filmed, and where I was pitching other ideas. It contained things no one should have had besides me . . . and the detective seems to think the stuff in it shows that I had a motive to kill Chad."

"What things?" Jeff demanded before Esther or I could.

"Papers." Charlotte heaved a sad sigh, and Yul took her hand. I might not like the guy much, but at least he was there for Charlotte. "I'd had some letterhead printed for our new reality show production company," she continued. "I used a few sheets for brainstorming—and they were in the package. One showed me as chief executive and listed some of our initial ideas—you need a lot so network execs can choose those they think'll work best. On another, I'd jotted down the most important rule from *Turn Up the Heat,* as a reminder: If I took up with Chad again, or there was even the appearance of our getting together, it would all be over. Then there was the schedule we put together, Yul's and mine, to figure out when Yul could meet with Chad without me present."

Esther leaned forward in her overstuffed white chair. "Why would he want to do that?" she asked her new client, though her eyes were on Yul.

"We'd heard Chad put together his own list of reality show ideas," Charlotte responded. "He wanted me involved since we were both reality show stars now, so he figured together we'd be dynamite. Too bad he didn't think of that before and dump Trudi when . . . Well, as it was, I had no intention of discussing ideas with him—his or mine. Too risky. I could lose everything. But Yul could talk to him, in case something he'd thought of was so wonderful that it convinced me to change my mind and give everything up for it."

I couldn't help a half-smile of skepticism.

She obviously caught it, for she continued, "Yeah, it wouldn't happen that way, but if there was something really good, I wanted to know about it. That way, if I couldn't work with Chad, maybe I could find a way to use his idea in a way that wasn't really stealing."

"Of course," I agreed, making no attempt to tame the irony in my tone.

She gave a small laugh. "I was so miffed with the guy I might not have cared if it *was* stealing, as long as I could get away with it."

"I figured," I said.

"Was there anything else in that package?" Jeff asked, his businesslike tone tugging us back to the essence of our discussion.

"I don't know if Detective Noralles showed me everything, but he let me read a photocopy of a note I'd written to Chad."

"You wrote to him?" Esther exclaimed.

"It wasn't the same as seeing him," Charlotte said defensively. "And I only wrote it to try to prove to the *Turn Up the Heat* producers that I wanted nothing to do with him. That's why I kept a photocopy. See, he'd shown up a couple of times and tried to talk to me directly. I warned him in the note to stay away or I'd have Yul make sure he did."

"I'll bet Noralles chose to interpret it as a death threat," Jeff said.

Charlotte nodded brusquely. "You know all that 'motive, means, and opportunity' stuff?"

I knew it well. The motive part was what kept me from

being arrested when my pet-sitting clients started popping up dead.

"Well, Detective Noralles thinks he's got it figured out. Motive: Chad lied to me about his girlfriend and also tried to spoil my winnings. Opportunity: The schedule showed times I'd be home but Yul wouldn't. Of course, neither of us was around when Chad was killed, but Noralles is ignoring that. He seems to think I agreed that Chad could come here, where I had access to the knife that actually killed him—that's the means."

A blade? That must have been what Noralles knew when he questioned Charlotte before. It made more sense than ferret fangs for severing a carotid artery.

"Not that they found the knife yet—or the detective wouldn't have asked me where I stashed it," Charlotte said. "Anyway, then I supposedly sprinkled Chad with ferret food to get them nibbling and to try to hide what I'd done. That's what the L.A. County Coroner apparently figures happened to him—stabbed first, ferret supper later."

"Did the detective give any more details about the autospy?" Jeff questioned. "Like, did the victim have bruises or other wounds besides the bites and stabs?"

"He didn't tell me," Charlotte said. "But I have the impression he's ready to arrest me."

"We'll see about that," Esther promised.

"But all this brings one big question to my mind," I said. "*You* wouldn't have mailed him those potentially incriminating papers. How would anyone else have gotten them?"

Charlotte shrugged.

"Could be the killer grabbed them when he was in the house the night he killed Chad," Jeff said.

"And mailed them to Noralles to make sure the detective's suspicions stayed on Charlotte," I agreed. "But shouldn't that make him even more suspicious that Charlotte's innocent?"

"Let's ask him," Esther said, and she went to get Noralles.

His response? "Sure, we've considered that the murderer may have sent that evidence to frame Ms. LaVerne,"
he said with a shrewd smile. "But Ms. LaVerne could have
mailed it herself to try to make us think someone else was
trying to frame her." He hurled a few more halfhearted
questions at Charlotte with all of us around—obviously no
longer an official interrogation. When finished, he agreed
to send Esther copies of the envelope and its contents, then
said snidely to Charlotte, "I assume your new responsibili-
ties won't take you out of town anytime soon, Ms. LaVerne. I'm sure we'll see each other again very soon."

"Then we will, too, Detective," Esther said smoothly.

Chapter Eighteen
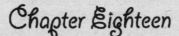

LEXIE AND I followed Jeff home. To *his* home, though I could make it mine if I accepted his unanticipated invitation.

Heck, it was mine when he traveled. And sometimes when he was home, when we hung out there together.

What was I going to do?

Act cool, of course, and collected, and stay that way all evening, while we both puttered about in his kitchen feeding the dogs, then ourselves. I even cooked that night, dipping into what little domesticity I had.

"Good chicken," Jeff said when we'd sat down at his round wooden table. I'd fixed a dish of my own creation, kind of—a combo of cacciatore and rigatoni, cooked with onion and zucchini and baked with provolone. It combined a bunch of flavors I particularly liked, and apparently it pleased Jeff's palate as well. Which made me feel relieved. And perversely, irritated.

If I moved in here, would domesticity dominate my need for independence?

Unfair, I chided myself. Playing chef tonight had been my idea. Jeff might appreciate it, but he certainly didn't expect it.

Another item to factor into my decision: Would I feel an unwanted but typically female urge to get at the man of the house's heart via his stomach? Unnecessarily, of course, since I'd already proven we were compatible while exercising much more interesting parts of his anatomy.

"Can I pick your brain?" I asked him—which wasn't the body part I'd been pondering. "About the Chad Chatsworth murder, I mean."

"Sure." He paused with his fork poised to spear more food and regarded me with interested blue eyes.

I gave a thumbnail recap of all I'd researched so far on Borden Yurick's computer, plus my queries of Charlotte, Yul, and the attendees at last night's strange soiree. "I don't know, of course, if all possible suspects were present, but that, apparently, was Charlotte's plan. Though whether she hoped someone would have so much fun that he'd stand up and proclaim his guilt, I couldn't tell you."

"Or she," Jeff said.

"Or she," I agreed. "In any event, it didn't happen."

"Sounds as if you're doing a good job of trying to help Charlotte. But you really don't think she's guilty?"

"You do?" I know my tone rose as if I was the one affronted. Or maybe his questioning me simply gave me an excuse for indignation. Which in turn would give me an excuse to thank him for his invitation and head back to my place.

He disarmed me with his sage, sexy smile. "I haven't formed an opinion yet, Kendra. I know why you have, though. Since you see Charlotte in the same situation as you were before, you'll do anything to make sure she's not railroaded." True. He'd heard me, same as Darryl had. "The thing is, you knew for sure you weren't guilty. Can you say the same about her?"

"Sure!" I exclaimed in staunch support of my poor tenant. "I think," I finished with a sigh. "I have to admit, if only to you, that Noralles's means, motive, and opportunity may have been met. But maybe someone else had them all, too. There is that anonymously sent package, after all."

"Someone else like your friend Yul? I assume the guy is at least smart enough to mail an envelope."

"Not *my* friend. Charlotte's." Once again Jeff had jumped right into the meat of what was on my mind. And I didn't mean chicken. "But he wouldn't have mailed that envelope, since its contents implicate her."

"So what about *his* reasons to kill Chad?" Jeff asked.

"That's easy. As her kept man—er, rather, assistant at her fledgling production company—he'd have all the same reasons she did to keep Chad away . . . permanently. Maybe after hearing his show ideas. Chad's presence could wreak havoc on all that nice money Charlotte was raking in. And Yul had another reason—Charlotte herself. She's his meal ticket. And most likely a lot more, if the way he looks at her now and then isn't just his wannabe actor skills kicking in. Chad was a good-looking guy, a charmer"—as I'd seen in my extremely brief acquaintance with him— "which might also have twisted Yul's testosterone. Sure, it could be him . . . but there are bigger and better reasons to doubt it was Yul."

"Let me guess," Jeff said, a grin easing the hard planes of his good-looking P.I. features. "One has to be the ferrets. They were Yul's, weren't they?"

"Yes," I agreed. "He wouldn't want to make it look as if—"

"His pets gnawed someone into oblivion," Jeff finished. "At least not if there was another way to protect Charlotte and him."

"Right. And then there's the fact it looks too obviously like him, if it's not Charlotte. Yul's intelligence is somewhat suspect, but I don't see even him committing murder where they live and trying to frame the ferrets to get the heat off them. And then worrying about his own behind enough to send a package to the police sure to sic them on his sugar mommy . . . it doesn't make sense."

Jeff nodded. "Yeah, but I'd suspect him over Charlotte any day." Once again, he and I were on the same wavelength. Which felt wonderful. Especially when he applauded my investigation efforts so far, interjecting a few ideas of his own and promising to check into them. And I knew he'd do it. I trusted the guy, his professional skills, and his judgment.

"I wonder," he said as we rinsed dishes and stacked them in his dishwasher, dogs prancing around as if hoping crumbs would miraculously appear on the floor. "I know Ned Noralles. I wouldn't be surprised if he's coming down so hard on Charlotte because he suspects them both. Either she'll crack, or Yul, guilty or not, will confess to save her. What do you think?"

I pondered for only a second before I said, "Maybe. But what if I'm right, and it's neither of them?"

"You know Noralles, too. He's a smart guy, but he takes the easy way whenever possible—whether or not it's the real solution."

"Then I'll keep on helping Charlotte. You, too?"

He grinned as he closed the dishwasher door. "If you insist, boss."

We didn't solve the murder that night. Nor did I tell him everything about Jon Arlen's treasure dilemma, though I related enough to tantalize him. "You're not representing the guy," Jeff said. "There's no attorney-client privilege. Tell me more."

"Only if you let me look in your client files. You're not an attorney, after all." And I was salivating about the possibility of sneaking a peek at the Philipe Pellera file.

"No, but I have my own brand of ethics," Jeff said with a smile and a shrug. "You stay out of my business, and I'll stay out of yours. Professionally, I mean."

"And nonprofessionally?"

He leaned down and locked lips with me till the dogs barked at us to break it up.

Though it was November and the days were growing shorter, we leashed up Lexie and Odin and let them lead us for their last outing of the evening, staying on the sidewalks of Jeff's flat neighborhood beneath the streetlights. Another advantage of moving in here, for in the hills around my house, cars too often zoomed around curves, streetlights were scarce, and sidewalks were utterly absent. And as a landlady who loved her leased-out house, I'd have to visit often to check on its upkeep anyway.

Heck, I was really thinking about this, wasn't I?

And later that night, after Jeff and I had engaged in erotic exercise in his bedroom, I lay awake for a long while, listening to lots of heavy breathing from the two canines, and a sexy, bare-skinned P.I. I didn't count sheep but reviewed, in my mind, a long list of pros and cons. Yes or no? Yes or . . .

I finally let my dreams take on the decision.

WHEN I AWOKE in the morning, I reached for Jeff. Or he reached for me. I wasn't sure which, but the outcome was the same: another energetic session of steamy sex.

Which caused me to dash off for my pet-sitting rounds with a cup of coffee in my hands and no breakfast in my stomach. I'd grab something from a fast-food drive-through when I spotted one on my way. I left Lexie with Jeff, since Odin and she were having a blast bounding around his backyard together.

I found myself singing to my canine, feline, and even reptilian charges. Good thing none could hold their ears. But hey, they had to be happy that I was in one heck of a good mood. I was especially friendly—and a particularly soft touch when it came to adding a little something extra to their breakfasts.

Would moving in with Jeff make my moods so munificent all the time? I'd bet the pets I tended hoped to find out.

This wasn't a Widget day, since it was a weekend. The active terrier pup had his owner at home to terrorize. That gave me a gap in the center of the day.

I found myself aiming the Beamer down the San Diego Freeway toward Palms. And then cruising the street where Chad had lived. Why? Hell if I knew. But I was pretty frustrated that I couldn't just haul out some helpful facts and hand them to Noralles to get Charlotte off the hook. Maybe Yul, too.

So there I was, creeping along Chad's street around noon on a Sunday, and I was just in time to see Trudi Norman exiting the apartment building where Chad had lived. She was followed by Chad's former apartment mate, chief geek Dave Driscoll.

As I said, it was noonish. But was it my imagination, or were these two just greeting the day? Trudi, at least, was fully dressed, in a T-shirt and denim skirt. She turned to. face Driscoll, who'd forgotten his shirt. His jeans were on, though they hung low over his hips. And though I parked in the nearest spot, which was a building away, I could tell the guy's build, though definitely on the skinny side, wasn't completely devoid of masculine muscle. How could I tell? Well, it helped that Trudi turned to him, ran fingers over his bare chest, then reached up to pull his head down for a big kiss.

Was this a case of two sad souls banding together in their grief over a mutual friend? Or had one of them decided that selfsame friend had been in the way of what was now, at least, becoming a beautiful relationship?

Perhaps there'd even been cause for both of them to divest themselves of the inconvenience of Chad.

Hmmm. They'd both been at Charlotte's suspects party last night, so I wasn't the only one who wondered at the possibilities of their being participants in Chad's demise.

I'd not had them in my radar when I'd dived into research yesterday at Borden's.

Next time, that's exactly where they'd be.

WITH TRAFFIC TERRIBLE on the 405 for no apparent reason, I took the long way around to spend less time getting back. As I headed up the Hollywood Freeway over the Cahuenga Pass toward the Valley, I glanced toward the north and the area known as Lake Hollywood.

The home of Jon Arlen's buried treasure.

Could I find a way to help the guy keep it? My legal research yesterday hadn't yielded a lot of hope, so good thing I wasn't about to regale him with lawyerly advice now. And even if I passed the ethics exam, I wouldn't want to pass along the unhelpful material I'd unearthed about digging up such stuff.

Surely there was—

My cell phone rang. It was Jeff.

"Where are you?" he asked.

I told him. I also let slip the interesting scene I'd witnessed at Chad Chatsworth's building.

"You want me to do a little extra digging into those two?" he asked me.

"Would you? Oh, Jeff, I'd really appreciate it."

"You'll pay for it, of course."

"How?"

"Think about it."

"Oh, I will," I said, then hung up. A big grin was pasted on my face, with no one there to enjoy it but me. I'd get home to the guy as early as I could, even as I imagined coming home to him all the time—at least when he wasn't on his trips out of town.

My phone rang again. I answered without peering at the caller ID. "You can't have found anything interesting on them this fast," I said. "Or are you just trying to make me uncomfortable as I drive?"

"Pardon?" shrilled an unfamiliar female voice. I stole a glance at my phone's display. Nope, not Jeff's number.

"Sorry," I said. "This is Kendra Ballantyne. To whom am I speaking?" I once again laid on my formal lawyer persona, even though I hadn't practiced law for months.

"Ms. Ballantyne, my name is Marie Seidforth. Fran Korwald suggested that I call you. I have a problem . . ." Her voice trailed off, followed by a sound that could only have been a sob.

"Hello, Ms. Seidforth?" I finally said. "Are you still there?"

"Yes," she finally wailed. "Please, help me."

Chapter Nineteen

IGNORING THE FACT I still couldn't give legal advice, the timing couldn't have been better.

I mean, unlike on the San Diego Freeway, the drive north to Valencia on a Sunday afternoon was virtually traffic-free. Plus, I was between morning and afternoon pet visits, so I had time to head there. In only half an hour, I pulled up to the guardhouse of the gated community where Marie Seidforth lived. I gave the guard my name and Marie's, and waited while he called to inquire whether I was an invited guest.

Soon the gate's arm lifted and I was signaled inside. "Two streets down and to the left," the guard instructed. "Poppy Place, number ten."

Good thing the houses were numbered, since there seemed to be only two or three housing plans in this development, all in earth tones with red tiled roofs. The streets were spotless, the yards small and landscaped, a pretty place if one was into cookie-cutter living.

I parked in front of number 10 and headed up its short walk. At a movement in my vision's periphery, I turned to see someone staring out the front window of the house next door.

I'd recalled what Fran Korwald and Jon Arlen had told

me about their friend Marie. This gated community was governed by a homeowners' association, and one member was giving Marie grief about the number of boxers she owned.

When I rang the doorbell, I was bombarded by barks from inside. Though the noise was muted by the house's walls, the sound still carried. If I lived next door and was a dog-hater, I might complain, too. Then again, I couldn't imagine myself ever despising dogs.

The woman who answered held one dog's collar and did a dance to keep the others behind the open portal. "Come in, Kendra," she said in a long-suffering tone that suggested this display of canine chaos was not uncommon.

I squeezed in and closed the door behind me, only then letting myself be rushed by a crush of tan and brindle boxer bodies. Fortunately, they all seemed friendly, wanting to sniff and lick me rather than nip off a limb or two.

"Let's go in here," Marie said. She was a slight woman, perhaps too small to be keeping these moderate-sized dogs. Her yellow shirt was man-tailored and tucked into brown slacks. She waved me into what looked like a living room, with a sofa, chairs, and a coffee table, surrounded by a variety of fluffy corduroy pillows that must have been doggy beds. The aroma suggested that accidents sometimes occurred and were cleaned up with citrus-smelling stuff.

I sat on an upholstered chair, only to have a boxer leap onto my lap. I was used to that with Lexie, but Cavaliers generally weigh less than twenty pounds. Boxers are a lot bigger—sixty pounds at least, I figured.

"Down, Manny," Marie commanded. "I like to name them after California beach communities," she said to me.

"Manny as in Manhattan Beach?" I asked.

"That's right." She leaned back on the sofa, waited until three blunt-muzzled boxers draped themselves over her, then sighed. She was blunt-muzzled, too, with jowls that sagged not unlike her dogs'. "I'm not sure what Fran told you, but in any event it's gotten worse. There's going to be a homeowners' association meeting in a few weeks, and I'll to be told either to get rid of my babies or to move. I can't afford to move. So . . ." Tears erupted from her eyes. "But how can I get rid of my dogs? They're my family."

"Is there a rule against having pets in the covenants, conditions, and restrictions recorded against the property in this community?" I asked gently.

"No, but there's a limit on the number of dogs in any one house," she replied.

"How many?"

"Two."

Seven surrounded us in this room. "Is this all of them?" I asked.

"No." She sighed again. "Vennie had a litter of five puppies a few weeks ago. They're all in the kitchen."

"Vennie for Venice?" I asked, as if that was relevant to the issue.

"Ventura."

"And are you going to place the puppies in other homes?"

"Most, but I wanted to keep one."

"I see." My turn for a sigh. "Marie, did Fran tell you that, though I'm a lawyer, I can't give legal advice right now?"

"Sure." As with Jon Arlen, she admitted that Fran had told her about my problems. She'd also read some about them in the news. "You were cleared of doing anything wrong, right?"

"Right." As I'd done often lately, I explained I still needed a passing score on the ethics exam I'd taken two days before. "It'll be weeks before I hear if I'll be reinstated. And you probably don't have weeks."

"No," she said sadly, sniffling. The sound must have galvanized her boxers to action, since those surrounding her stirred, and the brindle one on her lap stretched up enough to lick her cheek. "Thank you, Seal," she said.

Seal Beach, I ticked off in my mind.

"Fran also told me that you helped her in a way that didn't require a law license. You came up with a brilliant scheme that helped her outwit that awful ex of hers."

"I don't know how brilliant it was," I murmured modestly, "but it did the trick."

"I'll say. And now I need something like that to get my miserable next-door neighbor off my case. She's stirring up the entire association. She's made it clear she wants to be elected president next year, so she needs an issue to get attention. I'm just unlucky enough to be it."

"What does she complain about?" I asked. Barking, I figured. The yard looked clean, at least from the front, so I didn't bet on doggie piles as being the subject of her protests.

"Well, they are a little noisy sometimes when they're in the yard, being watchdogs. But that's true of all dogs. Best I can tell, she just is a stickler for following all rules exactly, even if there's no harm done by violating them."

"Does she have any pets?"

"She had a cat, but it was old and passed away a few months ago. Of course she blames that on me, too—like my dogs barked it to death." Marie looked at me hopefully. "Do you think you can help me, Kendra?"

"No guarantees, but I'll see what I can come up with. Meantime, do you have a copy of the CC&Rs and association rules that I can borrow? If I find legal arguments for you in them, you'll have to hire someone else to assert them on your behalf, but I'll be glad to explain them to whomever you choose."

"Okay. I'll pay you in any case."

"No, thanks. It'd be too close to accepting payment for the unauthorized practice of law."

"But—"

"I'll be in touch." I gently urged Manny to move off my lap and onto the floor.

"Would you like to see Vennie and her babies?" Marie asked as I rose.

"I'd love to."

After extracting herself from her dog sandwich, she showed me to the kitchen. On the floor, behind a metal fence, a pretty brindle boxer lay to one side. Around and over her, a pack of exuberant puppies engaged in mock enmity, growling and gnawing on one another. They were small, short-coated, and altogether adorable. "How cute!" I exclaimed.

"Aren't they?" Marie beamed as brightly as if the babies were hers. Which they were, in a manner of speaking. She opened a back door and let a bunch of dogs into the backyard. Then she handed me the paperwork I'd pressed her for and led me into the entry again. "I'll be eager to hear from you," she said.

"I'll see what I come up with, but you can't count on me solving this," I told her seriously. "Just in case, you might start seeing what good homes you could find for most of your dogs and pups."

"I know," she said weepily. "But surely I can keep more than two."

"We'll see," I said.

As she closed the door behind me, I darted a glance next door. The same nosy neighbor, probably Marie's adversary, was gardening in her front yard. Or perhaps she was simply spying. She was younger than Marie, maybe mid-thirties, and she wore tight jeans and an even tighter frown. "Hi," I called, then approached her. "I'm Kendra Ballantyne, a pet-sitter." I pulled out one of my cards and placed it in her unresponsive palm. At least her fingers folded over it.

"Are you going to be watching Marie's dogs?" she demanded in a tone that suggested it would be the straw that broke the homeowners' association's back.

"Not yet," I said. "But she told me you recently lost your cat. I just wanted to express my condolences."

Her eyes misted up. Maybe she wasn't a friendly neighbor, but the woman was human after all. "Thanks," she whispered. Then, more strongly, she said, "Do you know, that woman never said a word. I blame her dogs for shortening Sagebrush's life."

Ah-hah. As Marie suggested, an excuse for her antipathy. But could I do anything to dissipate it?

"How?" I asked.

"They chased the poor old thing every time he got into Marie's yard."

"I see. And was he an invited guest?"

"He was a cat," she snapped, as if that explained everything.

"And they're just dogs," I countered quietly, hoping she would be as understanding as she expected of me.

Of course she wasn't. "Yes, at least nine of them," she barked. "And our CC&Rs only allow two. If I were the president of the association, I'd have enforced the rules long ago."

"And you're interested in becoming president now?"

"What business is it of yours?" she demanded.

"None," I said, placing my palms up placatingly.

Obviously, this conversation was only making her crankier, but at least I now had some knowledge about her take on the situation. "See you next time," I said cheerfully, then turned and headed for my Beamer.

ONE MORE QUICK stop before evening rounds: Avvie Milton's. Though she wasn't leaving town for another couple of days, I'd promised to drop by to meet Pansy, her potbellied pig, and learn the routine for tending her.

Avvie lived on the city side of Coldwater Canyon, a little farther than I generally liked to go for pet-sitting, since it meant more time on the road between stops. But this was Avvie. Our friendship had frayed after all the twists and turns it had taken. Even so, we'd been close before and I still liked the intelligent young associate—despite her lack of common sense for staying involved with Bill Sergement.

Her place was small and set into a hillside. I had to make sure the Beamer's parking brake was well set before I ventured out and up to the pale blue home's front door. I rang the bell. No dogs barked. But when Avvie opened the door, a little black-and-white Lexie-sized creature bounded toward me. It had tiny cloven feet and a long snout, and its fur was wiry.

"I never really thought of a pig as having hair," I told Avvie immediately. "Guess I always pictured the pink-skinned Porky cartoon character."

"Most people do, I think," Avvie said. "Isn't she cute? Pansy, meet Kendra." The little creature looked up, as if she understood. "She's very intelligent," Avvie told me. I believed it.

Avvie showed me around her house, which I hadn't visited in years. She'd apparently developed an affinity for antiques. Most of her stuff, though well maintained, looked old—lots of carved wood and cherry-colored velvet.

Pansy's special sleeping place was in the corner of the living room. A futon had been fixed up for her with pillows and blankets on top. A person could have crashed there comfortably.

I learned from Avvie that potbellied pigs lack the gland that tells them when their tummies are full.

"Like a lot of people," I observed. "Me among them, sometimes."

She laughed. "Anyway, I'll write down exactly what to feed Pansy and when—pig food, plus salad. She also gets yard time for exercise."

"Should I walk her?"

"Interesting idea. I've never tried it . . . I'd say no, not this time. You have to watch to make sure she's not attacked by any dogs, since she has no way to fight back."

I got Avvie's house key and a list of instructions. "Make sure you give her lots of attention," Avvie said. "She'll need mental stimulation. She's used to being alone during the day when I'm at the office, but then she wants me to sit with her and hold a conversation. You'll see."

"I won't be able to spend long periods with her," I cautioned Avvie. "Not with all the other pets I have to see to."

"I'll only be gone four days this time," Avvie said. "This will be an experiment to see how it goes. If it doesn't work out, then I'll have to find someone to sleep here when I'm gone. Unless you think you'd be able to . . . ?"

"It'll depend," I hedged. Before, if I needed to stay overnight at another pet-sitting client's, I'd simply done so. But now, I might feel inclined to do it less, if I became Jeff 's and Odin's permanent in-home pet-sitter.

I'd need to make that decision sometime within the next few hours. Wouldn't I?

Well, not necessarily. I could ask for more time, and Jeff would simply have to accept that. If he didn't, that would supply me with my answer.

Right now, I was inclining toward the affirmative. If I inclined any further, I might fall right into it.

I said goodbye to Avvie, then headed off hurriedly to handle my evening visits.

It was nearly seven thirty when I finally finished and headed for Jeff 's. On the way, I picked up some of our favorite Thai takeout—a celebratory dinner? I wasn't sure, but I grabbed a bottle of champagne, just in case.

I was eager to see Jeff, to talk logistics and longevity and lots of other stuff I'd want to know before giving him my answer. Even if I was all but certain what it would be.

Yes! shouted my libido. After visiting Avvie, my mind had returned to those days when I'd had Bill Sergement as a lover, and had been positive afterward about my own really poor judgment when it came to men.

But Jeff was different. He was independent, and prized

my independence, too. Our careers were complementary but we weren't competitive about them. He'd helped me when I needed it, butted out when I needed that, and gave me lots of good loving—which I was discovering I always needed.

I trusted the guy and cared for him, a lot. It was too soon to know if I loved him, but . . . That could be coming, too.

So, I eagerly parked the Beamer under the light in his driveway beside his Escalade, grabbed the handles of the plastic bag filled with Thai food, and hurried up the front walk. I used my own front door key, the one I had for when Jeff was out of town.

And stopped when I heard voices. One was female.

No time to go back out and ring the bell. The dogs had discovered my presence and, barking, barreled through the house toward me. As they leapt on me eagerly in greeting, I stooped long enough to pet them. When I looked up, Jeff was entering the entry from the steps down to his sunken living room. "Kendra, hi," he said in a tone I didn't recognize. And I didn't hear the warmth and welcome I'd expected that evening.

Behind him was a woman, who was tall and slender with the features of a fashion model—all cheekbones and eyes and a mouth so pouty it fairly pouffed. But her perfection was marred by redness around those eyes and a sag to her slim shoulders.

Who was she?

"Hello," I said when Jeff didn't jump to introduce us. "I'm Kendra Ballantyne." Shifting the handles of the plastic bag I held, I approached her with my hand held out, dodging when Jeff seemed eager to obstruct my approach.

"Hi," she said in a soft, perfect voice, her expression unwelcoming and wry. "I'm Amanda Hubbard. Jeff's wife."

Chapter Twenty

"Ex!" EXCLAIMED JEFF before I asked any questions.

As if I could anyway. Even as a litigator, confronted with confounding witness revelations, I'd never felt so tongue-tied.

I'd been pet-sitting for Jeff for months, and sleeping with him for a substantial part of that time.

He'd never even hinted that he was married.

I supposed that *was* was the operative word, if his blurted-out syllable was intended to divulge that they were divorced.

"That's right," Amanda agreed, as if she saw what I was thinking flash in neon on my face. "We were divorced a year ago." Her head bent as if she remained in pain, causing her long golden waves to frame her pretty face even further. My hair had once been an attractive artificial color like that.

They'd divorced only a year ago? Then had Jeff bounced into bed with me on a slightly delayed rebound?

I noticed my knees were quaking, but damned if I was going to beg to sit down, especially here, where we all remained crowded in the entry. Instead, I knelt to hug Lexie, who sat before me and stared up, head cocked in concern. Even she seemed to see what I was thinking.

I wished I were among the many mind readers around here, for my brain had become blank.

My pup's kindness was quickly distracted by the aroma of food in the bag I'd rested on the floor, so I rose again before she could reach in and help herself.

"I see," I finally said inanely to the two humans. "Well, I think Lexie and I will be going now. Hope you brought your appetites." I held out the bag to Jeff.

"No." He inserted himself between the exit and me without accepting what I proffered. "Amanda's here because she's in trouble." Speaking of trouble, I saw something that reeked of uneasiness slide along Jeff's brow. Embarrassment? Irritation that his deep, dark secret was now outed for all to know?

"That's right," Amanda said as if following a cue. Her reddened gray eyes grew even wider, and they filled with tears. "It's a stalker. A man I used to date—after Jeff and I split, of course—has been calling me at home and at work. Showing up at my house, and even tailing me in my car." She sighed unevenly. "The authorities haven't been much help, and I've been so scared . . . I thought Jeff might be able to do something. He's in the security business, after all."

"Of course," I acknowledged. "He's quite good at it, I understand." She'd know that, but once I began babbling, I couldn't quite stop. "There are lots of legal possibilities. I'm sure Jeff'll help you find the right one and get your problem straightened out." While I remained twisted inside as if he'd tied my arteries and veins in knots around my most vital organs.

He'd been married. He'd never bothered to tell me that minor piece of background information.

Well, so what? I hadn't told him, either, about my damned dalliance with Drill Sergeant when I'd started working at the Marden firm—though he'd uncovered it while conducting the investigation he'd helped me with before. Nor had I told him of other, briefer affairs I'd engaged in occasionally post-Sergement—all of which had convinced me even more completely about my lack of intelligence when it came to mixing with men. Or about other things from my past that I'd considered irrelevant.

So why was I surprised that I'd flubbed it yet again?

It wasn't as if I'd asked Jeff to detail his past liaisons, either. Still, an ex-wife was a bigger secret than a little indiscretion here and there.

It's probably all in the past, I reminded myself. That's usually what an ex implied.

But if so, what's she really doing here? my inner gremlin gibed.

And did I really want to know?

"Tell you what," I said. "I don't want to intrude while the two of you discuss security. I'll take one of the entrées, and you can share the rest—the champagne, too. Jeff, call me next time you're heading out of town and need me to keep an eye on Odin." I knelt once more and gave that adorable Akita a hug, all the while maneuvering to keep the food away from both canines.

"You don't need to leave. Really." That was Amanda exhorting me.

"That's right," Jeff agreed. "At least join us for dinner."

And then head home after hearing them rehash old times together?

Since they were divorced, maybe those old times were the worst, but even so, it would hardly help my digestion.

"Thanks anyway," I said. I dug into the bag and extracted a small box without checking its contents. Then, grabbing Lexie's leash from the floor, I feinted left, then darted around Jeff to the right and headed out the front door.

I SWORE CEASELESSLY at the droves of other drivers who dared to weave into my path as I hurried the Beamer home. At least I forbore from hurtling hand signals at them, which in L.A. could only get one into hot water—or possibly an early grave.

Poor Lexie assumed I was angry with her, for she sat cowering on the passenger's seat, her long black ears bent back on her head.

"It's not you, pup," I reassured her when we stopped for a light. I petted her comfortingly, but she didn't seem convinced. Maybe that was because I spat out a stream of invectives when someone dared to make a left turn in front of me when the light finally turned green.

"I can't complain too much about the timing," I confided in Lexie. "I mean, I just might have told the slimy, secretive bastard tonight that I was considering moving in with him. Before I even knew that he'd already been there, done that, and walked away—from a wife, yet."

Of course I didn't know the circumstances. She could have walked away from him.

Did it matter?

Could I be overreacting?

So what if I was?

We finally reached our street. Fortunately, I slowed by habit when faced with the hills and turns. Otherwise, I might have slammed right into Lyle Urquard, who was barreling down as if he'd lost his bicycle brakes. As it was, he slid to a stop, but at least this time neither he nor his bike toppled over. I waved and kept going.

I didn't need to use the electronic control when I reached our gate. It was already ajar. *Damn it all, Charlotte and Yul,* I yelled inside my skull. *Isn't it about time you start paying attention to the terms of the lease?* I wasn't sure I could stomach more parties and ferrets and open entries just now, even for the lucrative rent I received.

At least I had the presence of mind to wait before confronting them. Maybe I'd cool down first.

I slid the Beamer through the open gate and into its reserved spot beside our garage apartment.

When we got out, I realized why the gate wasn't closed.

Charlotte and Yul were at the front door to my big, adored, rented-out abode.

With them was Charlotte's lawyer and mine, Esther Ickes.

And accompanying them all was the unwelcome un–peace officer, Detective Ned Noralles.

NORALLES HAD BEEN leaving alone, which was a good thing.

Since I didn't want to be alone just then, I sat with my tenants and attorney in the kitchen of my leased-out home for nearly an hour longer while they continued recapping the awful interrogation I had missed.

"How that terrible detective could imagine I could hurt anyone, let alone kill them by knocking them in the head, then slicing them open . . ." Charlotte still wailed as we all leaned on the large wooden table at the end of the room, sipping strawberry margaritas that Yul had made.

The man had some use after all.

"Not just anyone," Esther reminded her. "Chad Chatsworth, the man who, by merely showing up on your doorstep one time too many, could have forced you to give up all your winnings. That could drive nearly anyone to take a stab at getting rid of the interloper."

The sweet little old lady who was also my lawyer looked up at me, obviously pleased with her awful pun. I smiled back. Or tried to. Like Charlotte, I wasn't exactly in a humorous mood.

"And I certainly wouldn't then cover him with food to make it look as if the ferrets killed him," Charlotte went on as if Esther hadn't interrupted.

I gathered from all this that Chad's official autopsy report was finally released to Noralles. Not that it was a huge surprise, after Noralles's prior conversation with the coroner and the revelation about a knife. The report confirmed that Chad hadn't died from ferret chews, but from a single slender knife slice to the carotid that caused the awful blood I'd seen all over, especially near his neck. First, though, he'd been knocked unconscious by a blow to the back of his head. A board from the wall of the den, knocked loose by the Hummer, had been the weapon. But he'd bled to death. No knife was found. The ferret frenzy was after the fact, though the body had been covered with food to encourage the little mammals to act. They were still mini-felons, as pets kept in California. Maybe even conspirators or abettors, obstructors of justice or the like. But they definitely hadn't murdered Chad Chatsworth.

Maybe they'd be allowed to live, though eventually shipped to another state. Since I was a pet person, that should have made me feel good. But at that moment, I felt too bad to anticipate feeling better.

Damn Jeff Hubbard anyway. And Chad Chatsworth for getting himself murdered in my house. And myself, for not avoiding all this awful chaos. And Ike Janus, since, despite his promise, there was still all that Hummer damage to deal with—probably after a huge confrontation with the insurance vultures. And—

"Kendra, dear, are you all right?" Esther bent over the table and touched my arm.

Hard to believe that such a dear little old lady, a grandmotherly type who fussed over friends and clients alike, was such a go-for-the-jugular lawyer. But I thanked my lucky stars that she was.

"I'm fine," I lied with a feigned laugh. "Though bloody murders tend to botch up my psyche a bit."

"Couldn't have happened to a nicer guy," muttered Yul. "But too bad it had to happen here." He was obviously emotional to string two near-sentences together.

"Did Detective Noralles suggest you might have had something to do with it?" I asked.

"Yeah," Yul said, swigging from his own stemmed glass.

"H-he said it was either one or both of us together," Charlotte stuttered indignantly. "I can't believe it, but he's made it clear he has nearly enough evidence to arrest us. Especially after the papers mailed in that damned envelope. That was why he suggested that I have my attorney here when he came to see me tonight."

"I'll probably have to find someone else to represent Yul," Esther said to me, shaking her gray-haired head. "Their interests are diverging."

"I'll say," Charlotte snorted. "Noralles suggested that Yul rat on me to keep his own butt out of prison." She lifted her head enough that her long black braid slid down her T-shirted back, and stared at Yul with huge blue eyes. "But of course he wouldn't do it."

But for a moment I saw something speculative in Yul's dark stare. Was he considering turning against his meal ticket?

"Of course," he said after a pause that was a bit too long. "We're sticking together."

But his attitude left me wondering. And the way Esther's concerned gaze met mine, I felt certain she was wondering, too.

Chapter Twenty-one

I'D PEEKED INTO the container of Thai food before heading down to conclave with Charlotte, Esther, and Yul. Good thing it had only held rice. Though I'd stuck it on my kitchen table, Lexie had helped herself. Not a single grain remained, and even the box, on the floor beside the garbage container, had been chewed.

"Bad girl," I scolded, but my heart wasn't in it. How could it be, when it had been so wrongly wounded earlier that evening?

I forced myself to eat wheat toast with a slab of sliced cheese, though my stomach somersaulted with each bite. And then I took Lexie out for her last walk of the evening.

Later, my phone rang as I stepped from the shower. I considered ignoring it, since I had a pretty good idea who it was, but I didn't want him to imagine I was moping over him. "Hello?" I answered, projecting perkiness into my tone.

My assumptions hit the bull's-eye as Jeff began, "Kendra, we need to talk."

"Oh, have you heard from a client who needs you to zip

out of town? I figured you'd hang around to help Amanda sort out her stalker problem."

"No, I'm not leaving town—not tonight. And yes, I'll be helping Amanda. But you and I need to talk. About us."

"We were, I thought. I'm Odin's pet-sitter, remember?"

"Kendra . . ." His voice grew into his sexiest growl, which made me regret everything even more.

"Next time you're planning a trip, be sure to call me," I chirped. "Enjoy what's left of your evening, Jeff. Of course, I'm sure you will." I hung up. He might be planning a passionate interlude with Amanda or not. I didn't care.

Or so I told myself as I lay sleepless and solo in my bed—except for the warm, snoring Lexie—till way late into the night.

DAYS PASSED. I'D like to say they sailed by gracefully while I had a great time with my pet-sitting, and nothing else on my mind. Not Jeff Hubbard and his poor, persecuted ex-wife whom he was trying to help—the one who'd slipped his mind during the multiple months of our acquaintance.

Nor the fact that I still had more than three weeks to wait before receiving the results of my ethics exam.

Nor even my concerns over Charlotte, who was certain she'd be arrested any moment by the diligent Detective Noralles. Her fears could have been well founded. The media thought so, for once again Chad Chatsworth's murder topped the front page and news at eleven. And six, seven, ten . . . in fact, all day long.

The coroner's report was the reason for the resumed frenzy. People found it fascinating that the ferrets were now proven not to be the real culprits in this killing. An assailant of the human kind had smashed and slashed Chad first, then tried to frame the ferrets.

Could it have been Charlotte? Sure, but I didn't think so. Yul was a better bet as far as I was concerned.

And I *was* concerned, now that I'd become fond of my overly huggy tenant. Plus, there was my personal bias against people who framed others for their misdeeds.

So, I went into high gear trying to help Charlotte. If my actions cleared Yul, too, fine with me. I'd nothing against him. I simply didn't like the strong, silent, and seemingly unintelligent type.

Of course, the type I did like hadn't proven to be very wise, either . . .

A fact I couldn't forget. Not with all the calls from Jeff I ducked. By Wednesday morning, he'd given up.

Which only made me feel worse.

Around ten A.M. on Wednesday, I stopped my Beamer in front of Avvie's for the last time before her return and prepared to play with Pansy. Despite Lexie's inherent friendliness, the little pig had seemed uncomfortable with her around, so I'd parked my displeased pup at home for the day. I hadn't left food on the table or anywhere else she could easily get it—unless she figured out how to open the refrigerator or pantry door.

I'd never before imagined that pigs had personality. Pansy did. She cavorted around Avvie's as energetically as if she were a puppy craving exercise. "Want to play ball?" I asked. I swear she understood and nodded her piggy noggin. I rolled a ball and she chased it, nosing it with her long, porcine snout. "Roll it here," I encouraged, and she did, chasing it as it came toward me.

Cute little creature, I thought. No wonder pigs had become part of L.A.'s pet culture. And now I could say with a straight face that I knew the way to care for them—sans porkery or sty.

When I finally forced myself to leave, I sat outside in the Beamer and followed up on some calls I'd made on Monday and Tuesday that had never been returned.

The first was to Philipe Pellera. When I'd seen Philipe sneaking out the morning after one of Charlotte's parties, I hadn't gotten the singing and gyrating hip-grinder to divulge the security problems for which he'd hired Jeff. He'd acknowledged, though, knowing Chad Chatsworth. Had even admitted to having been fired by Chad from reality shows not yet in production. A motive for murder? Getting Philipe to talk intrigued me. Better yet, maybe he'd sing out what he knew, confession or not—complete with sexy dancing. Now that would be an interview worth waiting for.

But he still wasn't answering his phone. I left another message without holding out much hope that he'd respond.

I'd counted on getting two for the price of one call when I phoned Dave Driscoll, but neither he nor Trudi Norman had answered, either. Even so, I called again.

A click. A female voice. A response! "Hello," the woman said, sounding as if she was eager to hear from me.

"Hi, Trudi?"

"Yes?" She sounded more tentative now. Whoever she'd been expecting, I didn't sound like him. I guessed it was a him—most likely Dave.

"This is Kendra Ballantyne. We met at Charlotte La-Verne's party."

She was probably deciding whether to be polite and say goodbye, or just hang up, so I thought fast.

"I'm going to be honest with you, okay?" I lied. "First, tell me if Dave is there."

She hesitated, which worked well, too.

"Okay, you don't have to say. But I know you've been seeing each other since Chad's death." I didn't mention spying on them in Palms. Instead, I continued, "I saw you leave Charlotte's together. The thing is, I know just what Charlotte is going through. Have you seen it on the news? The poor thing is getting desperate. I don't think she killed Chad, but I don't think Dave did either, do you? Anyway, to save herself, Charlotte is pointing fingers at a lot of people Chad knew, maybe to confuse the cops, or maybe because she has genuine knowledge. I met Dave. I doubt he did it, but the cops seem to be zeroing in on him as another viable suspect."

"Oh, no!" Trudi wailed. "He's not here, Kendra. What can I do?"

"Meet with me," I said. "I can be at Dave's in half an hour. We'll talk, and then we'll see. Okay?"

"Let's meet somewhere else," she said without asking how I knew where Dave's place was. She suggested a location.

I didn't give her time to change her mind. "See you soon."

I hung up. And then I aimed the Beamer toward Palms.

WE MET AT a diner on Santa Monica Boulevard. It had been carved out of the bottom of a decrepit older building, and managed to resemble a quaint, fifties-type establishment notwithstanding its modern prices.

Of course I'd have to pay. I'd done the inviting, after all.

No matter what she'd been conniving with Chad, Trudi had struck me as being a wholesome-looking escapee from middle America. Except that now, Hollywood had apparently gotten hold of her. No longer was she makeup-free save for lipstick. Her freckles were hidden under a layer of base and a swath of artificial blush. Her pale brown eyes didn't disappear into her head, for they were enhanced by a load of liner and eyelashes mounded with mascara.

She hadn't, however, done anything to the mousiness of her brown hair. Maybe that was because she could wash all the rest off easily enough when she headed home to her dad's nursery.

I commenced our caucus with a little tap dance. "I hope you won't go scare Dave about this," I told her, "since I think Charlotte's strategy is to bring in as many possible suspects as she can in the interest of confounding the cops. Dave was Chad's roommate, so he's an obvious choice to drag into the confusion." *You, too, as the girl Chad left not far behind,* I thought but kept it to myself. "The thing is"—here I really winged it, basing my prattle on what Charlotte and Philipe suggested—"she seems to think that Chad was consulting with Dave on some reality show ideas of his own. Dave was delighted to be included, but when Chad made his move to force Charlotte to lose everything, he also knew Charlotte's name might make his show actually work. She wouldn't talk to him, of course, but her friend Yul told her Chad offered her a more-than-half interest in anything they earned, just to grab her attention. If so, that could have made Dave mad."

"Well, sure he was mad," Trudi said ingenuously, sipping her strawberry shake. "Who wouldn't be? I mean, I loved Chad, but I saw him for what he was—a user. I'd have accepted him that way, warts and all. Taken him back even after Charlotte dumped him right in front of a TV audience of millions."

But had *she* let him go in the first place, given their reputed conspiracy? And had she offed him when he still went after Charlotte, then sicced the ferrets on him?

"He'd only been Dave's roommate for about eight months. I've gotten to know Dave a little since coming here to find out what really happened to Chad"—so that was her articulated rationale—"and I can tell he believed everything Chad told him, poor guy." She lifted her hands, and I noticed her nails now were polished bright red. "Not that I think Dave was angry enough to kill Chad, you understand. But he was finally beginning to see Chad for what he was."

"A louse?"

She scowled so much that she suddenly looked older and evil, despite how I'd previously pegged her as the wholesome sort. "No. Not Chad. He was just . . . Well . . ." She waved her hands again, this time helplessly. "He was just Chad."

And now, thanks to being Chad, he was just dead. But I still didn't know for sure who'd made him that way. Though I now had no compunction about keeping both Dave and Trudi way up near the top of my suspect list.

BUT WHAT WAS I going to do with that little list? I decided to keep it to myself, even when Charlotte came speeding out of the house as I parked the Beamer in its spot.

Her braid was bushy, her blue eyes red and round, and I anticipated she was about to impart some terrible news.

In a way, it was. "I'm having a party tonight, Kendra." Her voice was shrill and a bit belligerent, as if she expected me to argue.

"Any occasion?" I managed mildly. I'd wondered a lot whether Chad Chatsworth's last stand at one of Charlotte's last parties was the reason for his demise. I suspected somehow that it was, whether for the obvious or a more subtle reason. Otherwise, why die here?

"Just because I can." Her eyes slunk into narrow lines that dared me to say she couldn't. "I'm still here and free and alive, even if that damned Chad can't say the same thing and I'm going to wind up being blamed for it one way or another."

"What do you mean?" I asked. "Have you heard something?"

"It's what I haven't heard," she moaned. "That detective is up to something, but he hasn't come with a warrant for my arrest. Yet. So, I figured I'd take advantage of borrowed time."

Okay, maybe I shouldn't ask. I wasn't her lawyer, and what she told me would hold no attorney-client privilege. But since I'd been doing some checking on her behalf, I really needed to know. And so, I asked for the umpteenth time, "Did you kill him, Charlotte?"

Her glare could have fended off a fire-breathing dragon

as she applied the same old answer. "Of course not. I might have been mad as hell at him for trying to spoil everything, but forget what I said before. I really had the hots for the guy. And even if I couldn't listen to him directly, from what I gathered he was trying his hardest to come up with a reality show idea to make us both gobs of money so I could have both him and riches, too. He even claimed he'd dump the old girlfriend once and for all. In a way, it was kind of sweet."

I remembered the row in my den the night of the party Chad crashed. Charlotte hadn't acted in the least like she thought him sweet then. But hey, what did I know? Everyone acted differently on their attraction to people of the opposite sex.

"I believe you," I said. "I've been looking into—" Not a good time to go there, not without info that could hand her some hope of staying out of jail free. "Into how to take care of a potbellied pig. They're really cute. I had no idea, but—"

"Then I'll see you tonight, Kendra?" This woman didn't even like Lexie. I had no idea how attached she was to the ferrets, but they seemed to have been Yul's. Obviously, she had no interest whatsoever in hearing about petite and playful porkers.

Which was fine with me, as it ended this conversation.

"Of course," I said.

DID I ACCEPT her invitation and go? Yes. Did I have fun? No. Did I at least achieve my purpose of pushing for answers from the usual suspects—er, guests—about Chad's murder? Yes to the pushy part, but no to getting any answers.

Oh, yeah, one good thing came of being present at the party: a chance to talk to Ike Janus about his insurance people. Once again, he promised to do some pushing of his own. And I believed it, like I believed someone would saunter over to me and confess to killing Chad.

Eventually, exhausted, I crossed the yard and mounted the steps to my apartment. Apparently Lexie was dog-tired, too, since she barely padded over to greet me before following me back to the bedroom and crashing on the bed while I undressed to shower.

The phone rang. I considered letting it roll over to the machine, since it was so late.

Was it Jeff? I didn't want to talk to him. On the other hand, I liked the idea of letting him know I'd just come in after one heck of a fun party, all wined up and mellow and getting along fine without him.

And so I picked up the receiver and said very sweetly, "Hello."

"Keep your nose out of the Chad Chatsworth matter, if you know what's good for you," said a voice I didn't recognize—probably because it sounded hollow and electronically enhanced.

Trying to keep my voice steady, I countered, "Who is this?"

The only answer was a loud thump as my caller hung up.

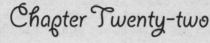

Chapter Twenty-two

THE DAMN VOICE definitely spooked me, but it didn't render me stupid. I immediately dialed *69.

Apparently the caller wasn't stupid, either, since caller ID was blocked.

I stood there for a good minute staring at the receiver. No, it was a not-so-good minute, since my thoughts swirled indecisively.

Should I take the warning seriously and leave Charlotte to save herself from a murder prosecution?

She wasn't exactly on her own. Yul was on her side. But the strong and silent Yul could actually be the killer, which would keep him from saving his sugar mommy's behind in favor of protecting his own.

Charlotte had Esther Ickes as her lawyer. That, at least was a good thing. But was it enough to save Charlotte?

Could I save her? I would never know, if I did as I'd been told and butted out.

Okay, then. I might be standing here quivering in my Reeboks, but I wasn't easily intimidated. Especially not when I thought I could help an almost-friend in imminent peril of being framed for something I didn't think she'd done. Fine. That decision was easy.

Next . . . should I notify the cops about the call?

What, and have Noralles tell me that, no matter what kind of creep the person who threatened me was, he—or she—had sent a sensible message? He, too, would rather my relatively well-shaped and definitely functional nose not be smack-dab in the middle of the Chad Chatsworth matter.

Speaking of noses, I was jolted out of my indecision by a cold, wet one applied to the hand free of the phone, which I'd let fall to my side. "I'm okay, Lexie," I told my pup, who regarded me with as much concern in the cock of her head and anxious glimmer in her deep brown eyes as if she'd understood the ugly call. Maybe she couldn't speak English, but she definitely comprehended all a dog could.

I pulled on jeans and a T-shirt, and carried my cell phone and my sharpest kitchen knife—which was still damnably dull—as Lexie and I engaged in our last actions of the night. I ensured that the outer gate was engaged be-hind us and triple-checked all the locks in my apartment. I wondered whether there was such a thing as an A–number one security system, complete with 24/7 monitoring, that could be counted on—assuming I could afford it someday.

To make sure I'd get at least a little sleep, I left my phone off the hook in the living room, so I wouldn't hear buzzing in the bedroom reminding me to hang it up.

I HAD A new potential client to call on the next morning—a guy referred to me by Darryl. Harold Reddingam, a con-struction company executive, lived in a home in North Hollywood with a couple of cats. November was edging toward December, so I didn't have a lot of sun to worry about as I left Lexie in the Beamer.

"My buddies don't need a lot of attention," Harold told

me after asking me in. He was tall and chunky enough to appear as if he belonged in construction, though he didn't look like a Harold or a man fond of felines.

Good thing for me he was, though, since he was heading out of town tomorrow for a week for an industry conference, and was willing to pay a premium to have me visit three times a day.

"Though you might not see them when you come," he told me, "they'll know you're here. That's what I care about—letting them feel like I haven't abandoned them."

They'd been invisible when Harold first invited me in. But once he'd called them as if they were pooches, they'd appeared in his den from different parts of the house. One, Abra, was a sleek, beautiful Siamese; the other, Cadabra, a fluffy tabby. Both arched their backs in similar ecstasy as Harold stroked them, and regarded me with twin expressions of disdain when I attempted the same.

"We'll get along fine," I assured Harold after he led me to the kitchen and showed me kitty food and the litter box.

After that, I leapt into regular rounds, visiting Pansy the pig, followed by some pampered puppies, and ending the morning with a call on Widget for his day's energy-burning gambol.

Finally I had a few minutes. Lexie and I beelined for Doggy Indulgence. I needed to talk to Darryl.

As if waiting for me, he sat alone in his office. I aimed a grateful wave toward Darryl's least likable assistant, Kiki, when she eased Lexie into a group of cavorting charges.

"That's different," I said to Darryl when I pushed my way into his office after the most perfunctory of knocks.

"What?" he asked.

"The color." Taking my usual seat on a chair across from his cluttered desk, I pointed to his skinny chest. He wore his typical Henley-style shirt with the Doggy Indulgence logo over his heart, but instead of green, it was red.

"Just needed a little change around here," he said,

peering at me playfully over his wire-rims. "Shake things up a bit."

"Go wild," I agreed.

"Yeah," he said. And then, "What's wrong?"

"Who said anything was wrong?"

"You're going to tell me, with that extra wrinkle between your eyebrows, that nothing is?"

"What extra wrinkle?" I reached for the offending spot over my nose.

"The one I haven't seen since you were being accused of murdering your pet-sitting clients every couple of weeks."

"You didn't tell me about any wrinkles then."

"You had enough problems. So, are you going to tell me?"

I told him about the threatening call.

"And you've been asking questions about who might have killed Chad Chatsworth?" At my nod, he asked, "And who've you been interrogating, Sherlock?"

"That's *Ms.* Sherlock to you." Since I valued Darryl's point of view, I ticked off on my fingers the various suspects from whom I'd sought information, futilely or not. "What do you think?" I finished.

"I think that, this time, you ought to let Detective Nemesis do his job."

"Noralles?"

"That's the one."

"But he's liable to arrest Charlotte."

"And your point is—?"

"You don't really think she's guilty." I stood and leaned over Darryl's desk.

"Who says?"

I shook my head. "I don't want her to be. She's begun to grow on me."

"I gather she began to grow on Chad Chatsworth, too, in front of millions of viewers—before she dumped him for money."

"I know. But the ferrets weren't hers. They're Yul's."

"They're the ones getting the shaft in this situation. First, accused of murder. Then, maybe they're only accessories, but they've also been seized. Best case, they're still going to be shipped to new homes—out of state."

"I know," I said with a sigh. "I've intended to visit them, too. Want to come?"

"Absolutely," Darryl declared.

THE EAST VALLEY Animal Center, part of the City of L.A.'s Department of Animal Services, crouched in a gaudy commercial area of mom-and-pop businesses and chain discount stores along Sherman Way in North Hollywood. Its reception building, squat and as aqua as the bottom of a swimming pool, lurked off the street, behind a parking lot and a line of palm trees and flag poles.

I'd never been there before. And I wanted never to go there again—after I'd exited the front building and followed, beside Darryl, the path of painted paws along the driveway toward the long metal warehouse containing the dog kennels. As members of the public wanting access to a building behind the main shelter, we had to walk the woeful gauntlet of captive canines. Some seemed blasé behind their chain-link barriers, lying on the concrete floor with hardly a roll of their sleepy eyes as we passed. Others sat at attention, wagging and woofing as if begging, "You'd love me if you got to know me. Get me out of here!"

There were even a couple of litters of little puppies. The impound forms fastened to the fronts of their enclosure stated they were unweaned, and their mothers, incarcerated along with them, were noted as lactating.

"They're so cute," I whispered to Darryl.

I noticed that my skinny, soft-hearted buddy was striding with his eyes full front, as if he wore a set of blinders. "Yeah," he said, his voice as sorrowful as I felt.

Not that I had any sense of mistreatment here. Each enclosure even had an opening to its own area outdoors. But all those poor, lonely pups, praying for a good home . . .

Think of Lexie, I reminded myself. _And the size of our apartment. And—_

Somehow Darryl and I made it to the end and through the doors, into a smaller area with desks and stacked cages on the concrete floor, and a few rooms opening out of it. One was the cat corral, in which kitties of all persuasions were layered in crates laid side by side and piled several high. It smelled riper than the doggy haven, but that could be because the room was smaller and didn't have the access—and commensurate ventilation—to the outside world that the canine area did.

"Can I help you?" asked a pleasant-faced man wearing one of the charcoal-and-blue-striped shirts of the shelter's staff.

We'd already checked in at the front area to explain our errand, and the attendant we'd spoken with had phoned someone back here. "We're here to see the ferrets," I told him.

"Oh, yes. Come this way." He led us out the back door and up some stairs into the next building.

What I saw surprised me—and that was even before I found the ferrets.

"Yul!" I exclaimed to the hulking hunk who stood at one side of the room, gazing into one of the stacked cages.

He turned to look at me. "Hi, Kendra," he said.

He wasn't alone. As we approached, I noticed the animal control officer who stood by his side—golden-skinned, Polynesian-featured, a badge on his khaki shirt. His name tag read KAALANA. The guy who'd walked us over here said something to him, then left. Our custody was now Kaalana's charge.

I introduced Darryl to Yul, then asked, "What are you doing here?"

"Visiting," he said in his basic brief-speeched style.

"He's here nearly every day at this time," Officer Kaalana confirmed. "And your reason for being here?"

"Visiting, too," I said. I didn't want to explain that I was Yul's landlady, which might imply, by my presence and interest, that I'd bought into his keeping illegal pets. "I was worried about the ferrets. Being by themselves, I mean. Whether they were lonesome." And how they were being treated, though I didn't say that. "I didn't realize Yul came to see them, too."

I faced their cage. Cages, actually. They were housed in two matching crates with solid plastic sides and metal grate fronts. The long, furry ferrets seemed to have adequate room, though they didn't look as comfortable as they had at home.

Two of those impound forms I'd seen on the dog enclosures were on the fronts of each double-occupancy cage. They had ID numbers, the kind of creatures they were—ferrets—and even their names, probably supplied to the shelter by Yul: Hamlet. Macbeth. Juliet. Regan. Ophelia.

I had no prior idea that their monikers were Shakespearean. Was Yul fond of the Elizabethan bard? Maybe his sensibilities ran deeper than his appearance suggested.

The kind of impound was noted on each form: OTC. Over the counter? And then there were the stamped signs on each. USE CAUTION. Because these ferrets had tasted human flesh? PERSONAL PROPERTY. They all belonged to Yul.

And most telling of all: EVIDENCE.

Which was better than stamping them as MURDER SUSPECTS.

"It looks as if they're being well treated," I ventured, watching Yul's reaction.

His dark eyes grew even darker. "Yeah. I guess."

"If there's anything you think needs to be done differently, feel free to tell the staff," Officer Kaalana said smoothly. "They're not too used to taking care of ferrets.

When we get custody of any, we usually call a ferret rescue organization immediately, but this situation is different. They're evidence."

"How long can you keep them here like this?" Darryl asked. He stood close to one of the cages, and the two occupants had their long little snouts pushed up to the bars as if they recognized an animal lover when they saw one.

"Till we're told otherwise by the court," the officer said.

"But the coroner's report said the crime they're accused of was committed by a human," I blurted. "Aren't they ready to be released yet?"

"Not as far as I'm aware."

"Why not?" Yul interjected. He turned angrily toward the officer, who stared coolly back at him.

"I won't be the one to make the decision," Kaalana said. "Personally, I like the little critters." He gave a wide grin toward the cages, but quickly turned back toward Yul. "But like I've told you before, Mr. Silva, they were impounded at a crime scene. If the court says we have to turn them over for humane euthanizing"—that ridiculously oxymoronic term again—"then that's what we'll do."

"Not if I can help it," stormed Yul.

"Which is why you're always accompanied while you're here." Kaalana turned toward Darryl and me. "The shelter has had people try to steal back their dogs who've been picked up for attacking neighbors. That's not something we're inclined to allow, especially when an animal could be dangerous."

"But they're not." Yul's tone had turned pleading, and he looked at Darryl and me.

This wasn't the time to get into my own investigation into who did what to Chad. All I could say to Yul was, "I agree. And we'll do all we can to clear them, okay?"

"Yeah. Sure." But Yul had turned glum again, and his back was toward us as he bent to talk to his little weasely buds.

Like the dogs we'd passed before, the ferrets seemed to beg for release, for they began issuing shrill little sounds, though less frantic than I'd heard in my home after the Hummer hit.

I wished I could help them. I wished I could help the slumping Yul.

Officer Kaalana walked Darryl and me to the door of the building. "I feel for the guy," he told us. "The ferrets, too." He shrugged his khaki-clad shoulders. "But what can you do?"

His question was rhetorical, so I didn't respond. "Thanks," I told him as we left, though I wasn't sure what I was thanking him for.

This time, I took Darryl's hand as we strode through the dog-filled shelter, needing his moral support.

"That was rough," he growled after we'd both climbed into his van.

"Tell me about it," I agreed. "And now I'm even more confused."

"Why?" he asked, his brown eyes especially somber behind his wire-rims.

"I'd hoped to clear Charlotte by finding out who really did kill Chad. I'd nearly talked myself out of suspecting Yul, but half hoped I'd learn something here to prove he did it after all. I'd already doubted he'd try to frame the ferrets except as a last resort. And now that I know he cares about them enough to visit them in their incarceration every day, I'm positive he'd do nothing to point the police toward them."

"So?" Darryl said.

"So now I'm totally convinced it wasn't Yul, and I sure don't think it was Charlotte. Who the hell killed Chad?"

Chapter Twenty-three

I DIDN'T SAY much to Darryl on the ride back to his place. Didn't have to. Driving his large Doggy Indulgence van with one hand on the wheel and gesturing with the other, he talked enough for both of us. That signified that my good friend Darryl had inverted into a demonstrably good mood.

What I didn't know was why. Not after that enervating visit. I, for one, felt exhausted.

"Have you talked more with Marie Seidforth?" Darryl asked.

Marie . . . ? Oh, the boxer lady boxed in by her community association's rules. "No," I said guiltily. "But I will. Her question's essentially a legal one. If I had my license back—"

"You helped Fran Korwald with an issue that could have been decided in the courts instead," Darryl reminded me unnecessarily.

"Right," I agreed. "And I'll try to help Marie, too."

"And Jon Arlen? Have you fixed his treasure hunt problem?"

"No, though I'm really intrigued and have been doing research whenever I can." I understood why the guy didn't want his snotty neighbor to benefit from his finding the cache of antique Spanish booty—even though it was on her property. The easy answer was to go all Solomon and split the baby, but Jon had indicated that he doubted the bitch next door would bite at that solution. She'd want it all.

So did he.

Something—or someone—had to change. And then there were all the extra complications that could occur . . .

"I'm hoping he can hold out till I get my license back," I said. "Assuming that's only another three weeks away."

"It will be. Meantime, anything you can do to help him?"

"I'm working on it." I'd even made one of my inevitable lists, throwing in research ideas relating to everything from real property issues to old Spanish land grants and off-shore salvages of treasure troves from sunken ships. So far I'd done more listing than researching, but I now had extra time in the evenings to dive into it, at least when I wasn't stepping over to Charlotte's for her latest soiree.

I wasn't, after all, keeping company with Jeff Formerly-Married-and-Murky-About-It Hubbard.

I glanced around to see if I recognized any nearby vehicles, as Darryl nosed his van into the Doggy Indulgence parking lot. The movement threw me off balance, even though I was wearing a seat belt, and my elbow hit the door.

"Ouch!" I cried.

"You okay?" Darryl said as he turned off the engine.

"I will be when the pain stops," I told him through gritted teeth. I looked up from where I'd been ogling my dented funny bone . . . in time to see a white car that had looked as if it was ready to follow the van into the lot speed up and hurtle down Ventura Boulevard.

"Hmmm," I grumbled.

" 'Hmmm' what?" responded Darryl.

"Did you see that car?"

"What car?"

"Obviously not. Then you don't know if it was following us as you drove back here?"

"No," Darryl said, "I don't." But he knew better than anyone how my mind maneuvered around matters real or imagined. "Look, Kendra, you're justifiably nervous after that phone call. Not to mention that you ignored it and went to the animal shelter to see Yul and his ferrets."

"Just the ferrets," I reminded Darryl. "I didn't expect Yul to be there."

"The point is, after being warned not to nose further into the Chatsworth murder, you still went somewhere related to it and dug in." He turned to me. "Whether we were followed or not, maybe you'd better butt out this time, Kendra, and let the police handle it. You're not even really involved now, like you were when you were a murder suspect."

"I know." I sighed as I unfastened my seat belt. "But I hate to think of anyone else going through what I did."

"Yeah, but this time you could be putting yourself in danger."

"I don't know for sure if we were followed," I allowed as I opened the van door, then turned back to Darryl. He unhitched his seat belt. "It could have been my imagination. But just because I may be paranoid—"

"Doesn't mean someone isn't out to get you," he finished with a smile that wasn't at all humorous, then shoved open his van door.

DESPITE LEXIE'S BEING in the midst of a great game of doggy tag, she seemed glad to see me. Even so, I decided to let her stay there and play while I headed to Borden Yurick's new digs to knock around with his computer and indulge in legal research on Jon Arden's behalf. And while I was at it, I'd look into community association law for Marie Seidforth.

"Hi, Kendra," said a voice from the doorway of the

empty office I'd usurped. I'd been at it for over an hour, and my eyes were crossing from lack of a break, so I was happy for the interruption.

It was Borden. "How's the legal business?" I asked.

"Growing," he growled. And a growl from the generally good-natured Borden was as surprising as a smile on a hungry grizzly.

"That's good, isn't it?" I asked. I'd swiveled in my desk chair—rather, *his* desk chair—to watch his slight frame, again clad in a Hawaiian shirt and light pants, slide inside the cubicle and lean against the desk.

"But I left that miserable Marden place so I could have fun practicing law. Taking my clients with me was only fair, but I didn't think I'd have to work so hard keeping them happy." He ran a hand through his unkempt silvery hair as if the answer to his problems could be swept through his fingers. His bifocaled gaze alighted on me. "When do you get your law license back?"

Unease skulked through me. I liked Borden. A lot. But if he was about to offer me a job, I was about to refuse it. Whatever would come next in my life, I didn't want to segue straight into a law practice like my prior job.

"It's still weeks away," I said in a voice that emphasized my actual regret about that fact.

"Well, we can talk later," he said.

"Right. Well, for now, I have to run. I have dogs waiting for walks and dinners."

"Of course. How enjoyable that sounds, Kendra." He sighed. "Take me with you."

Startled, I met his wizened gaze, only to see him wink. I grinned. "Tell you what. I'll convey your regards to my charges—before I clean up their normal little surprises of the day. Most are housebroken, but then there are those delightful few . . ."

"Have fun, my friend." He hastily left the cubicle I'd commandeered with a little wave.

I didn't stay much longer, though I spent a few minutes jawing on gossip with Borden's gregarious receptionist, Mignon.

I'd found some interesting stuff online, mostly relating to property ownership and such, to add to what I'd already learned on Jon Arlen's behalf. Some intersected with material I had researched for Marie Seidforth, who owned her home in the association-encumbered development.

Too bad I could offer neither legal advice.

Yet.

I finished my rounds as efficiently as I could, including a stop at my new client Harold Reddingam's house, where I got only the barest glimpse of his supposedly sociable cats.

I'd headed for Darryl's, picked up a worn-out Lexie, and aimed the Beamer for home when my cell phone rang. I glanced at the caller ID and almost swerved. Jeff Hubbard's number shone up at me. I considered letting the call roll into voice mail.

Better yet, let him roll into a nice, big vat of—

Now, now, I admonished myself. I was bigger than that. As graciously as if I'd felt gifted by his call, I popped open my phone and said, "Well, hello, Jeff."

"I need you, Kendra," he said. "Fast. Please, can you come over to my place now."

MY PRURIENT FANTASIES fled as soon as I got to Jeff's.

Fortunately, his dear Amanda was absent.

Unfortunately, what he needed me for was to watch Odin for the next week while he skipped town on an emergency assignment.

"I'd have called someone else if I knew anyone who could do as good a job as you," he said with a placating grin as I watched him pack. We were in his bedroom, and he wore a tight black T-shirt and jeans. Both of those particulars, under other circumstances, would have resurrected my most libidinous ideas, especially the way the snug stuff hugged him in the right spots as he moved. "When I get back, we'll spend some time together. Talk over this situation. I want you to understand exactly what's up between Amanda and me."

"Then there's still something between you?" I asked sweetly, seething inside. "Something *up*?" As if it was any of my concern. I stood at the window with arms folded, trying to look cool as I peered into the backyard and watched our canines cavort.

"No!" he exclaimed. "Not like that, but . . . Like I said, she needs me. She's being stalked."

"What's she doing while you're out of town on this rush assignment?"

"She's with her parents for now. They live way out near Bakersfield."

So why couldn't she have done that before to get out of her stalker's line of sight, instead of burdening her ex-husband?

"Since her stalker is one of her ex-boyfriends," he continued, "I referred her to a lawyer I know who can get a temporary restraining order fast, then follow it up by an injunction against the guy contacting her."

"Is the lawyer anyone *I* know?" Why was I feeling extra irritation over the fact he hadn't even phoned me for a referral? I knew lots of good lawyers who could handle that kind of case, even though I myself couldn't for at least the next three weeks and one day . . .

"You might know him." But the lawyer's name wasn't familiar. Not that it really mattered.

"You know, of course, that someone set on stalking is likely to ignore both a TRO and an injunction."

"Of course. But if so, I can get the cops' attention to pick the guy up for ignoring them."

He didn't say *she*—Amanda—could get the cops' attention, but *he* could. Damn.

But what difference did it make? We weren't in a committed relationship, let alone a cohabiting one. And the fact he'd been married in the past? What did it actually matter?

I only knew it did.

"Great idea," I responded as perkily as a skillful salesperson intent on impressing a recalcitrant customer. "And what if I told you I'd received a threatening phone call?"

Where had that come from? I hadn't intended to reveal it to Jeff at all, let alone now when he couldn't do a thing about it.

It wasn't as if I, like his ex-wife, really wanted his expert opinion. Was it?

In seconds, he stood in front of me. His hands gripped my shoulders. His blue eyes turned into squinting pools of pugnacious male power as he demanded, "Did you?"

"Did I what?" I asked innocently.

He wasn't buying it. "Come off it, Kendra. Did someone threaten you or not?"

"Well, kinda." I was much too aware of the clasp of his fingers on my upper arm. Their grip was causing a chain reaction inside my body that suggested that we hadn't had sex for several days, so how about now . . . No way! "Yes," I finished, pulling forcefully away. "I was told to stay out of the Chad Chatsworth investigation, but that only made me want even more to figure out what happened. Maybe when you get back, I'll take my dog-sitting services out in trade."

I stopped for a second as I saw his expression segue into the lust I'd felt a short while before.

"My expert pet-sitting for your expert investigation services," I clarified.

"Right," he said. "Assuming you're alive when I get back. Kendra, didn't you learn your lesson before?"

"Sure did," I said. "Danger's a good aphrodisiac." Oops. Judging by his even hotter gaze, I was really playing with fire. "What I mean is that a little danger went a long way.

When I was the one being framed, I even caught the perpe-trator and cleared myself. And now, I'm just trying to help Charlotte."

"We'll talk way before I get back," Jeff said. "I'll call you while I'm gone."

But just then, he only had time to pat Odin and Lexie goodbye and head for the airport.

Except that he took just enough time out to grab me into those strong P.I. arms of his and give me a kiss I wouldn't forget while he was gone.

I wondered whether he'd said his farewells to his ex-wife the same way.

Chapter Twenty-four

TIME TRAVELED ON. So did I, in the Beamer. Right now, I'd aimed it toward Forest Lawn Cemetery in Glendale. No Lexie with me at the moment. I didn't think dogs were encouraged to attend the memorial park. Besides, she would probably get bored.

It was Sunday. Several days had passed while Jeff was away, and Lexie, Odin, and I had enjoyed relatively uneventful housemate status. I'd received no more nasty phone calls, no sense of some white car dogging the Beamer's tail. I didn't even do much digging into Chad Chatsworth's demise.

Not that my mind stayed away from that particular mess. If Charlotte didn't do it, and neither did Yul, then who? Certainly not those Shakespearean ferrets.

I'd pondered that question a lot as I drove between pet places all weekend. My next opportunity to test my suppositions and suspicions would occur in approximately half an hour.

At Chad's local memorial service.

Trudi Norman, the girl he'd schemed with and who'd followed him here—now nearest to the top of my suspect list—had planned this little commemoration of Chad's life, or so Charlotte had told me when she'd informed me of the upcoming event. Then, Trudi was to accompany his body home, where it would be interred.

I recalled that she'd once worked for her father in his nursery business in Nebraska. So had Chad. Would he therefore be planted by . . . ? No, I decided not to go there.

Instead, I turned onto Barham Boulevard, and soon began the curving descent toward Forest Lawn Drive. The Beamer's windshield wipers, on full throttle, barely kept up with the downpour. Water ran in rapids down the sides of the street. L.A. didn't do well in the drainage department. Despite the fact there was a rainy season every year—some rainier than others—apparently the Department of Public Works hadn't figured out how to design a sewer system to keep up with the typical annual flow.

At the bottom of the hill I made a right turn and kept going. Till I hit the traffic jam. It appeared that all of L.A. had decided to come this way today. Because of Chad? Couldn't be.

Only I had to eat those words when I finally got to pull into the Forest Lawn entry. Somberly dressed attendants under black umbrellas halted all cars. The young man who spoke with me nodded knowingly as I rolled down the window and let the rain in. "Are you here for Mr. Chatsworth's memorial, ma'am?"

Ma'am? I'd dressed in black for the occasion, but I didn't look that old. Did I?

No use telling the polished and professional funeral person that his polite greeting had insulted me. "Yes," I replied brusquely.

He pointed up the hill—behind a long line of other vehicles. "The Wee Kirk o' the Heather Church. You may park along the street."

"Thanks."

The wee kirk actually looked like an old-fashioned

small-town church, with beige stone walls, a steeply sloped slate roof, and a bell tower in front. Lots of people lined up on the walkway, umbrellas open, as they waited to get in. I joined them, recognizing quite a few beneath the mobile canopies—everyone from my neighbors to attendees of Charlotte's parties.

I finally reached the door, closed my umbrella, and slipped inside. The place was quite pretty, with wooden beams connecting the vaulted ceilings, and lights dangling from rafters and glowing in sconces along the walls. Behind the altar at the far end of the church there was a lovely stained-glass window.

Not a bad spot to commune with one's Higher Power while celebrating the life of a guy who'd gone calling on his first. Assuming one could find one's way through the onlookers.

Caught in the stream of people, I felt myself being swept toward the front—not a good place to be if I wanted to watch the mourners and scan for two-faces and crocodile tears. I sidestepped into the closest of the polished wooden pews and looked around.

Spotting someone I thought might be handy to sit with, I braved the wave of people and slipped a few rows back, trying not to dampen any seats with my dripping umbrella.

"Hello, Detective Noralles," I said. "I'd always heard it was a good idea for the authorities to be present at a crime victim's funeral, since the guilty party often attends, too."

"You heard right, Ms. Ballantyne." His smile was wry, and then his gaze started sweeping again over the people pouring in.

"Call me Kendra. After all we've been through together, I'd say we know each other well enough to be on a first-name basis."

He didn't miss a beat or stop his scrutiny. "Right. You can call me 'Detective.'"

I couldn't help it. I laughed. Not the most polite thing to

do at a memorial. I put a lid on myself fast. "Okay, Detective Ned. I've got a question for you."

His lack of response didn't deter me.

"I've heard that Trudi Norman will be taking Chad's body home for burial. Is it wise to let her out of your jurisdiction? I mean, I have to assume she's on your suspect list."

"Not that it's your concern, Kendra, but we know where she's going. And that she'll be back."

"Really?" That surprised me. "Why?"

"Because she's inherited Chad's interest in his reality TV show development ideas."

I wasn't astounded by the concept, but I'd have been flabbergasted if Noralles had been that forthcoming. The voice that spilled the info didn't belong to the detective. It was Tilla Thomason's, and the shrill tone shot the same kind of pain through my head that I get from taking a drink of something too cold.

The detective turned to see who'd spoken. His brown eyes looked as chilly as that same kind of uncomfortable drink. "And you are—?" he said to Tilla.

She introduced herself and her husband, Hal, behind her. "I recognize you," she finished. "You weren't the police officer who interviewed us, but I know you're looking into what happened to poor Chad. Right on our street. Terrible."

Noralles swiveled toward me and asked, "The Thomasons are your neighbors?"

I nodded. My back was to them, and I rolled my eyes, signifying I'd disown them if I could.

"Where did you get your information, Ms. Thomason?" Noralles asked.

"Oh, it's what everyone's saying," she said.

Before he could ask who "everyone" was, Tilla pushed closer to me as she moved down the pew to admit a few more of our neighbors. Just in time, for the organ music that had been playing a quiet dirge suddenly perked up into something louder to capture the congregants' attention. A minister stepped up to the microphone on the altar. Asian in appearance, he looked about the age Chad had been— late twenties—and he was nearly as good-looking as the guys who came to Charlotte's parties.

I wondered idly if he was an actor playing the role of a man of the kirk. He introduced himself as Reverend Lee.

The good thing was, he spoke of Chad as if he really had known the guy. Maybe he had, for he said he usually officiated at services at a church in Palms, the area where Chad had lived.

His part in the service was short. After describing what an extraordinary young man Chad had been, how he'd been cut down in the prime of his life and would never realize all his far-reaching goals, the reverend ceded his place on the pulpit to Trudi Norman. She wore a short black dress with long sleeves. Tearfully, she related how honored she'd been to grow up with Chad, how much she'd loved him and wanted to marry him, but had known he had to follow his dreams, and so she had followed *him*. And now she would take him home . . . and return to achieve all those dreams in Chad's name.

Apparently Tilla's sources hadn't been whistling "Hooray for Hollywood."

After finishing her tribute, Trudi headed back to her seat between Dave Driscoll and Philipe Pellera. I'd assumed her chief comforter would be Dave, but it was Philipe who stood, handed her a handkerchief, and hugged her before she sat down.

A few other friends rose and delivered sad eulogies. Then Charlotte stood alone before everyone. She'd donned a charcoal pantsuit, conservative for her. The bow at the bottom of her long braid was as black as her hair.

The crowd had been exquisitely polite, even before. Now, there wasn't an iota of noise—except for the drumming of the rain hitting the roof and driving sideways at the windows.

"I'm so sorry," was what she started with, and I could have shaken her. It sounded not only like an apology, but an admission as well.

But then she continued by talking about how she wished she hadn't been put into such a crazy situation by fate and the producers of *Turn Up the Heat*. She'd actually loved Chad, she said, and would have adored seeing whether their fledgling relationship could develop into one with a future. But in the pseudo-reality of the reality show craze, she'd had to make a decision, and it had forced her to turn her back on Chad.

"Which I wouldn't have done, except for certain extenuating circumstances." She stared icily at Trudi before returning to her tribute. "Even so, I felt sorry I had to hurt Chad on national TV, despite how he'd hurt me. I wished him well, and hoped he felt the same about me. If only things could have been different . . . but now I have to live with the *reality* of what happened"—she stressed the "R" word—"without Chad."

She choked on a sob at that emotional ending, and then sat back down beside Yul. I wondered how he felt after hearing Charlotte say, in front of this throng, how much she'd cared for Chad. On the other hand, he'd been the winner of her affections after she won the money, so he'd been the true last man standing, even before Chad could no longer stand at all.

I glanced at my dear friend, the detective. Did he buy Charlotte's accolade? It had sounded pretty self-serving, even to me. Still, I thought it was true.

I couldn't tell what my pew mate thought, though. His expression stayed stoically somber.

At the end, Reverend Lee took over again, saying a short prayer for Chad's soul and wishing him, and everyone here, peace. He then invited the entire assemblage to another Forest Lawn structure for a snack.

I remained with Noralles while the others filed out. Was

he studying their faces, too, to see if anyone looked too self-satisfied to be ignored? Of course, it wasn't that easy. Trudi shuffled down the aisle while hanging on to Dave. If she'd worn any of her newly discovered makeup, it had all been washed away by the rain or her tears. Her pallor was more pronounced as it contrasted with her freckles, but her small chin was raised as if to confirm her courage.

Dave looked pasty, eyes huge and wet behind his wire-rims. He clasped Trudi's hands as if holding her grief at bay. They passed without looking at who still occupied the pews.

Soon Charlotte filed out beside Yul. She still looked sad. Yul didn't. He didn't look pleased, either, but I kind of wished he'd appeared a little more grief-stricken so Noralles would knock him off his suspect list, too.

There weren't many people left in the kirk when Noralles started to exit, followed by me. And the Thomasons. Only then did I notice Lyle Urquard, Phil Ashler, and even Ike Janus. My neighbors had joined the mourners. Because the guy had died on our street? Because they were all celebrity stalkers? I didn't ask.

I saw at the reception that the next-to-the-last guy to get canned by Charlotte, Sven Broman, had come. Of course, the singer with the oh-so-Latin hips, Philipe Pellera, was there, too. I also recognized one of Chad's former neighbors, Helene. No baby with her, though.

Then there was Detective Wherlon, one of Noralles's cronies whom I'd met when he helped try to pin some murders on me. Noralles and he stood in a corner surveying the crowd.

I took a different corner and did the same. As I watched, I saw Trudi and Dave glued to each other as well-wishers offered condolences to her.

Charlotte and Yul hung out by the bar, also hanging on to each other as they seemed to be politely shunned by most mourners. A few, though, mostly neighbors like Tilla, Hal, and Lyle, appeared to offer support.

For a rueful moment, I regretted not having someone there to help me through this sorrowful situation. Not that I'd known Chad well enough to grieve deeply, but even so, watching to see if anyone gave him- or herself away as a murderer was fraught with tense emotions. And memories, as I recalled only too well being in a similar position to my tenants—suspected by all, no matter how much people pretended to believe my story.

Impulsively, impelled by being alone, I stepped from the crowd toward the rest room corridor. I withdrew my cell phone from my purse and pushed in an often-used number.

Jeff 's.

I felt as deflated as a beach ball gone holey as I got his voice mail. Since I'd called his cell, I knew he'd notice he'd missed a call, so the message I left was perky, about how well Odin was doing with him gone.

It implied I was doing great, too.

Wasn't I?

Of course. And next time I heard from him, I'd tell him all about this memorial, and who my main suspects were now. I figured I could do as good a job with my investigations as he did with his.

Of course, I hadn't figured on the next occurrences in this odd and lethal loop of events.

Chapter Twenty-five

FIRST ODDITY: PHILIPE Pellera walked me to my car.

Me, and not Trudi, despite how he had comforted her at the memorial. Which made me supremely suspicious.

Though I had no problem spying on those who'd shown up for the memorial service, I didn't want to intrude by pouncing on anyone and picking his brain right there. As a result, I hadn't planned on speaking to Philipe, who still hadn't returned my calls. Apparently he had no problem speaking with me now.

"Hello, Kendra." His Spanish-accented voice was soft as he joined me in line with the crowd filing out. "You have called me, but I am so seldom at home."

"You could give me your cell phone number," I said, softening my presumptuousness with a smile.

"Ah, but then there would be no mystery between us. You could reach me anywhere." His closest hip did one of its legendary thrusts sideways, toward me, though more subdued than in his music videos. Still, it touched me, reminding me of the *anywheres* I could reach Philipe, given his cooperation.

Yeah, and he'd be one of my better selections, if I

signed him on in the lover department. Right up there with Bill Sergement and, now, Jeff Hubbard.

At least with him, I'd be the envy of thousands of screaming female fans. Exactly what I needed.

No, what I really needed was for Philipe Pellera to stop obfuscating what info he could send my way, and answer a few questions.

We were out of the reception hall now and in the overcast air of the small parking lot. Though the precipitation had tapered off, both air and ground were damp. People meandered by, talking softly, sending curious—and from the women, envious—glances our way.

Charlotte exited in an assemblage of our neighbors, pale, strained, and for one who craved reality show fanfare, displeased to be the focus of media attention. A consortium of reporters awaited the mourners' exit from the post-memorial reception. They flashed cameras in Charlotte's face, shouting questions she bravely ignored while staring straight ahead. Lyle Urquard steadied her on one side, and Ike Janus the other. Yul remained in the rear of the procession, also snubbing the newshounds.

I watched this performance for a minute, then turned my attention back to Philipe. How could I extract the info I wanted from him? I had a sneaky hunch that simply asking about his relationship with Chad Chatsworth, and whether he had motive, means, and opportunity to murder him and frame the ferrets and a few humans, wouldn't yield an up-front answer. Not from this tall, dark, and flirtatious hunk who obscured all he didn't want found out behind his bumps and grinds.

I decided to be as devious as I assumed he was.

"It's about the reality show you were working on with Chad before he fired you," I said, taking a large leap of faith. But heck, all these people who were friends with Charlotte and Yul seemed to have reality TV, if nothing else, in common.

"You, too?" he barked, glaring down at me, his dark eyes gone vicious. Like probably ninety-nine percent of the women he came in contact with, I hadn't paid much attention to his face as I'd studied him. Of course, I'd noticed those bedroom eyes before, as they fit quite appropriately with his sexy, suggestive moves. But I'd not really noticed how the shadow of his blue-black beard emphasized the hollows in his cheeks, or how his white teeth looked long and feral. Of course, I might not have noticed the latter even now if it hadn't been for his gargoyle-like grimace.

"Me, too, what?" I asked calmly, keeping my uneasiness covert under his glare.

"Did you also receive an early payment for your part in the show? Chad did not tell me that was in his plans."

I had no idea what he was talking about, but he'd obviously had a beef with the man we'd just memorialized so affectionately. I only had to understand why. What payment? What show? The one Trudi Norman had apparently conspired in and consequently inherited? How could I ask without giving my obliviousness away?

"No!" I exclaimed. "Do you mean some people got paid early?" I merely reflected back what he'd said, but it maddened him all the more.

"You did not know? What did he promise you? How were you to help Chatsworth pitch his best show idea with enough zing to entice Charlotte into working with him?"

We'd stopped in the parking lot beside a car befitting a megastar like Philipe: a Mercedes convertible that conceivably cost as much as my mega-mortgaged home. A bright yellow one, to attract the attention of music fans and traffic cops alike. My Beamer was one car away, and the car in between was backing out.

Philipe stared down at me, not moving or speaking but obviously awaiting my answer. Okay, what could I say? How could a suspended lawyer turned pet-sitter pitch a reality show?

Of course, Philipe didn't necessarily know my background. But since I'd gossiped at Charlotte's parties about him, I couldn't be certain he hadn't engaged in some of the same about other guests.

"I expect to have my law license restored in about two weeks," I finally told him. "I've been called a shark and a lot worse in the courtroom, so I believe Chad actually wanted me for my bite."

I grinned, revealing teeth that had been the stuff of expert orthodontia when I was a kid here in L.A. That was before my parents had split with so much force that my dad had ricocheted to Chicago with a new family, and my mother bounced to D.C., happily unmarried and practicing law for the U.S. government.

And why had my mind taken off on such an incongruous tangent? Because in some inexplicable way, this irritable, intense music star reminded me of my hotel mogul brother, Sean. Not that Sean, who now lived in Dallas, tossed his hips around like Philipe. But somehow I spotted, behind those piercing, prying eyes, an anomalous vulnerability, as if the adulation of fans wasn't enough without feeling himself successful.

That only came for Sean with the addition of a new hotel to his collection each year. And for Philipe? Perhaps it was the addition of yet another area of show biz in which he gained recognition. Not just singing and gyrating and starring in music videos. Maybe the guy also wanted to be revered for making mucho money in reality shows, too.

"Really?" he asked me now. "You were to be Chad's lawyer? I had thought, since you were in the news for finding the person who made you look like a killer, that Chad would use your fame. Or maybe he'd want you to help choose candidates to be on his show. You would help screen them for who would not get along together. Maybe even do things that were not totally legal. That would make such interesting television."

Wow! What was this reality show that Chad had invested so much of his life into—the best of his ideas that had in some manner probably led to his death?

And so much for Philipe not knowing much about my briefly sordid background.

"Why did you ask about my involvement if you knew the truth?" I told Philipe, adding extra width to my grin.

"Then it is true? You are well known for solving murders, and you know people."

There was something more to all this, something Philipe had yet to share with me.

"What's really going on?" I asked.

"It was these people at the service in there." He leaned toward me as if trying to make sure whoever "these people" were, they couldn't hear. Which was unlikely anyway, since the parking lot had all but emptied as we stood there speaking.

"Which people?" I prompted.

"Charlotte," he confided softly. "And Yul, because he backs her in all she says. Hypocrites. They wanted to have nothing to do with Chad's new production, but now that Trudi and Dave have hired me, for the money that I am worth, they are angry."

"Then you're one of the people who got paid early?" I was getting so confused that I wished Chad was around to question. But then, if Chad had been around to talk to, I wouldn't have been having this weird conversation.

"Well, of course." He smiled. "The show is now sweet Trudi's, and she wisely wants to keep me involved, even after Chad once tried to fire me. You see?"

Not really, though I attempted to sort it out. I wasn't sure where the funds originated, but Trudi, who'd inherited the show, would be willing to spend the money up front to make sure it was a success.

Might she have killed Chad to take over total control of his most promising idea—and to keep Philipe involved?

Might Philipe have killed him, perhaps conspiring with Trudi, so he could stay with the project and get paid up front? They'd seemed pretty tight inside the kirk.

It appeared that my answers were hurtling me to a whole heap of more unanswerable questions. But I had lots of new material to stick on my suspect lists. When that list got long enough, I'd notate it for Noralles.

Then that single-minded detective wouldn't be able to ignore that there were a lot more suspects in Chad Chatsworth's murder than Charlotte, Yul, and five little ferrets.

"What exactly was this wonderful idea Chad had for a reality show, Philipe?" I suddenly blurted, knowing that I was giving away that I had not been part of Chad's plan. "His best one. The one that you're all working on now?"

"He didn't tell you? Well, I will hint without giving it away. But imagine people who are famous, or who have been made famous by circumstance whether they wanted it or not, brought together to compete in a game in which winner takes all." He grinned at me, then slid into his car and started the engine, not looking at me again.

I stood there and stared as he pulled away. I still didn't know what Chad's surefire super idea, culled from his list of possibilities, had been.

But I did know one thing: Philipe Pellera, still involved and paid in advance, might have gained a lot more from not having Chad around.

Did that mean he'd murdered Chad for it?

THE NEXT ODDITY? Well, I was pondering my conversation with Philipe as I drove from the cemetery and headed toward the Valley. I went through Burbank, since it was on the way and I needed a caffeine fix. I aimed for a Starbucks in the Empire Center.

I slowed as I saw a familiar car parked along the side of Victory Boulevard. A sports model, on the expensive side, though not as snazzy as Philipe's. The one usually parked underneath me as I slept over the garage.

Yul's.

We weren't far from Forest Lawn, so it was no huge surprise to see him. Since I'd talked neither to Charlotte nor Yul after the memorial service, though, this seemed an opportune time to compare notes. Had they seen anything — or anyone—there that stirred their suspicions in Chad's murder? Of course we could chat later, but our suppositions would be fresher now.

I pulled past him and braked the Beamer, aiming it into the nearest parking space. I headed back along the partially dry sidewalk toward Yul.

And saw that he was alone in his car. No Charlotte? I'd figured she'd need Yul's emotional support after such a sad experience at the memorial. Besides, how was she getting home?

Well, that I could learn later. Right now, I had something else on my mind. I walked slowly in the shadows, near the storefront, as I watched Yul.

No longer clad in coat and tie, he talked animatedly on his cell phone. Not just listening. Not just blurting out a word or two. But actually chattering, or so it seemed. His mouth was moving. The hand not holding the phone was, too. It waved at the end of his long arm along which he'd rolled up the sleeve of his dressy white shirt. His facial expressions also punctuated whatever he prattled about— dirty blond brows alternately arcing and lowering, mouth baring teeth, then frowning.

In other words, Yul looked alive.

Hmmm. I didn't really know him, of course, but I thought I'd had him pegged. Rather, he had Charlotte pegged, as her gorgeous, silent gigolo.

What had gotten him talking?

And if he talked this much while alone, why didn't he when people were around?

Maybe I didn't know him at all.

But I would. I'd figured the none-too-intelligent ferret lover nearly as much of a framee as his lover Charlotte. His apparent change in character didn't mean he wasn't.

Yet not long ago Charlotte had been frightened because Noralles had found some potentially incriminating evidence in an anonymously mailed envelope, including a copy of the note that threatened her reality show reject. It also contained descriptions devised by Charlotte about her own new reality show ideas. Charlotte didn't know how anyone else could have gotten the package's contents.

Yul could have, of course. What if he had been in cahoots with Chad, behind Charlotte's back? What if he had shared his ladylove's latest reality show ideas with the guy she'd rejected—instead of getting that same reject to cough up his ideas for Yul to relay to Charlotte? Chad could have threatened to blackmail him, and—

I laughed a little at myself as I stealthily returned to my car. All this speculation, a shifting of my suspicions back onto Yul, just because this guy I'd concluded was innocent was speaking on a cell phone?

I was probably way off base. And yet, this latest oddity niggled nastily at the most suspicious synapses in my brain.

I'd already planned to spend more time on Borden Yurick's computers doing research. Googling I could do at home. But now, I intended, on the more sophisticated databases, to look up every iota of dope on everyone I thought could have killed Chad, to root out anything unusual in their backgrounds. The cops had probably already undertaken such a search. My turn, now.

And the first person I'd dig into would be Yul.

BUT NOT TODAY. After the memorial, I had to get busy seeing to my many pet charges. Since it was Sunday, I didn't have to worry about Widget. Though romping with the rambunctious terrier wasn't on my agenda, more than half a dozen dogs and cats, including Harold Reddingam's friendly felines Abra and Cadabra, awaited my attention. So did Pansy, the adorable pig, though Avvie would be home later that night. At least Milt Abadim had gotten home, so I no longer had to check on my pal Py the python.

Eventually, I was ready to head home. Or at least my temporary home-away-from-home. The place I'd been invited romantically to move into permanently.

Until I'd learned of Jeff Hubbard's perfidy.

I sighed as I headed the Beamer back through the Valley. Maybe I really had overreacted. Ex meant ex, as far as I knew. And if the experience had been unmemorable, maybe Jeff wouldn't have thought to mention it. Or maybe it had been too horribly memorable for him to talk of.

But either way, why was he helping dear Amanda to deal with her stalker?

Too much cogitation made my mind spin. I'd shelve the subject for now. After all, with Jeff out of town, I didn't have to consider his offer, or him, except to take good care of Odin and his house.

I'd nearly gotten to Jeff's when I recalled I had forgotten some files at home, stuff on my Chad Chatsworth investigation. I could get them tomorrow, but I had a feeling I wouldn't sleep well tonight. Not after my discussion with Philipe, my spying on Yul, my fretting about Jeff, and mostly, my consideration of Chad's memorial, and the many potential murder suspects there. Maybe sifting through notes that so far led nowhere would be soporific enough to let me doze.

Mentally sending a message to Lexie and Odin that I'd be there soon, I had the Beamer bear right, toward the hills.

At my place, I used the electronic eye to open the gate. There was no sign of any other car—neither Charlotte's nor Yul's. Evidently they'd driven separately to Chad's service. Where were they now? Not my business. But at least this day of mourning Chad hadn't been Charlotte's cue to toss another shindig.

I parked in my usual spot beside the garage, then headed for the wooden stairway to my upstairs apartment.

Since I was in a hurry, I started quickly up the stairs. But as I stepped on the third step—or was it the fourth?—my feet slithered out from under me.

I grabbed frantically for the handrail. Got it!

Only as I tautened my hold, the railing was slick and slimy beneath my hand. In no way did my action steady me.

Instead, I tumbled headlong back down the stairs.

Chapter Twenty-six

PITCHING BACKWARD, I shoved out my hands, snatching at whatever, wildly attempting to break my fall.

Except there was nothing to grasp but humid and useless November air.

I smashed hard onto the pavement and felt as if I broke something, all right. Not the fall, but a bone. Or two. In my butt. Maybe my arm.

Pain slammed through me. I may have screamed. I wasn't sure, though I heard something shrill.

I sat there, stunned. Waiting for the agony to ebb enough for me to stand and assess the damage. Only I couldn't stand just then. Nor did the pain abate, not for a long while.

I half lay, half sat, immobile in the shadows of the late fall evening. The light at the top of the stairs came on as dusk grew to dark.

The hardness of the driveway spread unyielding beneath me. No one came to see what was wrong. Charlotte and Yul apparently were absent. Only a minimal number of lights were on in the house, probably those set on a timer to suggest to the stupidest thieves that someone was home. No neighbor was close enough to mark anything amiss over here, except maybe Phil Ashler. But no windows in his house across the street spied directly at my garage, even had he been home staring out.

My teeth started to chatter, though the throbbing mess that was my body began to stop hurting so badly. A sign of shock? I breathed deeply and forced myself to cease shivering.

I glanced around to see if my purse was within reach, considering whether to call 911. What, and let the world know that klutzy Kendra Ballantyne couldn't even climb her own stairs without falling flat on her fanny?

Shame suddenly outshone the pain. Instead, I assessed the damage. My butt ached and would doubtless be bruised, but where I'd landed had been padding, not bone. It would be okay.

And the hand that had hit nearly simultaneously, and the arm to which it was attached? I was a little less sure whether they'd suffered damage. When I tried to bend both, they hurt, but not enough to make me scream.

Still, I remained there for a few moments longer before carefully turning to rise to my hands and knees.

Which was when I realized the driveway was dry beneath me.

It had been raining earlier, when I'd been at Chad's service. The sky had wept in a dreary drizzle later, too. But not for a few hours—I hadn't had to dry doggy paws when I walked my canine clients.

So how, then, had my steps stayed so wet? My hands, too, now, as well as my dressy dark slacks that I hadn't bothered to change all day?

The dampness I felt from fingers to feet was slick, even oily.

Oily?

Carefully, I stood and stumbled toward my stairway. Its wood shone, reflecting the sheen of the dim outside lights. I touched it.

No way had this slippery sliminess fallen from the heavens. No, someone had slathered it onto the steps and handrail, to ensure that anyone climbing up would lose traction and tumble down. Just as I'd done. And who else besides me would be expected to scale this stairway this night? Lexie? Maybe, but the texture of doggie paws would cope with the oil without causing a canine catastrophe.

No, this skullduggery was deliberate and not intended to injure a dog.

It had been planned particularly for me.

"No HOMICIDES HERE tonight, Detective Ned," I said to the most familiar of the cops who'd shown up after my 911 call. "So why are you here?" I sat in the driver's seat of the Beamer, the door open. The first cops to arrive had set up floodlights and had begun to conduct a crime scene investigation.

Did greased wood collect fingerprints?

"I recognized the address." Noralles stared down at me with what looked like sympathy in his dark, usually expressionless eyes. I wondered fleetingly if this African-American flatfoot ever went off duty. Or whether he slept in his inevitable dark suits. He'd probably been wearing the same one earlier, at Chad's service. "And I gathered this could be an attempted homicide." He nodded toward where guys from the L.A.P.D.'s Scientific Investigation Division were taking samples of the slime I'd slid on.

Considering that his supposition was most likely true, I shuddered but tried not to let him see it. "Maybe," I said as carelessly as I could. "Or a nasty practical joke gone bad."

"Any idea who might have done it? And don't tell me it's more ferrets. I might bite, though, if you say it's some former ferret owners."

I shook my head. "Not Charlotte or Yul," I said

vehemently, though more convinced about the former than the latter.

Why had Yul acted so different from his typical taciturn character earlier?

"Maybe, but they still could have set up Mr. Chatsworth and let someone else stop their nosy landlady from solving the murder." He stroked his smooth-shaven chin. "Now if my department made a habit of disposing of meddling citizens, I might be a suspect in that myself." He lifted a dark brow as he smiled speculatively.

I couldn't help it. I laughed.

"Not funny, Kendra," he said, though his voice stayed lighter than the usual grouchy growl. "Even if I didn't like it, I could understand your butting into our investigation of murders when you were a suspect. But right now, you're off my radar and I figure you want to stay that way. You're not a suspect in Chad Chatsworth's murder, but I can't say the same for Ms. LaVerne or Mr. Silva. My investigation indicates your relationship with them is as landlord and tenants, but you're interfering as much as if you were related." He gazed at me quizzically. "You're not, are you?"

"No."

"And you're still not practicing law, so they're not your clients, correct?"

"Correct."

His formerly friendly stare segued into something malevolent. "If you're doing this because you think you're smarter than the L.A.P.D. in general, and me in particular, I'd suggest you concentrate on your pet-sitting, Ms. Ballantyne."

I blinked under Noralles's sudden switch of mood. "All I want is justice, Ned," I said, not liking at all how my statement slipped out as a shaky whisper.

"You'll like it better if you stay alive to see it. Finding out who killed Chad Chatsworth is an official investigation, and we're still gathering evidence. Someone besides me apparently doesn't like your nosing around—someone with an interest in shutting you up." I opened my mouth to offer my opinion, but he waved it shut with his officious hand. "Butt out, Kendra," he finished, "before things really get too slippery for you."

NORALLES HAD MORE to say to me before we parted company.

By then, I'd waited for the SID team to let me climb my stairs again, more carefully this time. They'd gathered what evidence they could, then kindly helped me scatter sand along the wooden stairs from a bag some landscapers had left long ago.

A few neighbors filtered through my open gate. Phil Ashler, for one, hadn't seen anyone do the nasty deed on my property.

Lyle Urquard left his bicycle on the edge of the street to check on me, but he hadn't been around to view who'd committed the vandalism, either. "Was Charlotte here?" he asked anxiously. "She wasn't hurt, was she?" He didn't seem overly concerned about me, but maybe that was because he could see I'd survived.

No sign of the usually nosy Thomasons, but Ike Janus parked his Hummer and checked what was happening, too.

A while later, after gaining access to my apartment, I used some strong household cleaner to take an initial swipe at eliminating the oil, aching with every snail-like motion I made. To my surprise, Noralles hung around and even helped a little.

As I finished all I had intended to do that night, he eyed me up and down. "You don't look so hot, Kendra."

"Thanks. I'd like to say the same, but I can't." I eyed him similarly up and down and waggled my brows à la Groucho. Was I flirting? Heck, I didn't know. Maybe the fall had knocked all common sense out of my noggin. Of course it had been my nether end I'd landed on.

Noralles laughed, then grew sober within the same thirty seconds. "I'll add a patrol along this street tonight."

"No need, unless you think the mad oiler intends to come back. I'm staying at Jeff Hubbard's." As his gaze intensified, I felt my face flush. "He's out of town," I clarified quickly. "Lexie and I are staying with his dog, Odin."

"Well, give me his address and I'll make sure there's an extra patrol there, too. This wasn't a random act of vandalism. Whoever did it knows you. And wherever you go, nasty surprises may follow."

I felt my knees weaken and grabbed on to the partially scrubbed stair rail.

"You need to be checked over," Noralles said. "I'll drop you at the St. Joe's emergency room."

Providence St. Joseph Medical Center in Burbank was the nearest major medical facility. But I no longer had medical insurance. Plus, what ailed me now besides ugly bumps and bruises couldn't be cured by emergency medicine specialists.

"Thanks," I said, "but I'm okay." I watched him watch me while I poured myself into the Beamer. He sat in his unmarked car while I backed out the driveway and used the automatic control to close the gate behind me.

And I repeated to myself as a mantra, "I'm okay," during my whole ride to Jeff's.

LEXIE AND ODIN seemed happy to see me. Or maybe their pleased wriggles and wags in Jeff's kitchen simply signified eager anticipation of dinner and their last walk of the evening. I didn't want to disappoint them but, after feeding them, led them only a short way on their leashes—making sure to stay on the sidewalk beneath the streetlights before turning back. Fortunately, Jeff's residential road was flat and straight. The idea of navigating a curving, climbing street like mine didn't sound inviting to my sore carcass.

And here, I could see anyone approaching for several blocks.

We soon went inside, and I fixed myself a short glass of wine, strictly medicinal. Then I settled down on one of the white sectional sofa pieces atop the bright, Southwestern-style area rug in Jeff's sunken living room. I turned on his wide-screen TV to watch a mindless sitcom to get my mind off my aches.

My cell phone rang, and I looked at its digital display. Avvie Milton's number. The last time I'd visited Pansy, her potbellied pig, had been earlier that evening, but by then it felt like a lifetime ago.

"Hi, Avvie," I said. "Are you home?"

"Yes, and Pansy's great. Thanks so much for taking care of her for me."

"You're welcome." I relaxed a little in relief. The way things had gone that evening, I'd half expected to be scolded for mistreating her pet in some unanticipated way.

"You sound funny. Are you okay?"

I didn't feel at all funny. And though Avvie and I hadn't been in touch much recently, we'd been good friends up until a few months ago.

A little to my surprise, and a lot to my chagrin, I found myself pouring out the night's misadventures to her.

"Oh, Kendra, are you okay? Do you want to come here and spend the night? What are you going to do?" And then, before I could spew out any answers, she said something that clinched my reply to her invitation, even had I been inclined to accept it. "You're not sticking your nose in the investigation of the Chad Chatsworth murder, are you? I mean, Kendra, you nearly got yourself killed the last time you interfered in a murder case, but at least you had a stake in that one."

She'd been bent out of shape then because of some fingers I'd pointed toward her, but at that point I'd been flinging out accusations against everyone to see where they

stuck. But that didn't excuse her interfering with my inter-
ference in this case.

"Thanks for asking," I said coolly and noncommittally.
"I'm glad Pansy enjoyed my pet-sitting. I'll get your keys
back to you soon." After a hurried goodbye, I hung up.

I hadn't much time to simmer over Avvie's intrusion before my cell phone rang again. The caller this time was the
man of this very house, Jeff.

After my last conversation, I had every intention of remaining unruffled and talking only of how much fun
Odin, Lexie, and I were having. Since Jeff and I were
hardly speaking to each other anyway, that shouldn't have
been hard.

Only it proved to be impossible. Jeff's voice sounded
calm and caring. His flight to Phoenix had been fine, and
so far his business meetings about the security system at a
major corporation's headquarters had gone magnificently.

"And Kendra," he added. "I miss you."

That did it. Whether he was a hypocrite or not about his
prior married state, I missed him, too. Damn it. And I
missed being able to share my problems with him.

So, once again, I found myself blurting out all that had
happened.

"Damn it, Kendra, listen to Noralles this time. He—"

That was enough to break the spell his voice had cast
about my poor bruised body. "He has his own agenda,
Jeff," I interjected irritably. "And I'm fine. Maybe even
getting closer to whoever really killed Chad Chatsworth,
and I'm making someone nervous."

"That's the point. Stay out of it. Look, I'll be home in a
couple of days. We can talk about it then, and I'll help
you—"

"Fine, Jeff. Thanks. Odin says good night. Lexie, too."
And then I hung up without saying good night.

I didn't need a macho security guy P.I. telling me how
to run whatever investigation I intended to make.

I didn't want Jeff Hubbard, the secret ex-husband, interfering in my life.

I didn't want . . .

And then I realized what I did want that I could get right here, in Jeff's house, while he was gone. He'd never know about it, so that would make it okay.

Well, ethically it wouldn't, but who would ever know but Odin and Lexie? And they'd never tell.

They did follow me into the guest bedroom, though—the one I'd slept in when I'd first started pet-sitting for Jeff, before I started sleeping *with* him. The one I should have moved into now, but hadn't. The room that doubled as a storeroom for boxes of some of his security company files.

The one that contained a carton labeled PHILIPE PELLERA.

That box was at the bottom of a stack of four. I made certain to put the others in order as I lifted them down, so when I returned them, they'd stay the same way. That job wasn't easy, the way my body ached at every move, but at least with all the walking and lifting I'd done that evening, I was even more sure I hadn't broken any bones in my fall.

To make it easier on myself, I sat on the edge of the bed rather than on the floor after scooting that particular box right beside me. And then I lifted its lid.

Chapter Twenty-seven

THE FIRST FILES on Philipe Pellera were much as I'd anticipated. They mostly contained data about his professional tours to U.S. cities. Jeff had assessed his security, found it slack, and made suggestions that Philipe and his entourage incorporated into their travel plans. They'd insisted that various venues where Philipe performed beef up security, too.

And no wonder. The voluminous files toward the back described a deranged fan who'd obsessively adored Philipe. Sitting on the guest room bed, I foraged through in fascination. Philipe had gotten an injunction to prevent the woman from even attending his concerts, since she always managed to dupe the guards into letting her up on stage with him. She didn't seem inclined to injure him but had attacked nearly every woman in Philipe's backup band and dancers, accusing each of trying to seduce her famous sweetheart.

Someone as obsessed as she was likely to violate any injunction, which she did. Worse, she'd come on stage and nicked a dancer in Philipe's troupe with a knife, eliciting streams of blood and panicking the audience members.

That was two years ago. Criminal charges were filed against the fixated Ms. Eileen Green. Civil, too, though she had countered with a claim of her own: Philipe Pellera had committed malicious carnal mesmerizing of female audience members, which had caused her to act in a totally uncharacteristic manner.

Not a tort I'd ever heard of, but the claim had apparently caused Philipe to drop his civil action, and both parties had settled sort of amicably. A newspaper clipping in the file indicated that Ms. Green had gotten off the criminal charge, too, with just a slap on the wrist of the hand she'd used to wield her knife: probation and community service.

Rehashing what I'd read, I put it all back as I'd found it. Most was public record anyway, so I felt less ethically challenged about snooping in Jeff's files.

Nothing there handed me greater insight on why Philipe might have had it in for Chad Chatsworth. Of course, I already knew Chad had fired him, so that could be a clue. So could the way Philipe comforted Trudi. And if Philipe had murdered Chad, that might be motive enough for him to frame Charlotte, Yul, or anyone else that would keep fingers from pointing toward him.

But nothing in the files bent those accusatory fingers away from Philipe, either.

So, I was back to considering Yul's uncharacteristic chattiness. I left Lexie and Odin together at Jeff's the next morning, which was Monday. After my early visits, I headed for Borden Yurick's offices.

His effervescent receptionist, Mignon, sat in her usual seat behind the big desk at the entry, where the hostess had once awaited diners at this former restaurant. Mignon was on the phone, nodding, and her auburn curls made small corkscrew motions about her face. She smiled as she saw me and waved her dangerously filed fingernails.

I waved back as I headed through the door into the suite's inner sanctum. My other hand held the file containing my suspect list in Chad Chatsworth's murder and their increasingly intertwining connections. I peered into Borden's office, but he wasn't there. In an empty cubicle with a window, I sat down and booted up the computer. I headed for the best legal database to which Borden subscribed, typed in my password, and dug in.

An hour later, the stuff on my suspect list had expanded further—sort of—and my head was spinning.

I'd gotten lots of data on nearly everyone whose backgrounds I'd researched that day. I knew about Trudi Norman's family holdings in her hometown. Chad's relations' resources, too. And how Dave Driscoll, the computer geek, had gotten into trouble more than once for hacking into multiple government information systems. He'd claimed to be doing it to prove how insecure they were, and had gotten off with warnings . . . so far.

Philipe Pellera's records were surprisingly scant on official databases. Or maybe that was just a comparative assessment, since in doing the usual Internet searches the hits on Philipe's name were astronomical. But other than his owning and driving a car, and maintaining a few business interests, there wasn't much on him. He owned no real estate, hadn't been arrested or even sued except in that Eileen Green matter, and he'd also been a witness in the criminal action against her. Otherwise, he had a legally uneventful history.

Same lack of exciting stuff on Charlotte, though her credit report was hurting till she won the riches on her reality show.

No, what really got my attention and caused my brain rotation was the one other person in this equation whom I'd attempted to psych out online: Yul Silva.

The problem?

He didn't exist—at least not before eleven months ago.

I tried variations on his first and last names. There were references to former celebrity Yul Brynner galore. Others to Silvas and da Silvas. The closest hits prior to last year did not light on men of similar age or background to Charlotte's Yul.

He had a California driver's license, and the red sports car he drove was leased. But those were the only records I found in these detailed databases.

No listing of his birth in any state.

Of course, a lot of stuff was verboten to visit in some states for privacy reasons, so it could just be that this guy happened to move from one to another in such a manner as to obfuscate any of the usual early-life info. Or he'd taken on a legal alias in anticipation of movie stardom.

Still, somewhere there should have been something linking his nom de guerre with his given name.

I needed to move along, and so I ended up by doing a final search on behalf of Marie Seidforth, the boxer lady, and Jon Arlen with the treasure-hunting Welsh terrier.

It didn't look good for Jon and Jonesy, and I had to tell them so. Finders keepers didn't usually cut it when it came to trespassing on someone else's property. Sure, I was a damned good attorney, and when I got my license back, I'd craft a great argument for Jon if he was my client. But even great arguments often didn't succeed in the face of unfavorable precedent.

And yet . . . As I read one more case about trespassing, I had a passing thought that I caught and held on to. There was one avenue I hadn't yet researched that just might yield something interesting on which to hang a potentially persuasive argument.

I did an online search for the website of a title company I'd used in litigation last year, called and asked for the title officer who'd been helpful before. I gave her the particulars and asked her to run a thorough title search.

Who'd pay for it? With luck, it'd ultimately be Jon.

As I HEADED out of Borden's offices, he was heading in. "How much longer now, Kendra?" he asked, a lopsided grin on his gracefully aging face.

I knew what he was talking about. "Two and a half weeks and counting," I told him—till the result of the MPRE came out and my law license would, hopefully, be restored.

"I'm counting on it, too," he said, smiling harder. I sighed inside, hoping I wouldn't have to burn more bridges behind me as I fled my old legal career.

"Great seeing you again, Kendra," Mignon called as I headed out the door.

In the Beamer, I did something that I hoped I wouldn't regret later. I called Jeff.

"I couldn't find a dratted thing on Yul Silva before last year," I told him. "Do you suppose Althea could check her resources for me?" She was his P.I. firm's middle-aged, motherly, and remarkably computer-savvy research techie.

"And how will you pay me?" I could picture his arch grin.

"In pet-sitting services," I replied primly.

"Fair enough." He sounded miffed. Had he figured I'd tell him, as I'd often teased before, that we'd work it off in bed?

And why did the thought of that—when all I wanted to do was ease myself out of this guy's life except as Odin's sitter—make me tingle in all the right places?

"Is it okay if I call and tell her what I need?" I pressed, hoping my inappropriate interest didn't tingle out of my voice.

"Sure."

This was a Widget-walking day, so after tending Harold Reddingam's cats, I headed there. When the terrier and I had tired out, I took him home and called Marie Seidforth.

"Can I come see you this afternoon?" I asked her.

"Sure. I'm so glad to hear from you, Kendra." That made me feel guilty, but I'd hoped to have great news before calling her again. "Did you find anything to help me fight the association? The vote's next week, and my damned neighbor's campaigning against me."

"I think we should talk about what I did find," I told her.

"Oh." Her sad tone suggested she anticipated my answer.

Well, I wasn't about to let her give up without a fight. In fact, I'd been chewing on an idea since my last visit with her.

An hour later, I pulled up in front of her house.

Damned if her nosy neighbor wasn't right there, in her yard. All alone. Weeding in her tight blue jeans, though her dark sweatshirt was loose.

The inspiration that had been percolating in my mind started bubbling full force. I got out of the Beamer and approached her.

"Hi," I said. Putting my hand out, I said, "I'm Kendra Ballantyne, a friend of Marie's. We met a week or two ago."

Her hand had a grass-stained glove on it. The shade was similar to the buttoned blouse I'd chosen to wear with my khakis that day. She looked down, then pulled off the glove and shook relatively amiably. Little did she know how much I was about to shake up her life.

"Hi," she said, looking at me suspiciously. Though the day was chilly, a sheen of sweat dampened her short brown hair. Obviously weeding was hard work, despite the way recent November rain had softened the ground.

"What's your name? Marie told me, but I'm afraid I've forgotten. Though I'm sure everyone who lives around here knows it. Marie says she's so pleased that you're thinking of becoming the new president of the community association."

"She's pleased? Are you kidding?"

I smiled sadly. "She told me how she regrets that the two of you haven't gotten along well. I'm sorry, what's your name?"

"Carline. Carline Mallotte."

"Glad to meet you, Carline. Are you going to be out here for a while? Marie said she wanted to talk to you."

Carline glowered guardedly. "I'll bet she does. Yes, it'll be some time before I'm done here."

"I've been thinking about our conversation about your poor cat—Sagebrush, wasn't that her name?"

"Yes, that was *his* name."

"Very cute. I love cats." Which was true, though my heart had gone to the dogs. "I'd like to hear more about him."

Though Carline eyed me suspiciously, those same eyes turned moist as she did as I asked. Standing there in her small front yard, she described Sagebrush. "He was silver with dark stripes. I got him from a shelter as a tiny kitten. He wasn't a persnickety cat but definitely liked things his own way."

I was glad it was November, so I didn't have to bake in the sun as I encouraged her to keep talking. She told me all I wanted to know about Sagebrush, and about half an hour more.

When she started to wind down, I said, "You must miss him."

The moistness from Carline's eyes trickled down her cheeks. "Yes," she acknowledged softly.

"Do you have any other pets?" I asked.

"No, I'm not like some people, who turn their homes into kennels." Her tone hardened once more as she alluded to Marie.

"I understand," I said smoothly, "but as a pet person, I can't imagine not having any around. Do you have birds or anything else?"

"No. I'm divorced and live alone."

"Oh." I drew that out in obvious sympathy. "That must

be particularly hard when you've loved a pet. Have you thought about getting another?"

"Maybe someday."

"A kitten? A puppy? You know, as a pet-sitter, I see all sorts of adorable animals all day. Some are so much cuter than others. Like . . . have you seen how sweet boxer puppies are?"

Her sad expression segued into a glower. "Ms. Seidforth hasn't exactly invited me."

"Wait here."

Would my not-so-subtle ploy work? Would Marie go along with it? I certainly hoped so. I headed to her door and rang the bell. Instantly, a chorus of canine cacophony rent the air.

"Hi, Kendra," Marie greeted me when her door opened.

"Let's talk," I said sans preamble. I headed toward her kitchen, with Marie and a pack of boxers trailing behind.

A few minutes later, Marie expressed dubiousness about the merit of my scheme, but agreed to go along. We headed back outside. And we weren't alone.

Carline was still outside her condo, kneeling at the front walk, though darned if I could see weeds in her yard.

"Hi, Carline," I said. "Come here a minute, will you?"

She stood and glared—mostly at Marie—saying not a word this time. Only—

I cued Marie with a glance, and she came forward, holding out a wriggling puppy in her arms. "Kendra said you might like to meet one of the pups," she said. I could tell from her tone that she struggled to stay civil, and she succeeded admirably.

At first, Carline simply glared at the small bundle of brindle fur. I took the pup from Marie and snuggled it, reveling in the rough little tongue that sanded my cheek. I laughed. "Okay, fellow, that's enough." I stepped toward Carline and held out the two-month-old puppy. "Care to meet him? I'd introduce you, but Marie hasn't named him yet."

When Carline stayed still for another instant, I shoved the puppy toward her. Rather than let the little creature fall, she put out her arms and took him.

The puppy did what puppies do—wriggled and snuggled and licked enthusiastically. Would that turn off a cat-lover like Carline?

I smiled in relief when she laughed. "Okay, okay, calm down." But she hugged him all the more when he didn't.

Marie took that opportunity to say what we'd discussed before dashing out here. "Carline, I know we haven't been friendly, and you're within your rights not only to run for the board but also to enforce our community rules. But there are things I've wanted to say to try to smooth things between us."

"Like?" Carline obviously tried to growl gruffly. Only the growl turned into a giggle when the puppy nibbled her ear.

"Your cat, for one thing. I thought Sagebrush was cute, and I felt so sorry when you lost him. I know you think stress had something to do with it, since he kept getting on my side of the backyard fence and my pups would run him out."

"That's right," Carline said, more irritably than angrily—a good sign, I hoped.

"Well, I don't know if I actually had anything to do with your loss, and I know it won't replace him, but Kendra said you're all alone—and I wondered if you'd like to hang on to that puppy to keep you company." She pointed at the bundle of wriggling boxer who had started burrowing into the top of Carline's sweatshirt. "He's from Vennie's latest litter, and he's so sweet that I've been looking for a really special home for him. I can't keep him and figure you'd be a great owner. Plus, I'd get to see him. What do you think?"

"You're trying to bribe me, Marie," Carline grumbled without giving back the pup.

"Yes," Marie admitted. "And I'm also willing to

compromise. I'll find homes for most of my dogs, but I want to be able to keep breeding puppies as long as I find them good homes when they're old enough. I'll have a lot around now and then, but I'll keep them down to three or four otherwise."

"That might work," Carline allowed.

"And as to your candidacy for board president, I'll help campaign for you around here as long as we've reached an agreement. Have we?"

I held my breath. The puppy wriggled so hard that Carline nearly dropped him, just as a car drove by. "No!" she cried, and hugged the puppy tighter. "You need some training, little one." And then she grinned. "And I'm just the person to do it. Okay, Marie. Let's give it a try."

I left them to discuss details, grinning all the way back to the Valley in my Beamer. I wished I had Lexie along, for at times I talked aloud to myself, and I'd look less loony if I discoursed with a dog. Oh, well. Who would know but me?

Had that been too simple? "Hell, yes," I said aloud in the privacy of my car. But I'd learned as a litigator that sometimes the simplest arguments were the ones that won over juries.

Had I been sure it would work? "Hell, no." Too often, cat people loathed dogs and vice versa. And Carline had evinced every likelihood of being a felineaphile and potential canineophobe.

But I'd caught a hint of lonely along with her resentment that day she'd glared as I'd left Marie's.

Could I be sure they'd become best friends? Hardly. But at least they'd taken a positive step toward healing prior animosity.

I'd done something similarly simple for Fran Korwald, and it had worked.

"Now if only I could solve Jon Arlen's problem that easily," I observed to the Beamer.

And Chad Chatsworth's murder, I added silently.

Chapter Twenty-eight

TIME ELAPSED, A few frenzied days filled with the usual pet-sitting routine.

I'd called Althea, Jeff's computer ace, and laid on her my latest quest: Find out about Yul Silva's past. I'd checked with her daily, but so far she'd come up as info-empty as I had.

I'd gone to my place to warn Charlotte about the slippery stairway and railing. She'd been justifiably shocked, and claimed to have no idea who could have generated such a slick booby trap.

While there, I'd asked where she'd met Yul, in the guise of gushing over the incredible origins of romantic relationships. He'd been a diversion brought in on her reality show, a gorgeous guy tossed into the mix to see if her head could be turned from the last men still standing.

"I noticed him right away, of course," she'd told me. "But at that point I was really interested in Chad. When I learned why Chad was really there, heard about his ongoing thing with that Trudi, well . . ."

She hadn't had to finish.

That evening, Friday, I sat at Jeff's kitchen table, the

dogs on the floor at my feet, as I checked over the voluminous lists I'd made containing my thoughts about Chad's murder.

But though the info expanded, the list of suspects hadn't: Trudi; Chad's and now Trudi's geeky but probably ambitious roommate Dave; swiveling singing sensation Philipe Pellera; and Sven Broman—though he was a long shot since, as he was the next-to-the-last guy standing before Charlotte had made her decision, I wasn't sure why he'd kill Chad once the show was over. I even checked out a few of the show's producers and production staff. And then, of course, there were Charlotte and nonexistent Yul.

I sighed. Maybe Jeff was right. This wasn't my area of expertise, despite my success when my own butt was on the line. I should leave solving murders to experts like Noralles. That's what Detective Ned would want, after all.

In your dreams, my brain shot back to the absent detective.

Would he arrest Charlotte? He hadn't yet, so even though she felt threatened, he obviously didn't have enough evidence to haul her in and support a successful prosecution. And despite how I'd come to revile the relentless detective when he'd been after me, I had to admit there'd been plenty of evidence indicating my guilt. Of course, it had been planted.

With Charlotte, there might be evidence, too, and she could be as much a subject of a frame-up as I'd been, but Noralles had either grown wiser, or whoever was framing her wasn't as good at it as my persecutor had been. Making nasty calls and greasing steps were another matter.

I sighed again—and heard the sound of a key in the front door.

Instantly, the dogs leapt to attention and, barking, barreled through the house in that direction. I followed, a huge smile on my face. Jeff was home. I could dump my ideas and frustrations on him, brainstorm a bit, and see where it all led.

Only it wasn't Jeff who entered.

"Hi, Kendra," said Amanda Hubbard. Last time I'd seen his ex, I'd been struck by how beautiful she was, though then she was fragile-looking and teary as she'd spilled her story of a stalker to the P.I. she'd been married to.

Now, her tall, slim body was clad in slender jeans and a fuzzy beige sweater with a rolled collar—the only part not clinging to ample curves. Her blond hair spilled over her shoulders. She carried a handbag, and an overnight case on wheels hummed over the hardwood floor behind her.

No fragility. No tears. No hesitation.

She had a key.

My cue to pack up and go home. "Your timing is good," I said, as if she didn't know. "Jeff's due back later tonight."

"That's right," she acknowledged. No apology for barging in, but hey, why should she? I was only Odin's pet-sitter.

"Well, since you're here, I'll take off. You can tell Jeff for me that we can settle up my bill tomorrow." Not that I'd want to see him then, or any other time.

Odin was another matter. Lexie would be crushed not to see her big Akita pal again, and I didn't need to give up a pet-sitting client just because he was apparently reconciling with his onetime wife.

"I'll be right back," I said. Passing the kitchen, I piled my files back together and stuck them into the briefcase I'd used to bring them here.

Despite the tumult that resulted from Amanda's earlier appearance, I'd gotten used to sleeping in more comfort here than when I'd stayed in the guest room. As a result, I bundled up belongings spread all over Jeff's bedroom, ignoring my embarrassment. Amanda could deal with changing the sheets on the bed if she chose.

As I tossed stuff into my bag, muttering imprecations against Amanda and her irritating ex under my breath, Lexie hung about my feet. My pup acted anxious, so I picked her up, hugged her, and said, "Looks like we're heading home again, kiddo."

I only hoped no one had spit-shined our stairway again.

GOOD THING I'D come home, I told myself when I spied the folded package in my mailbox and saw who it was from: the title officer. I'd have some titillating material to read in bed that night—as long as detailed real estate documents turned me on.

I wouldn't consider what else I could have been doing in bed if I hadn't had to come home. Or whom I might have been doing it with. Or how turned on I could have been . . .

I unpacked, then took Lexie back downstairs for her late-night constitutional. No problem navigating the stairway. No one had messed with it again.

But I was still aching and kept my defenses on overdrive, as this was where someone had sabotaged my own surroundings to injure me. Or worse.

I pushed in the code to open the front gate, then jumped when I heard a sound behind me. Lexie lunged on her leash and began to bark.

"Good girl," I told her. If someone intended to harm me, the more noise accompanying it, the more likely that a neighbor would hear and intervene. Or at least call the cops.

Only— "Hi, Lexie." It was Charlotte. "Hi, Kendra. I wasn't sure when you'd be home, but I've been watching for you. Your friend Detective Noralles has been nosing around again." Under the dim security lights, she looked scruffy, with sunken eyes, old clothes, and a haggard expression showing premature lines in her skin. Hunks of hair escaped from her habitual long braid. "He said he'd gotten another anonymous tip and needs to talk to me about it. I made an appointment with him for Monday, and

I'm bringing my lawyer Esther along. Your lawyer. Our lawyer." Her long sigh was a soft shudder that only remotely resembled a laugh. "Anyhow, I'm throwing another party, tomorrow night. It might be my last. Can you come?"

Yul would surely be there, and I could buttonhole him and ask the questions for which neither Althea nor I had found answers. Some of my other murder suspects would probably be there, too. Sure, I was still sticking my nose where it didn't belong, but I still believed that my pretty, erstwhile effervescent tenant was being railroaded.

Just maybe, I had one more chance to get that particular train off the track.

MY PHONE RANG at ten that night. I figured I knew who it was even before I saw the caller ID, and once again considered letting it roll to voice mail. But that would be the cowardly way. I was a litigator. No way was I lily-livered or spineless. Not a single part of my anatomy was anything but gutsy.

So I answered. "Hi, Jeff. Welcome home. I trust that Amanda and Odin got along okay after I left. I'll fax you my bill tomorrow. I think I know how much time Althea spent doing computer research for me, so I'll deduct that at the rate of—"

"Bullshit!"

"I don't know how to calculate that currency," I continued smoothly, proud of my unaffected aplomb. "But I'll try."

"Look, Kendra, I'm sorry I didn't tell you I'd been married. I didn't think it was important, since I'm divorced. And if you think I'm a jerk for making that assumption, then . . . well, hell."

I swallowed the spiteful rejoinder my lips had started to form. He had, after all, apologized. Kind of. His ending sort of spoiled the effect, which lent justification to my staying incensed.

"I definitely didn't invite Amanda here tonight," Jeff continued. "She left as soon as I got home. She said I'd helped get rid of her stalker and wanted to thank me personally."

I decided to respond solely to that last, significant statement.

"I'm sure she did." The sweetness that streamed from my tone must have smelled great, for Lexie sat up where she'd slept at the foot of my bed and slithered up to lay her head on my arm. She licked me, then looked up with her tongue lolling as if it awaited something luscious.

Or maybe she was simply sensing my miserable mood and trying futilely to make me laugh.

"Look," he said. "I have catch-up work to do at the office tomorrow since I've been out of town. Can we grab dinner together tomorrow night?"

"Amanda, you, and me? I don't think so."

"Only the two of us," he shouted, as if raising his voice would somehow erase the mistaken impression from my mind.

Only the impression I had was far from a mistake. Amanda was moving back in, one way or another.

She'd had a key. She probably had his alarm code, since she hadn't hesitated about heading right in.

"No, the four of us," Jeff corrected. "We'll walk the dogs and talk after we eat."

"Sorry," I said. "I've been invited to a party tomorrow night. Maybe another time. Right now, I'm beat. Pet-sitting can be tiring, and following it by pretending to be pleasant to someone I hadn't even known existed . . . well, that's even more exhausting. Good night, Jeff." I hung up before he could jump in with more unwelcome suggestions.

I wondered for a long while afterward, though, where

Amanda was while Jeff invited Lexie and me for a frolic tomorrow.

I didn't really want to know.

SINCE SLEEPING WAS an occupation that eluded me, I instead read the title report that had been messengered to me that day.

"Well, what do you know!" I exclaimed as I ploughed productively through it. Too bad it was well past midnight, too late to call Jon Arlen, in case I'd awaken him.

Thank heavens for e-mail. I booted up my computer and sent Jon a message instead: "Interesting development in the matter I'm looking into for you. Let's talk tomorrow."

Though I wasn't set up for an instant message, I got a reply almost immediately. "Anytime. Is it something good?"

"Good enough to convince your neighbor to talk to us," I responded, then went once more to bed. Tomorrow would be an interesting day.

Chapter Twenty-nine

I LEFT LEXIE at home that morning, not looking back at her sad face as I crept carefully down my steps. As I did every day now since last Sunday's scary fiasco, I checked them out before proceeding. Today, they weren't slick.

Neither was my mood. Poor Lexie had gotten used to keeping company again with Odin during the day, and now I'd had to leave her alone. But I didn't dare bring her on my late-morning mission, and I wasn't sure I'd have time to stop either here or at Darryl's to drop her off.

After nearly a week, the bruising on my body had fortunately faded, as had the related pain. I faced the morning's routine and my round of dog walks with more spring in my step each day.

Or I would have today if I'd maintained a mind-set that stayed far from Jeff Hubbard and his key-carrying ex.

Damn! No way would I let that frustrating man make hash of a perfectly good mood. I forced myself to consider instead how I would present the potentially excellent news I had to Jon Arlen. Despite all good intentions, I was running late when I reached Jon's home by Lake Hollywood, along the hill beside Barham Boulevard. It was one-story, small, gray stucco and nondescript except for an elderly gnarled oak that dominated the front yard—rather amok for property possessed by the proprietor of a tree-trimming company like Jon Arlen.

I wondered how old the oak was. Had it been witness to the situation I was about to mention to its owner?

Okay, Ballantyne, wrap up the whimsy.

I heard his Welsh terrier, Jonesy, bark in response to the doorbell, and the bearded ball of energy nearly bowled me over when Jon opened the door.

"Kendra, come in," Jon said in his regular raspy voice. As I followed him straight inside to the cozy living room, I considered how disproportionate this large, casually clad man was to his relatively small home.

A decanter and mugs sat on a square coffee table before the faded plaid sofa, and Jon poured us each some coffee as I took my seat. Jonesy joined me till I darted him a dirty look. Not that it made him cower, but he leapt down, licked my leg, then took his place on the chair, crowding his more welcoming master.

Though I took a polite sip of the strong brew when Jon handed me my mug, I put it down and wasted no time before pulling out the papers I'd brought. "I haven't fully researched the implication," I told him. "At best, you can keep the treasure. At worst, someone else altogether winds up with it—possibly the government. But since neither you nor your neighbor are likely to want that, what I've found should at least make it more palatable to her to palaver with you first, if she's got any sense at all. Tell me her full name."

"Beatrice Flores." The way his thick, stubby fingers plowed through his short curly hair suggested that she gave him a headache. Beatrice the Bitch is what he'd called her before.

"Interesting. Her last name suggests a Latina heritage, which might work against you here."

"Figures. With her, I doubt anything'll work *for* me."

"Do I detect a history here you haven't told me about?"

Jon gave a careless shrug that suggested I'd scored a hit. "We met at a neighborhood party when she moved in last year. Went out a couple of times."

"Then what?" I asked.

"Then she started getting possessive and I stopped taking her calls."

Interesting. "So this squabble could also be based on hard feelings."

"Could be. Only—"

"Only what?"

"Only I missed her after a while. I asked her out again a month or so after we broke up. That time, she snubbed me."

"I see," I said, and I did. Hmmm. That added a new dimension to this trespassing situation. "Let's go over the papers, then I want Jonesy and you to take me to the yard and show me where he dug up the loot."

Fifteen minutes later, we headed down a small hall and out a door to the backyard.

The area was along the hillside, and it wasn't fenced. Neither were most neighbors' yards, which had undoubtedly led to the current dilemma. The trees here, mainly eucalyptus and walnut, looked better trimmed than the front yard's oak.

"Over here." Jon headed down the hill, through the unkempt weeds behind his home onto property with short, green grass shadowed by a white multilevel house that looked architecturally advantaged. He'd dumped a damsel with that kind of good taste? Too bad.

With a happy yap, Jonesy bounded onto a path amid abundant landscaping at the foot of the hill.

As I hurried to join Jon and Jonesy, I heard a noise behind us. A woman in pressed linen pants emerged from the house, preceded by a sand-colored mutt of a dog that made Jonesy look like a midget. The dog barked at the same time the slender, scowling lady yelled, "What are you doing there?"

"Showing a friend where Jonesy found the treasure," Jon replied mildly, following the script we had discussed inside.

"It's on my property. It's my treasure, and I want it back," the obviously riled property owner responded.

"Hi, Ms. Flores," I said, extending my hand as she reached us. "Jon told me how pretty you are, and he was right. Oops. I think I spoke out of turn." I ignored Jon's scowl meant to shush me, continuing, "Too bad things didn't work out between you. It would have made things easier."

"What are you talking about?" she demanded as icily as if my comments had carried us to Antarctica in midwinter.

"I have something for you." I reached into the envelope I'd brought outside and handed her a copy of some of the chain of title info I'd shown Jon.

She shrank back as if I'd tried to stick Pansy the potbellied pig in her hand, or maybe Py the python. Her short black hair ruffled in the mild November wind.

"I think you'll find this interesting," I told her. "By the way, have you hired an attorney yet?"

"No, but believe me, I will," she said stonily.

"I believe you will do anything that'll—" Jon began before I stepped in front of him to hide his angry expression.

"Jon's made it clear," I interrupted, "that he regrets how badly things turned out when you were dating. In fact, he's said how much he still misses you. But that's another story."

I felt fury radiating from Jon and motioned him to silence by sticking my hand behind me and flicking my fingertips.

"Meantime," I continued, "I need to let you know that I'm a lawyer, though I'm not acting in that capacity right now. But let me tell you what I've learned by doing a little research."

I described the fascinating facts I'd found. It seemed

that the property behind both of their houses, as well as many others in that area, had been part of an old Spanish land grant that showed up on the chain of title. It had been a roadway, and today it would be considered an easement reserved for the benefit of the Catholic Church or the government, or both.

That was where Jonesy had dug up the treasure.

The reserved rights had never been vacated, so arguably the government succeeding the Spanish one could have kept the same interests. Under today's law, a person couldn't obtain property by adverse possession or gain prescriptive easements—legal ways of stealing property of others simply by using it—of property interests owned by governmental entities and not even equitable easements applied where there were no improvements to the part of the property in question. As a result, California might in effect own that strip of land. The treasure could be the state's, and not Beatrice's or Jon's.

Or the coins might be deemed lost property. In that case, Beatrice might be considered their trustee until their true owners could be found—descendants of the Spanish settlers who buried it there. If that was the decision, said descendants would undoubtedly descend en masse to make a claim once word got out—genuine or illegitimate.

There was a good argument, of course, that the treasure belonged to the ostensible owner of the property where it was found—Beatrice. Of course, when Jon asserted his finders-keepers argument, he might be the one to prevail.

Years of litigation later, after the value of the treasure was already spent on the lawyers, the court would decide who owned the coins—one or both of them . . . or someone else altogether.

Wouldn't it be better to share it, to act as a cohesive unit to fend off the inevitable claimants if word got out that the treasure was found? And assuming the world learned about it, imagine the extra wealth that could be won, from talk shows, interviews, book deals, and all. The two of them could form a terrific team to handle it . . . together.

I watched her face as I talked. Glanced at Jon's, too. They looked equally dazed. I'd told Jon what I'd found, not what I intended to say about it or any of the rest.

"Nothing's absolute, of course," I finished. "And please don't think I'm giving either of you legal advice, just telling you the way I see things. But I really think it would be in the best interests of both of you to talk this out, reach a compromise."

I looked at Jonesy, who was doing his schtick of digging on the property that was the subject of this discussion. Only this time, he wasn't alone. Beatrice's dog, too, had entered into the game.

"Why don't we have dinner together tonight to discuss this?" Jon asked Beatrice tentatively. "My treat. Have you been to Dalts since the last time we were there?" He named a trendy restaurant in Burbank not far from there.

"No," Beatrice said. She was silent for a moment. "Sure. Why not? If we can reach an amicable solution, I'm all for it."

So was I. I took my leave soon after, a huge grin on my face. Could this be the onset of a rekindled romance or two—Jonesy and the larger sandy dog, and Jon and Beatrice?

Even if it was simply a start to renewed neighborly détente, I was all for it.

As to the legal implications—well, I hadn't totally overstated the potential quagmire. I wished them both luck—and hoped they'd hire me if they needed a lawyer when I was practicing once more.

I DASHED TO Darryl's when I was done at Jon's, and told him all about what I'd accomplished.

"Good job, Kendra," he enthused, standing near the

front desk with his back toward the chaos that was his doggy resort on a Saturday afternoon. "I've heard Marie Seidforth is ecstatic, too, over how you helped solve things with her neighbor and their community association. And even that stud fee situation, where the small claims action was filed. You knew that'd get the breeder's attention so she'd talk. In fact, you seem to be specializing in getting people to talk to one another."

"Yeah." I'd realized that, and all I'd done had seemed somewhat simple. It wouldn't always work, of course. I was certain of that. But still, I supposed that even the most fractious people sometimes craved compromise that let them save face and feel they'd aced an argument. And where the result was a new pet, or sharing of a small treasure—hey, why not?

"I think I've discovered my own form of ADR," I said. I'd considered this some after I'd helped Fran Korwald figure a solution for her pug custody dilemma. "When used relating to legal matters, that usually stands for 'alternate dispute resolution.' "

"But yours—let me guess," Darryl broke in. "It's 'animal dispute resolution.' "

"You got it! Maybe I can run with it even more when I get my law license back."

"Which is when?"

"Less than two weeks," I crowed optimistically.

"Can you make a living at animal dispute resolution? Or will you go back to litigation? And most important, are you going to keep on pet-sitting? I'm asking that since my clients keep requesting referrals."

"Stay tuned," I told my long, lanky friend. "I'll tell you first, whatever I figure out."

"Interested in grabbing dinner with me tonight?" he asked.

It wouldn't be a date with Darryl. That wasn't the nature of our friendship. "Rain check," I told him. "Charlotte's having what might be a pre-arrest party, and I intend to be there. I really would like to figure out exactly who and what got those ferrets munching on Chad Chatsworth, preferably before it's too late for Charlotte."

"I remember when you complained about your tenant almost as much as you complained about your ex-lover Bill Sergement," Darryl said with a grin.

"Whoever accused me of being consistent?" I said. "I'll tell you all about what happens when I drop Lexie off here on Monday, okay?"

"I didn't know she was coming," he said.

"Neither did I, till now." I gave his skinny bod a big hug, then hurried out to speed into my late-day duties.

LEXIE WAS DELIGHTED to see me. After we took our walk and I fed her, I rushed to get ready for Charlotte's murder suspects' soiree. Time for one of my dressier informal outfits: silver sweater over a long multicolor skirt that swished as I walked. I doubted my makeup would stick me on the pages of *Elle,* but what the hell? It enhanced what I had. I'd kind of gotten used to my hair in its natural nondescript shade of brown, but I combed it back and stuck on some dangling earrings. I stuck a comb, some emergency cosmetics, and my cell phone in a small purse.

I left while Lexie was eating, so she'd pay less attention to my latest defection. As I prepared, in open sandals despite the crisp November air, to span the enormous distance between my humble abode and my unhumble, rented-out home, I saw Charlotte standing in the backyard between the two structures, near my swimming pool that was now off-limits to me. Despite the fact that her party was imminent, she was all alone—not like the ultrasociable hostess. I headed in her direction.

"Hi, Charlotte," I called through the wrought-iron fence. She looked up from the tiled deck about the pool fast, as if I'd startled her. Though her snazzy purple tunic and matching pants had obviously been donned for the party, her pale face reflected anything but a party mood. The shadows from the ample landscaping didn't help.

"It's awful, Kendra," she responded in a halting rasp.

"What is?" I asked.

"Yes, what?" echoed a male voice from behind me. I turned to seek out its source. Lyle Urquard, the mad bicyclist, had left his cycle at home and had cleaned up rather well for this latest party. His charcoal shirt looked silky, and his black slacks barely suggested the contours of his bulging belly. He looked concerned, as his out-jutting lower jaw sagged in a frown.

"Is everything okay, Charlotte?" chirped Tilla Thomason. She and her husband, Hal, plus others from the neighborhood gang, had flocked through the open front gate after Lyle.

"Sure," Charlotte lied with an obvious effort to be cheerful. "Let's go inside."

As we all followed her in through the kitchen, I had a sinking feeling that tonight's festivities would seem more like a wake than a gala.

And I intended to grill Charlotte till I got the reason why.

Chapter Thirty

Before I caught up with the crowd, my cell phone rang. "So why the heck did you bring it, Ballantyne?" I muttered to myself, knowing the answer even as I checked out the caller ID.

"Hello, Jeff," I said stiffly. Since I'd headed home after the Amanda-and-the-key affair, I'd heard from him often. Wasn't sure whether I wanted to. But tonight was a good time. "Sorry I can't talk to you now. I'm just on my way to a party." *Enjoying my social life sans you*, was my unspoken gibe.

"Another of your tenant's shindigs?" he asked. "I'd like to crash one, one of these days."

"Without an invitation?" I responded breezily. "Let me tell you all the interesting research I recently did on trespassers. It's not a good idea to become one. Are you going out of town anytime soon? Lexie misses Odin."

"I've got something planned for the end of next week, but—"

"Great. I was wondering why you called. I'll be glad to pet-sit. We'll talk before you leave." And I hung up.

I'd handled that as I'd intended to. Friendly, professional, not suggesting a smidgen that the Amanda bit was still bothering me.

So why did I feel as if Jeff had heard all the stuff I hadn't said? I sighed. *Get over it, Kendra.*

When I finally entered my leased-out house, Yul was in the kitchen adding the finishing touches to cuisine for guests craving calories: chips and melted cheese for nachos, fixings for French dip sandwiches, and a couple of different kinds of quiche. The aromas that encircled the room and all who passed through suggested impending paradise for the taste buds. And for those eschewing rich and fattening fare, there was a tray of finger-sized veggies and dip.

Charlotte stepped around the food and headed for the bar, and the rest of us followed.

I noticed, as I grabbed my drink, filled my plate, and headed for the heart of the revelry, that the big UGLY ROOM sign was back on the door to the den. Obviously it was off-limits for this gathering. A good idea, since a murder scene wasn't a prime venue for a party.

"Next week, I promise," said someone standing beside me. Ike Janus, in a sporty sweater tonight instead of a suit, held a wineglass in his hand and a hang-dog expression on his bespectacled face. "The insurance company assured me you'd have a check then."

"Thanks," I said, recalling how I'd thought he was can-do enough to get this done a hell of a lot faster. Of course, a murder had slowed the situation down. Still . . . "I'd love to get the wall fixed." Though even doing that and redecorating wouldn't keep me from remembering all that had happened in that room.

A short while later, we all gathered in the black-and-white beast of a living room. Mostly, it was the same mob of people present when I'd partied here before: Charlotte and Yul, her showbiz friends including Philipe Pellera and Sven Broman, and the same stable of neighbors. Each established clique again sat on its own side of the room—neighbors on one side, and celebrities and wannabes on the other.

Charlotte's red carpet had really rolled out that night. Trudi Norman and Dave Driscoll were there again, too. Dressed in a skimpy, shimmering shirt and slacks, and made up like a model, Trudi sat on the sofa between Philipe and Dave. I wasn't sure which she was with. Or if she'd come stag with the sole purpose of latching on to one or the other, for she seemed to cozy up first to Philipe, then turn to Dave before he ran for another drink to drown his sorrows.

I'd have spent more time studying those suspects if it hadn't been for Charlotte. She seemed to hold court at a side of the room as she downed one glass of Smirnoff after another. How did I know her choice of vodka? She kept the bottle on the area rug on the floor beside her, lifting it often for refills, not even bothering to pretend to water it down with juice or anything else of a lesser proof.

At first only Yul and Sven seemed to be the recipients of whatever she whispered about. Sipping my own clear liquid beverage—solely soda water, as I wanted my wits at full throttle—I nonchalantly edged toward that end of the room. I needn't have bothered with subtlety, though, since the volume of Charlotte's voice grew louder with each passing swig.

"Yes, it was that terrible," she said, standing with a lurch as Yul steadied her by grabbing an arm.

Though her handsome hunk had dressed well in a muscle-hugging ski sweater over designer slacks, something I didn't recognize sizzled in his somber expression. Apprehension? Anticipation? No, it was more than that. Something that suggested even more intelligence than I'd imagined as he listened with apparent alarm to what Charlotte said.

"That damned detective, Nor . . . Nor . . . Nor . . ."

"Noralles," I supplied to end her sloshed stammering.

"That's it. He insisted that I come to his stupid police station today. Of course I brought Esther, but it didn't go well. I hadn't told her . . . Well, now she knows, and she said she's still my lawyer and she'll help me anyway. But how on earth did that damned detective learn any of that?"

"Any of what?" Yul asked the exact question that had slipped to the tip of my tongue, his tone soft and placating while his eyes studied her with both caring and wariness.

"He told me more about that latest tip," she responded, not quite on point. "Someone phoned it in anonymously and untraceably this time, or so he said. If he knew whether it was the same person as sent the package, he didn't let me in on it, but it probably was. The question's still 'Who?' "

More important, "What tip this time?" I asked.

"About the reality show ideas Chad came up with," she said. "The one he was really pushing—and getting buzz about—was about bringing in people for an American Idol kind of show, showcasing talent and awarding the winner a recording contract. Only everyone would have been checked out in advance, and each contender would have had something in his or her past he wasn't proud of. Something hidden. Of course, it would come out on the show. The point would be to see reactions, and the viewers would vote which loser should win the prize of big bucks."

"Which they could use to hire a lawyer to defend them from whatever charges were brought for what they were hiding," I muttered loud enough that everyone could hear it.

I was surprised—or maybe not—to see Charlotte turn stark white against the blackness of her hair and purpleness of her pantsuit. Her blue eyes were huge. "How did you know?" she rasped. "Were you the one who gave Nor-whatever the tip?"

By this time, the respective cliques about the room had grown silent, everyone listening to this exchange. Some people had risen to gather around. Tilla Thomason, looking even chunkier than usual in a muumuu festooned with enormous yellow flowers, appeared all ears. I wondered that she didn't already have her cell phone stuck to her ear as she bleated out gossip to everyone she knew, and to many she didn't.

Lyle Urquard stood right behind Charlotte, not far from me, though I stayed within her line of sight so I could ask her questions. Lyle squirmed as he stared at her—and seemed to glare daggers sharp enough to saw off the arm Yul had stuck around her shoulders.

Interesting, I thought. Our klutzy neighbor seemed to have a crush on reality star Charlotte. I should have realized it before. He always seemed so friendly toward her.

Charlotte was still staring, so I said, "I didn't give Detective Noralles any tips. Did he bring you in to question you because he thought you were stealing that reality show idea?" And then the truth butted me in the gut. "No, he brought you in because of something in your past you were hiding, right? Because Chad came up with this idea and ran with it since he knew something about you. Was he blackmailing you so you'd work with him to make his reality show career a reality? Or did he just want to humiliate you the way you humiliated him by dumping him in front of millions of viewers?"

The party crowd about us began to chatter. Maybe that was a good thing, since despite what Chad might have wanted, I had no interest in humiliating Charlotte in public, even in front of a small group like this.

Charlotte simply nodded. Yul drew her closer. "Everyone has something in their past they wouldn't want broadcast everywhere," he said in an entire, astute, and sensitive sentence. I'd been right about a different look in his eyes tonight.

What was he hiding? Obviously, it had to do with who this man with no recorded past really was.

"What's yours, Charlotte?" asked Tilla Thomason.

"Yeah, Charlotte," said Trudi Norman. "What's your deepest, darkest secret?"

Dave Driscoll tried to shush Trudi. Philipe Pellera asked, "Did that detective know your secret?"

Before I could tell them all to take their big mouths on the road, Charlotte answered. "He did," she said sadly. "I'm sure he's just getting his ducks in a row to arrest me for killing Chad." She sighed and took another swig of vodka. "It won't be the first time I was arrested."

"I'm not your lawyer, Charlotte," I said, "but if Esther was here, I'm sure she'd tell you not to talk about it."

"We're all friends here," she said. Maybe so, but I'm sure the buzz from her drink made everyone seem like better buddies.

"Do you want me to call Esther and have *her* advise you to shut up?" I asked, not liking the edge to my own voice. But I'd handled clients who'd stuck even small feet in their mouths in manners that made their cases go south in seconds.

"No," she replied. "I guess you're right. But you know what? I don't feel like partying anymore."

Silence sliced the air, and then Yul said, "Time to clear out, everyone. Thanks for coming."

SINCE THIS WAS my house and I hadn't far to go, I made sure I was last to leave. "You're okay?" I asked Charlotte.

We stood by the entry, watching the last partygoers go through the gate. Yul was in the kitchen wrapping a lot of leftovers.

She nodded. "I need to get out of here, though," she said sadly. "Even though we can't get in while it's being rebuilt,

Yul's taking me to the Griffith Park Observatory. I like it up there on its hilltop. Open space, a wonderful view of L.A., and lots and lots of sky." She sighed. "I have a feeling my life is going to get cramped into just a few feet of jail space soon."

"Did you kill Chad?" I had to ask—for the zillionth time.

She shook her head. "I can see why Noralles is suspicious, after that tip and because he knows my past. The records are sealed because I was a juvenile, but I was arrested for a hit-and-run when I was sixteen. I'd only just started driving when I turned a corner too fast and hit a mother pushing a stroller in a crosswalk. They were hurt, but thank God they weren't killed. I was so scared I ran away. But I turned myself in, worked hard as a waitress so I could pay as much as I could toward their hospital bills, and did community service."

"And Noralles thinks you'd kill Chad over that?"

"It's not the image I want to portray while starting my reality show career."

"But it's not—"

"Ready to go, Charlotte?" Yul had come from the hall toward the kitchen, still wiping his hands on a wet paper towel.

She nodded.

"What about you, Yul?" I blurted out. "You said everyone has something they don't want people to know about. How about you? Like, what's your real name?"

His glare could have singed away superglue. "Have you been checking up on me?"

"Where'd your single-syllable replies go?" I countered.

Charlotte swept across the entry and pulled Yul into her arms. "I know about him, Kendra. It's not what you think. And don't try to help me by telling the detective it's Yul. Esther Ickes has referred him to his own attorney, but he didn't do anything, I swear."

"And what about you, Yul? Do you swear you have no fatal secrets?"

"Bite me," he said, and swept Charlotte out of the house.

IRRITATED THAT MY tenants, no matter how miffed at me, had left without locking up, I took the time to check the front and back doors. All was fine.

Except, as I headed out, I heard something. A shrill something. A familiar shrill something.

Ferrets?

How could that be? The little critters were incarcerated way out in the Valley.

Even so, I headed for the den. Now, *that* door was locked.

Good thing the key ring I'd put in my little purse contained the keys not only for my apartment door, but also for the ones here. Even when I'd rented the place out, I'd always had aspirations to take it back and live here again. The keys kept my hope alive.

When I opened the door, I found myself rushed by two furry ferrets. They seemed smaller than the five who'd lived here before, and they were loose.

"Yul!" I shouted into the empty hall. "What the hell are you doing? Even if these guys aren't mini-murderers, they're still illegal." I'd have to put him on official written lease-conforming notice as quickly as possible. *Bite me,* he'd said. Maybe he'd been hoping his illicit animal friends would hear and instead bite *me.*

No, that wouldn't happen. I knelt and lifted the friendly little ferrets, who'd already started exploring my feet. Warm and wriggly, they slinked over and around the long sleeves of my silver sweater—and then one actually slipped inside.

"Hey, pervert!" I cried. "You must be the male of this

pair." I managed to pull him out, then placed both ferrets on the floor. This time, they hurried across the room to a crate that was low to the ground and contained a lot of ragged towels. Was that a sock I saw hanging off one end? Could be these critters were little thieves.

That didn't make them, or their kind, killers.

"You're awfully cute," I said as I took one more look before locking the door behind me. "Too bad you're illegal."

AN HOUR LATER, I lay half-asleep in bed. Could Noralles's tip actually lead to the killer? A reality show that would unearth the untenable pasts of its contestants. That didn't mean its creators, or others on its staff, would be exposed.

Or had Chad made it clear he intended it as a vehicle for revenge?

Who knew?

And what was I going to do with this new pair of ferrets? Was Yul a ferret junky, craving the little creatures, unable to survive without some about?

I didn't think I'd stirred, but suddenly Lexie, who'd been lying sound asleep beside me, rose and stood at attention.

My little black, white, and chestnut Cavalier started growling way deep in her throat, a menacing sound that could have come from a much bigger hound.

"What's wrong, Lexie?" I asked in a whisper, only garnering a deeper growl from my edgy dog.

My lights were out. I didn't put them on, though I did don the robe I'd thrown over a bedroom chair.

I looked out a window.

A light was on in the house.

No biggie. Charlotte and Yul could be home.

Only I'd been enough awake that I'd have heard their car pull into the garage underneath my apartment, if it had arrived there.

The light moved. A flashlight?

I intended to find out.

I wouldn't call the cops, in case there was a perfectly innocent explanation, like maybe my tenants had come in without my noticing and one was now creeping through the rooms with a flashlight so as not to disturb the other, who was already sound asleep.

Right.

Well, just in case, I did call Jeff. Woke him.

Fortunately failed to hear Amanda's voice.

"Stay put till I get there, Kendra," he ordered.

"See you in a bit," I responded without assent.

I wouldn't take the stressed-out Lexie, despite her being the one to alert me. She'd only alert the prowler, too.

I threw on jeans and a T-shirt. I happened to have a can of Mace in a purse, and I fortunately found it in the dimness of the streetlight that spilled into my front window.

And then, locking Lexie in the back bathroom so her barks couldn't be heard as well, I started down the stairs.

And stopped and blinked before continuing, carefully, for I'd been struck by a sudden bit of insight.

After all I'd seen and heard that evening, I had a feeling I knew whom I'd find there.

I believed I knew the identity of Chad's killer.

Chapter Thirty one

WHAT I DIDN'T know was why the killer was again on the prowl in my house. I'd find out eventually, after I'd maced and trussed the murderer, and waited for Jeff and the posse he was bound to round up.

What I hadn't anticipated was that the killer anticipated *me*.

I'd no sooner sneaked into the kitchen door than I was grabbed from behind. I had my Mace poised to spray, and I turned my hand to aim it over my shoulder. I only got out a useless spritz before my hand was hit by something hard. I shrieked at the sudden pain, and the can tumbled from my damaged fingers to the floor. The clatter on the tile only called my attention even more to my precarious position.

I might not have taken this person seriously before, but I'd have to now. Bad enough I'd been subjected to bruising when my stairway was made slick and slippery, but I was in greater danger at the moment. Life imprisonment without parole or the death sentence, whichever, wouldn't be worse if the person threatening me was punished for one murder or two.

"Hello, Lyle," I said sweetly as I turned in the darkness

of the room that had so recently been the scene of a party. "How nice of you to drop in."

He was backlighted by a soft glow through the arched doorway from a light he'd left on in the house. His body was long and lanky from this angle; no sign of his prominent stomach that stood out in profile. I couldn't see the expression on his face but figured he wasn't smiling.

I certainly wasn't.

"I tried to keep you out of this, Kendra." His voice twisted into a childlike whine that sent tiny ferret feet of horror tiptoeing up my spine.

"I know, Lyle," I said as evenly as my trembling body could manage. "The phone call, the oil on my stairs . . . And I never knew before that you had a white car, the one you used to follow me. I always associate you with your bicycle."

"I like bicycling better than driving," he confirmed.

Could I keep him talking long enough for the cavalry to arrive? Assuming it did. Maybe I was only grasping at straws to believe that Jeff, with whom I'd been quarreling, would appear to save me from my own stupidity. He had warned me to stay in my nice, safe apartment with Lexie. But I had to pretend I was as proficient an investigator as he. And now I was liable to pay.

If so, at least I could go with the knowledge of Lyle's acts and their motivation. Would I go happy? Not exactly.

"You're the one who mailed the package to Noralles, aren't you?" I asked. "The one that contained Chad's reality show ideas, Charlotte's and Yul's schedules, the note from Charlotte that looked like a threat, and the rest." I inched around so Lyle did, too. This way, I could see him better in the light.

I didn't like the way his eyes glowed so insanely.

"Of course," he acknowledged with less of a whine. "That detective questioned me, you know. I was worried at first, but I think the cops questioned everyone in the neighborhood, especially those who came to Charlotte's parties."

Too bad he hadn't arrested Lyle on the spot. Of course, I hadn't suspected him either. But Noralles was the expert. And despite his having suspected me in another situation, he had definitely struck me as being smart.

Still, Lyle . . . ?

"Where'd you get the papers you sent?" I asked, curious.

"From inside the house and their cars. I took my time, looked around during days they were gone and you weren't here, went through their files and collected things I thought would help. I used gloves—no fingerprints." Not the bicycling gloves of his I'd seen before, then. They'd covered his palms, not his fingers. "I made copies and snuck the originals back. There was no problem getting into the house after the Hummer hit it, of course. Or into their cars, either. I'm a locksmith, you know."

I'd heard he was in construction. Close enough, I supposed. "Nice touch, mailing the package from near the studio where Charlotte's reality show was filmed. No one would imagine anyone who lived around here sent it."

He shrugged slightly. "I get to that area often. Since I met Charlotte, I've picked up work at the studio whenever I can. They need locksmiths a lot. I make sure of it." He smiled a scary, self-satisfied grin.

Charlotte hadn't mentioned seeing him at the studio. Then again, Lyle wasn't exactly as memorable as a lot of men she met in her showbiz milieu.

"So why did you mail those documents to the detective?" I inquired as composedly as if we conversed about the climate.

"The idea was to send things to keep him from suspecting Charlotte, not make him jump on her more." He sounded miffed.

"I understand," I fibbed. I mean, why would a threatening note from Charlotte get a cop thinking she'd had a bone to pick with the recipient when he turned up dead?

"I figured that something demonstrating that Yul was

part of Charlotte's company—like that stationery listing him as a manager—would tell the cops he had more reason than having the hots for her to make sure everything went okay with the business," Lyle continued earnestly. Good. The more he talked, the safer I felt. For now. "The stuff about Charlotte and Chad never being able to see each other, and the note from Charlotte warning him to stay away, were evidence that Chad was harassing her. Yul would want to stop that. Their schedules showed that Charlotte wasn't always with that S.O.B. Yul, so he could kill Chad without her knowing. But that detective didn't get it."

"Yeah, Detective Noralles can be obtuse, especially when he thinks he has all the answers," I said in pseudosympathy. "I learned that the hard way, too. So . . . the murder weapon." I might as well get all the answers I could as I stalled for time. "Where did you hide the knife?"

He looked abashed. "It was a special one, with a real skinny blade. It came from a set in my house so I had to get rid of it. It's at the bottom of some poured concrete at a construction site where I worked for a while."

"Very wise," I said with a simulated smile, hoping I sounded admiring. Maybe building the guy's ego would keep me alive a little longer. And right about now, every extra moment seemed of momentous value. No sign of a weapon in Lyle's hand, but I still felt definitely endangered. "What was your reason for phoning him with that last hint, though—about secrets from the past—if it wasn't to implicate Charlotte?"

"Like the other stuff, to point him toward that asshole Yul!" Lyle exclaimed. "He was the one with the past worth hiding. That's why I came back tonight. I followed Charlotte and Yul into Griffith Park. Instead of coming home tonight, they got a room at the Universal Sheraton. This'll be the last time they spend the night together. I'll make sure of it." He took a step toward me that made me feel he'd make me pay for the affront he figured Yul perpetrated by hanging with the woman Lyle thought he loved. At least that's what I figured his motive was.

Which was how I'd at long last determined the murderer was Lyle. Jeff's ex, Amanda, wasn't the only one in my life lately who'd been victimized by a stalker. Philipe Pellera had been followed by a crazy fan. And around here, I'd started noticing how often Lyle looked at Charlotte with big puppy-dog eyes. Too bad I hadn't realized before that they obscured his pseudowerewolf persona.

Humoring the beast inside, I said, "She should be with you, right? I kind of thought that was the case."

"Of course. She's pretty and smart, and needs that jerk out of her life so she'll see I'm the one for her."

"So how would you convince her by coming here to-night, when you know they're not home?"

But *I* was home, and he'd known that from the party. Obviously his brazenness was building. Why?

As I waited for his response, I inched toward the open archway. At least then I'd have an entire house to hide in—assuming I could flee first.

"I brought back some stuff I'd taken before about Yul and his past, since it has to come out now. Did you know Yul was nothing but a big, fat tub of a freak until last year?"

I let my incredulity lunge out. "That gorgeous hunk?"

"You, too, Kendra?" Lyle grabbed my arm and clamped down. "He had you fooled?"

Only then did I see the small but sharp knife in his other hand. I'd thought him unarmed—my unobservant error. And now that he held my arm, I was in even bigger trouble.

Especially when I considered what really killed Chad—a lethal slice to his neck.

"Guess so." I winced under his grip and my burgeoning fear. I was compounding one mistake on top of another, and wasn't sure how to fix any of them. "Tell me the truth about him, Lyle. I'd really like to know."

"His name isn't Yul Silva. It's Stanley Smith. He used to be a three-hundred-pound, spectacle-wearing waiter in Beverly Hills. Know how I knew? He was stupid enough to laugh about it on his cell phone one day, right outside there in the driveway. I'd been biking by, saw him, and stopped to listen, and he didn't even notice me. I don't know who he was talking to, but he admitted to whoever it was that he'd lost all that weight and changed his name not to become a big successful Hollywood star, but to find himself a rich woman to sponge off. When I heard, I checked him out—his old self—and found a bunch of stuff about him at the places he'd worked, his driver's license, lots of evidence. That's what I just brought over here and hid. I was going to call that cop and leave him another tip. Maybe the third time he'd get it right."

On some level, I admitted to myself that I admired Yul. I mean, if Lyle was right and he'd remade himself into an irresistible hunk with the express intent of being a successful lady's lover, I'd tip my hat to him for ingeniousness and perseverance. Assuming I had a hat.

And a life, after this night—an even bigger assumption.

At least my brain was regenerating despite my fear, and pumping out a few, if feeble, ideas to get me out of this mess. I was a lawyer. A litigator. Animal dispute resolution notwithstanding, I lived by my wits and my ability to talk myself out of any terrible situation.

Yeah, in a courtroom, where my enemies were the opposition attorney and an occasional asshole of a judge.

Throwing in the towel isn't in your nature, Kendra. Time to kick myself in the butt to keep going. Too bad I wasn't a contortionist. Instead, I used the best weapons I had: my mouth and mind. My mind reminded me of another time when I'd been in danger, and it gave me an idea. Would it work? I'd find out.

"So you killed Chad to frame Yul?" I asked so conversationally that we could be chatting about Lyle's proclivity for sliding onto the street from his bicycle.

"Partly, but he needed to go, too, for Charlotte's sake. That reality show idea about digging up skeletons in people's pasts? I actually talked to Chad awhile after that party of Charlotte's that he crashed, the one where she threw him out."

"Sure." I knew which he meant: the one just before Lyle murdered him. I kept that to myself.

"He told me he'd gotten into that show *Turn Up the Heat* mostly because he wanted to make it big in reality TV himself, but he was really bummed out when Charlotte dumped him—though he admitted to me he planned to do the same to her. He had to. His girlfriend Trudi would have blabbed all over if he hadn't. He knew afterward, though, that to get anywhere he'd have been better off with Charlotte's cooperation, and she refused to even talk to him once she learned about Trudi. That's when he came up with that idea of a show that would use stuff from people's pasts. Charlotte and he had gotten close enough at some point that she'd admitted the hit-and-run accident to him, and he intended to use it against her unless she agreed to work with him. To help my poor Charlotte, he had to go."

Right here, in my house. Lucky me. And Chad . . .

"Fortunately, that Yul jerk had something in his past he'd want hidden, so he had a good reason to kill Chad, to stop that stupid show idea," Lyle continued. "I figured I could get rid of Chad and Yul, too."

Now that the guy was talking, he obviously didn't want to shut up. Which didn't bode well for my long-term future, unless he liked the idea of leaving a witness. Still, the longer he talked, the longer I lived.

"At least it should have gotten rid of Yul. I pretended to be him and invited Chad here that night to talk. Told him to come right in when he arrived and wait in the same room where Charlotte and he talked at her party. I'd already sneaked in through the wall the Hummer hit and opened the door for him. Then I made it look like Yul got those nasty little pets of his to kill Chad. I refastened the plastic when I left so they couldn't get out."

"Clever," I said admiringly, still pondering my idea. Would it work? I wouldn't know unless I tried. "Especially because ferrets really are nasty creatures. They do kill people, you know."

"They do?" He sounded astounded. "They're awfully small for that. I figured it would look that way, though, with their food all over Chad's body after I stabbed him in the throat. They chewed on him, didn't they?"

I nodded, not attempting to conceal my shudder. "Yeah. I saw that when I found Chad's body. I really thought at first that they'd killed him." I didn't believe it for long but didn't tell him that. "I'd read 'Sredni Vashtar' for a class when I was a schoolkid. Some literature that was."

"What is it?" he asked.

As I had a lot lately, I related the story of the orphan kid and his plea to his pet ferret.

"Wow," Lyle said. "I made a great guess, didn't I?"

"You sure did. And the thing is, once ferrets have the taste of blood, they lust after it. They become real killers, and it's nearly impossible to stop them." That part I made up. Vampire ferrets? Move over, bats.

"No! Wow."

By this time, I'd managed, by sidling slowly as we spoke, to move around enough to make it nearly to the inner hall, with Lyle facing me in the kitchen. The table and chairs were between us.

Time to make my move.

Screaming at the top of my lungs, I grabbed the nearest chair and flung it on the floor in front of me, blocking Lyle's ability to grab or stab me easily. Then I fled down the hall.

"Bitch!" he shouted. I dared a glance back and saw his shadow move. Bicycling had made his legs limber enough to leap over obstacles as pitiful as a kitchen chair.

I screamed again and headed for the closed door to the den.

I hadn't locked it again earlier. What was the use, with all the party guests gone? I'd intended to confront Yul with the room's contents again first thing tomorrow morning.

Now, I was grateful I'd had so much foresight. Not that I'd envisioned how that act would aid my future. I hoped.

Lyle grabbed my arm again as I reached the door, all but wrenching it from its socket. In the dimness, I watched him raise the knife in his other hand.

"No!" I shrieked, and aimed a kick at the spot most strategic for subduing a menacing male.

Lyle's turn to scream as I wrenched free and threw open the door. I flicked on the lights and was thrilled to see furry movement along the floor. I heard shrill, excited squeals and shouted, "Sic him, ferrets. Kill!"

"No!" Lyle shouted. "They're at Animal Control."

"Not now," I taunted triumphantly, hoping that the plastic still hiding the Hummer hole in the room was as easy to unfasten as he'd implied. Otherwise, if Lyle didn't flee based on my tale of ferret vampires, I was toast.

But these ferrets were apparently scared by the sudden commotion. They dashed toward us as we scuffled at the door. "No!" Lyle shouted again. He stood still, brandishing his knife at his small, squealing assailants. I prayed for their safety.

"Get him!" I shouted as the ferrets still scampered in confusion. One headed toward Lyle. I held my breath. Would he hurt it?

It climbed onto his sports-shoe-clad foot. He sliced down with the knife. I launched myself at him to knock him off balance. The ferret ran up his leg.

Lyle screamed, shook the small animal off, and fled down the hall.

In time for me to hear what I'd hoped for—the familiar voice of Noralles: "Police!"

Chapter Thirty-two

A LOT OF people besides pet-sitters work on Sunday. Some even work in the middle of Sunday night.

Cops, for example. At three in the morning, they were all over my home, along with the Scientific Investigative Division people, collecting evidence to prove my allegations against Lyle.

It helped that he actually had done as he'd said, and planted evidence against Yul in the bedroom the former obese waiter Stanley Smith shared with the lovely reality show diva Charlotte LaVerne. Lyle had been smart enough to wear his gloves earlier to minimize fingerprints. But he'd taken them off before confronting me in the darkened kitchen. His prints were all over the knife he'd brandished at the ferrets and me.

Right now, I sat outside on a deck chair overlooking my swimming pool, singing out answers to the many questions Detective Noralles slung at me.

Jeff sat beside me in another chair, holding my hand. No matter what he'd done in the past, what he'd hidden, he had come through in the latest pinch. He'd hied over here as quickly as his Escalade could carry him, using his cell phone to alert Noralles on his way. He'd rallied with the cops outside before they'd broken in to end the felonious fracas inside, for they'd heard my screams and Lyle's, and probably the ferrets', too.

"So after you got him to admit killing Chad Chatsworth, what happened, Ms. Ballantyne?" With my permission, Detective Noralles was recording my statement.

"I ran," I said. "And screamed. And then I confronted him in the middle of the house, where I defended myself by kicking him in . . . er, the genitals."

I heard both Jeff and Noralles suck in their respective masculine breaths, sensing their sympathy for Lyle, but hey, it had been either him or me.

A chilly November wind wafted over us, but it wasn't what made me shiver.

"And then what?" Noralles asked.

"Then is about when you came in and hollered 'Police!' "

While Noralles helped take Lyle into custody, I'd taken custody of the ferrets and secreted them in a dog crate I used for Lexie, upstairs in my apartment.

And then we all pretended they'd never been there.

Jeff's hand was warm in mine, which helped me recount the ugly stuff I'd suffered through that night.

He was kind enough not to say "I told you so" or call me stupid for ignoring his warnings and heading into the prowler-occupied house.

He did, however, tell me I couldn't always rely on animals and the element of surprise to save my life. "You'd be a lot better off not getting into these predicaments in the first place," he said.

I couldn't disagree. It'd happened twice now, though. Hopefully, I'd never learn if my luck would hold a third time.

When Noralles, SID, and the balance of the official team finally bailed out later in the morning, I called the Universal Sheraton and asked for Charlotte LaVerne's room.

"Who is this?" demanded a sleepy, irritable female voice.

"It's Kendra, Charlotte," I said, and proceeded to relate all that had just transpired.

"Kendra, are you okay?" she shrieked, then followed it up with, "We'll be right there. Don't go anywhere, okay? Oh, Kendra, that's terrible. That's wonderful. See you in a few." She hung up, and I figured that if she'd been here, I'd have been subjected to one of her more hysterical hugs.

The former Stanley Smith and she arrived half an hour later, looking disheveled, as if they'd just been awakened and had tossed on their clothes. Sure enough, Charlotte hugged me. I'd already been brazen enough to make coffee in my own former kitchen, and we all grabbed mugs and adjourned to the garish black-and-white furnished living room to talk.

"Then it's over?" Charlotte exclaimed when I'd finished.

"Looks that way," I said, eyeing Jeff. He'd stood as we'd spoken, leaning against the wall with arms crossed, even as he continued to hold his cup in one hand and lift it now and then to his lips. His expression stayed inscrutable. Was he mad at me? I hoped not. For this moment, I truly wanted a truce.

A while later, we all promised to stay in touch and share info. And then I went up to my apartment with Yul to retrieve his ferrets.

"Sorry, Kendra," he said as I handed them over, taking them out of Lexie's crate. My dog was fascinated by the little ferrets, standing up with her paws against Yul's legs. They clearly wanted nothing to do with her, though, staying on their master's chest and shoulders.

"They're illegal here," I reminded him. "As if you didn't know."

"Yeah, but I have a thing for them," he said.

Although I'd mentioned all that Lyle had divulged about Yul's mysterious past, I hadn't waited for the subject of the revelation to respond. Yul said now, "What Lyle told you was true, to a point. I purposely made myself over. I grew up in L.A. without much ambition, but being a restaurant server in Beverly Hills gave me ideas. So, I went on a diet, did some bodybuilding, and started auditioning. Then I met Charlotte. I know what it looks like, since I haven't made it in Hollywood yet, but my intent is to be a valuable part of her reality show production company."

"No need to explain to me," I said, though I was glad he had. "But what's with that strong-and-silent image of yours?"

"A habit I'm trying to break. Not the strong part, but the silent. I became good at keeping my mouth shut while waiting tables. Listening is a whole lot more valuable when you want to learn something. But now I think I have stuff to contribute, too, so I'll be sure to talk about it more."

"Good deal," I said, then finished, "And the ferrets?"

"I'll take care of them," he said with a sad sigh.

"You do that. Oh, and from what Ike Janus said, I should actually have the insurance money to repair the den soon. After that, maybe we can fix it up to be more ferret friendly."

Yul's gloom was immediately gone. His smile displayed gleaming white teeth that I figured were part of his makeover. "Really?"

"As long as you don't let anyone know," I cautioned. "And if you get into trouble with them, you'll need to indemnify me and hold me harmless." Okay, so I was still a lawyer. His eager verbal agreement was probably worth the paper it was written on. If I got into trouble as an accessory, then so be it.

After all, those endearing little critters had saved my imperiled life.

A SHORT WHILE later, I gathered up Lexie, and she and I adjourned with Jeff to his house, where Odin greeted us all with gusto.

Did I join Jeff in bed? Well, sure, but just to sleep. Really. We had a lot to discuss, but that wasn't the time to do it. Or anything more recreational.

Besides, Amanda's presence still dominated the place . . . even though she wasn't there, nor did I hear her key in the door.

The next day, the media went mad over the latest development in the Chad Chatsworth murder. I had to duck dozens of reporters, but that failed to keep my name out of the news.

I talked to Darryl, who chewed me out but good for putting my butt on the line that way.

Sitting outside on Jeff's back porch for most of the day when not pet-sitting, I watched both dogs romp in the backyard while Jeff stayed inside to do admin work for his P.I. firm on his computer.

I took calls on my cell phone from others I knew, like Avvie Milton, who called to say how glad she was that I was okay—and that I could keep her keys for now since Pansy needed pet-sitting services again next week. And Bill Sergement, Avvie's boss and lover who was also my onetime boss and lover, called, too. He was also happy to hear I was all right.

Then there was Borden Yurick, Sergement's former partner. "Did the legal research you did at my office lead to all this excitement?" he asked.

"In a way, though I was mostly researching a couple of quasilegal matters."

"Quasi?"

"Well, as you know, I can't actually practice law till I get my license back." I took a swig of bottled water, then told him of the excellent outcomes I'd helped to reach in Marie Seidforth's and Jon Arlen's matters.

"Do you really think a public easement established by the Spanish that long ago would have any effect today?" Borden asked skeptically.

"It doesn't matter, as long as the parties think so, or that the government or the former settlers' descendants could have a claim. I got them to at least start talking, hopefully negotiating a mutually satisfactory solution." With a little potential romance tossed in to sweeten the situation.

"Without litigation?"

I heard what I thought was an accusation in the other lawyer's voice, but refused to get defensive. "Hell, yes," I said. "I may be a temporarily defrocked litigator, but these days I like the idea of trying to work things out peacefully."

"Even if it keeps you from getting a fee?"

I sighed. "Sure, Borden, though someday—"

"You're my kind of lawyer, Kendra," he interrupted, sounding gleeful. "When you get your license back, I want you to come work for me. Okay?"

I hesitated. I'd feared this offer was forthcoming and wasn't sure how to respond. I didn't know how I'd practice law now, but it definitely wouldn't be like life at the Marden firm. "We can talk about it," I said carefully.

Borden laughed. "How about you can practice whatever kind of law you want, bring in your own clients, and help me with those I bring in? I'll make you a full partner—in a limited liability partnership, of course. That way, our ability to harm each other economically, or be harmed by my retired friends who'll help us out, will be minimized."

Hey, that actually sounded enticing. Still . . .

"And if I want to continue pet-sitting on the side—which takes up some time?"

"Fine."

"I've kind of liked researching people's problems with their pets and helping them hammer out amicable solutions. Animal dispute resolution, so to speak. What if I become a . . . pet advocate?"

"Fine."

Too good to be true. But hey, Borden had reportedly left

the Marden firm because he'd lost his marbles. And if that worked in my favor, what the hell?

"I'll come and talk to you about it," I told him. "See what we can work out."

"Fine," he said yet again. "And when is it that you get your law license back?"

"If all goes well, in less than two weeks," I told him.

Did I dare hope, this time, that all would go well?

Epilogue

OKAY, I HAD to insert an epilogue. I mean, I figure anyone interested in these latest exploits might also be interested in whether I passed the ethics exam.

Of course, anyone who'd read this far would already anticipate the answer. Hell, yes. I knocked the top off it.

And got my law license back at last.

Did I accept Borden's offer to join his firm? Absolutely. I mean, what lawyer worth her litigator's skills wouldn't want to practice law in a way that was fun?

Freedom! Flexibility! A senior partner who might be a modicum mad, but hey, who of us hasn't had a fleeting urge to chuck all that's onerous and start over again, smelling the roses along the courtroom corridors? Metaphorically, of course.

So what came next? I won't spoil it for you, other than to say I now had a corner office at the former restaurant on Ventura Boulevard.

And with the sensible solutions I'd helped Fran Korwald, Marie Seidforth, and Jon Arlen achieve, I was certain I'd found a new calling, especially when I could leap into a courtroom to argue in a lawsuit, too.

Pet advocacy. Not just for the pets, but for their owners as well. Animal dispute resolution.

Would solutions always come so easily and work out so well? They would if I could help it, though realistically I knew I'd have a few failures now and then.

Did I intend to give up pet-sitting? Hey, I'd been having the time of my life learning all about potbellied pigs and pythons as well as cats and dogs. Scaling it down, though, might be obligatory once I plunked on my advocacy hat and took up tilting at legal windmills for my new breed of clients.

Then there were Yul's ferrets. I pretended that the two in my house weren't there, at least for legal purposes. When I popped in now and then to see how my tenants were getting along, I included their pets in my social call. After all, the ferrets had helped me deal with a damned difficult situation with Lyle. And they'd actually never given me any trouble, notwithstanding how I'd maligned them with a vicious reputation as minivampires.

They still resided in my now fully restored den. Yes, Ike Janus finally got his insurance company to come through.

As to the five ferrets who'd been arrested, I intended to exercise my pet advocacy on their behalf. Lyle had set those poor ferrets up for a fall. They'd stay incarcerated until his trial, since they remained extraordinary evidence. But at least they'd been exonerated as killers. When they were no longer needed around here, I'd ensure they were handled appropriately by a ferret rescue organization.

And if, someday, Yul happened to find five extra ferrets hunting for a home . . . Well, if Charlotte and he were still my tenants, we'd see. But my inclination was to plead ignorance.

What would I do about Jeff Hubbard, P.I. and sometime secretive S.O.B.? That remained the chief conundrum of them all. Especially since Amanda came crying back to him yet again when I was present, claiming the stalker remained on her trail. Maybe it was true. Maybe not. But if I kept Jeff in my life, I'd still have Amanda to contend with. And I'd no doubt she intended to try to keep Jeff in *her* life any way she could.

Could I handle it? Did I want to?

Well, I didn't have to decide everything at the same time I commenced this newest chapter of my life.

And when it came down to it, Jeff wasn't the only one in this fledgling relationship who hadn't tossed onto the table every little skeleton from the past.

So, as long as Odin needed pet-sitting, and Lexie and he remained pals, and as long as I needed the services of a premier P.I., preferably gratis, I decided to keep on seeing him.

For now, at least.

"Hey, Kendra, are you through daydreaming yet?" demanded Darryl. I'd brought Lexie to the Doggie Indulgence Day Resort to play, so I could enlighten Darryl about the latest events in my life, and he'd had to leave me in his office while he greeted a new canine client.

I stood up from the comfortable chair facing his cluttered desk, and Lexie bounded into the office after him. "Sure am," I told him. "You got any more customers here with legal problems relating to their pets?"

"Do I ever!" he said. "Come on into the kitchen for a cup of coffee, and I'll tell you the latest."

It was a lulu, and I couldn't wait to meet the poor pet owner and sink my teeth into his doggy dilemma.

Meet Kendra Ballantyne.

Former high-powered litigator.
Hollywood pet-sitter.
Crime solver.

Sit, Stay, Slay

By

Linda O. Johnston

Canned from her L.A. law firm, Kendra
Ballantyne is now a freelance pet-sitter. When
her clients start getting murdered, Kendra
fears she's being set up. Aided by sexy
detective Jeff Hubbard, she's got to find out
why, and fast, because this killer's animal
instincts are downright dangerous.

0-425-20000-0

Available wherever books are sold or at
penguin.com

pc992